MURDER IN MATRIMONY

Also by Mary Winters

The Lady of Letters Mysteries
MURDER IN POSTSCRIPT
MURDER IN MASQUERADE
MURDER IN SEASON *

* *available from Severn House*

MURDER IN MATRIMONY

MARY WINTERS

SEVERN
HOUSE

First world edition published in Great Britain and the USA in 2025
by Severn House, an imprint of Canongate Books Ltd,
14 High Street, Edinburgh EH1 1TE.

severnhouse.com

Copyright © Mary Honerman, 2025

Cover illustration by Yuxi Liao and jacket design by Piers Tilbury

All rights reserved including the right of reproduction in whole or in part in any form. The right of Mary Honerman to be identified as the author of this work has been asserted in accordance with the Copyright, Designs & Patents Act 1988.

British Library Cataloguing-in-Publication Data
A CIP catalogue record for this title is available from the British Library.

ISBN-13: 978-1-4483-1549-9 (cased)
ISBN-13: 978-1-4483-1866-7 (paper)
ISBN-13: 978-1-4483-1550-5 (e-book)

This is a work of fiction. Names, characters, places and incidents are either the product of the author's imagination or are used fictitiously. Except where actual historical events and characters are being described for the storyline of this novel, all situations in this publication are fictitious and any resemblance to actual persons, living or dead, business establishments, events or locales is purely coincidental.

No part of this book may be used or reproduced in any manner for the purpose of training artificial intelligence technologies or systems. This work is reserved from text and data mining (Article 4(3) Directive (EU) 2019/790).

All Severn House titles are printed on acid-free paper.

Typeset by Palimpsest Book Production Ltd., Falkirk, Stirlingshire, Scotland.
Printed and bound in Great Britain by TJ Books, Padstow, Cornwall.

The manufacturer's authorised representative in the EU for product safety is Authorised Rep Compliance Ltd, 71 Lower Baggot Street, Dublin D02 P593 Ireland (arccompliance.com).

Praise for the Lady of Letters Mysteries

"A charming mystery"
Kirkus Reviews on *Murder in Season*

"The follow-up to *Murder in Postscript* emphasizes Victorian
social customs and society. Fans of Dianne Freeman's
'Countess of Harleigh' mysteries will enjoy"
Library Journal on *Murder in Masquerade*

"Enjoy the charming characters, a touch of romance,
and an unexpected denouement"
Kirkus Reviews on *Murder in Masquerade*

". . . [A] refreshing libation of mystery, wit, and Victorian
society, with a twist of romance"
Dianne Freeman, Agatha Award-winning author,
on *Murder in Masquerade*

"A delightful character-driven historical mystery for fans of
Katharine Schellman or Dianne Freeman"
Library Journal Starred Review of *Murder in Postscript*

About the author

Mary Winters is the Edgar Award-nominated author of the Lady of Letters historical mystery series, two cozy mystery series, and several short stories. A longtime reader of historical fiction, Mary set her latest work in Victorian England after being inspired by a trip to London. Since then, she's been busily planning her next mystery—and another trip! Find out more about Mary and her writing, reading, and teaching at marywintersauthor.com.

For Amy Cecil Holm, who thought up the perfect title for this novel. Thank you for your many years of friendship and support.

ONE

London, England

1860

> *Dear Lady Agony,*
> *Many successful matches have been made this season, and several couples wish not to delay their nuptials. I, for one, do not think they should have to. However, my mother's friend believes a hasty ceremony is to be avoided at all costs. She says an engagement of six to twelve months is a must. Is it?*
> *Devotedly,*
> *Tiresome Traditions*

> *Dear Tiresome Traditions,*
> *It's the time of year when the word* wedding *drops from many young lips. The fans have been fluttered, the waltzes have been danced, and the garden paths have been walked. All that is left are those two little words young hopefuls long to say: I do. Left to themselves, the words are inconsequential, hardly worth the space they take up, but put them together, and one makes a lifetime commitment. How many will utter these words at the end of the season? How many will wait until next spring? As long as the couple is in love, I do not believe it matters. I eagerly await the number, whenever the date. Dearest readers, I know of one already.*
> *Yours in Secret,*
> *Lady Agony*

As Amelia Amesbury glanced at friends and family gathered in her drawing room, she was excited for the future. The Amesbury name had been cleared from controversy, her sister Margaret Scott was fully recovered, and Simon Bainbridge had admitted his feelings for her not more than a fortnight ago. She was melancholy, yes, to see her sister depart for Somerset tomorrow, but she was also relieved to return to her schedule, which would include answering an influx of letters addressed to her secret pseudonym, Lady Agony.

Since Edgar Amesbury's passing, she'd responded under the alias in one of London's foremost penny papers. No one would have guessed that a widow to one of the greatest fortunes in the city was the authoress of the agony column, a space where correspondents poured out their problems in hopes of solutions. They knew she was a peeress; she signed her letters Lady Agony with a capital L. It was one of the reasons her column was so well read. However, the knowledge did not conform to their idea of what a lady should be. A lady should not deign to work anywhere— a penny paper, no less—and they were as curious about her reasons as her unconventional answers. Lately, they wanted to know how she happened to catch and release the Mayfair Marauder. One correspondent had even become quite obsessed, yet she didn't allow the complication to dampen her excitement.

The answer was much less complicated than they suspected. The truth was Lord Drake, the man whom she christened Mayfair Marauder in her letters, was a good man in a bad situation. His father was ill, and anyone who'd been through a long, debilitating illness with a relative would understand how desperate one could become in the situation. It was hard to see someone suffer day after day. Amelia knew that firsthand from her short-lived marriage to the Earl Edgar Amesbury. He, too, had a progressive illness that took him just two months after their marriage, and Amelia would have done anything in her power to bring him peace in his final moments. For Lord Drake that meant saving his ancestral home. He wanted his father's last breath to be taken in his beloved Cornwall estate, and indeed, he'd achieved his goal of keeping his father in his much-loved castle.

The story of the Mayfair Marauder, as all stories of human interest, intrigued her readers a good deal and would intrigue them more if they knew it was a peer who had stolen and then returned the most precious jewels in Mayfair. The story, however, would not be told by her. She'd promised to never reveal his identity if he returned the jewels. He'd kept his end of the accord, and she'd certainly keep hers—no matter how many correspondents called for his name, including A Concerned Citizen, who vowed to reveal her real identity if she did not share the name of the Mayfair Marauder. But she'd dealt with blackmail before and most likely would again. She refused to cow to the demands then, now, or ever.

"I, for one, shall miss you, Miss Scott." Lady Winifred Amesbury snatched the last strawberry tartlet from the tray in the drawing room, where they were enjoying tea with Lady Tabitha Amesbury, Marquis Simon Bainbridge, Margaret Scott, and her new friend, Captain Fitz.

Amelia smiled at Winifred, who was Edgar's niece and charge. Amelia loved her as much as a daughter. Of course Winifred would miss Margaret, better known as Madge. Her sister had indulged her every whim.

"Who will play with me in the garden?" continued Winifred. "Or pop popcorn? Or race horses?"

At the last comment, Amelia jerked her head. *Race horses?*

"You have *dear* Amelia for that," Madge returned, emphasizing the bit of flattery. "She knows how to race horses as well as I do. You only have to encourage her." Madge winked a pretty hazel eye at Amelia. "Besides, I might be around more than you imagine."

Plunk went Aunt Tabitha's teacup onto her saucer. As silent as the room grew, it might have been a window shattering. Tabitha Amesbury was Edgar's aunt and the sole surviving Amesbury besides Winifred. When it came to the family's reputation, she had exacting standards, taking it upon herself to be judge and juror of all household undertakings. "You'll keep in touch, certainly," said Tabitha with a placid smile.

Madge's eyelashes fluttered in the direction of Captain Fitz. "Oh, we'll be keeping in touch." She covered a chortle with her hand, looking very unlike the girl Amelia had grown up with, the girl who liked trousers, fishing, and tinkering. The girl who could fix a worn hinge or wheel before you could say Jack Robinson. The girl who *did not* flutter her eyelashes.

Amelia darted a glance at Simon, who caught her look. For a single second, she forgot Madge's confusing behavior and lingered in the green grasses of his eyes. She could live in a countryside that color, and she didn't like the country that much. She loved London—the city, the smells, the scenery. The Thames could grow rank, true, but nothing compared with the scent of a nut or oyster seller setting up his cart for the day, or the sound of foot traffic on Pall Mall, or horses' hooves in Hyde Park, or the shades of faces that made up the crowd on Derby Day.

Yet she would give all that up to live one day in those green, green eyes.

Simon turned to Lady Tabitha, perhaps with the idea of appeasing her. The Bainbridges and Amesburys had been friends for ages, and if anyone knew a word that would comfort her, it was he. "I've discovered keeping in touch with family is so important. I only wish I'd discovered it sooner."

"It is of utmost importance," Lady Tabitha replied, her pronunciation as correct as her posture. "Mrs. Scott will be overjoyed at her daughter's return."

Overjoyed might be an exaggeration, thought Amelia. Madge had arrived in London under a veil of criticism from the citizens of Mells. She had broken the arm of a man who had attempted to kiss her without permission, only to be accused of murdering a man she danced with at Amelia's ball. The real murderer had been brought to justice, but it had taken many difficult weeks to expose the culprit.

"I don't disagree with you." A second chortle dropped from Madge's lips, and her cheeks grew as pink as her auburn hair, which was brighter than Amelia's and possessed its own kind of energy. Like her freckles, it gave her the appearance of just coming in from a walk on a winter's morning. "Mother will be overjoyed with our news."

The room grew three degrees cooler, as if a ghost had floated in from the open window and hovered behind Amelia's shoulder. This couldn't be what she thought it was. Only two weeks ago, she and Simon had affirmed their feelings for one another. He had admitted to her occupying his every thought. If her younger sister preempted their budding romance with a

MURDER IN MATRIMONY 5

declaration of love, she would be the first one to grab Tabitha's cane—ebony with a regal gold timepiece—and rap her over the head with it.

Captain Fitz, who was a thoughtful man with a calm head in a crisis, looked very little like his reputation today. The flush of color when he smiled at Madge, which was continually, extended to the roots of his blond hair. Even when he lifted his chin in serious reflection, he appeared the same smitten suitor. "The truth is, we called on you today for a specific reason."

Winifred jumped out of her chair, the tartlet falling on the floor. "You're getting married!"

And there it was. *From the mouth of babes . . .*

"Yes!" Madge joined her, clasping her hands and jumping up and down. "We are!"

Forgetting his attempt at seriousness, Captain Fitz chuckled, and Amelia couldn't help but smile, too. Marriage was happy news, and despite having her own romance preempted, she was delighted for the captain and her sister.

Amelia stood and hugged Madge. "Congratulations."

Simon took the captain's hand and gave it a hearty shake.

Only Tabitha remained silent. Eventually she said, "Congratulations to you both. I must say the news isn't entirely unexpected. I imagine you will be married next June."

"Oh, no." Madge shook her head, and several pieces of auburn hair dislodged from a hasty coiffure. She would have left it habitually undone if their mother had allowed her. Hairpins she considered a menace, heels were intolerable, and woe betide the person who suggested tightlacing. "We cannot wait that long. We want to be married this month."

"This month," Tabitha repeated.

"This month?" Simon questioned.

"This month!" Winifred squealed.

Amelia closed her eyes and counted to ten, then twenty. Leave it to Madge to expect miracles and her older sister to perform them. Yet she was leaving for Mells tomorrow . . . Perhaps she would take her ardent nuptial plans with her. "I don't know if Mama will be able to plan something that quickly.

The traveling season is winding down, but still, the demands at the Feathered Nest are plenty."

Captain Fitz and Madge exchanged a secret look.

"Actually, Lady Amesbury, my family lives in London, and we are considering marrying here." Captain Fitz swallowed. "It would mean a lot to my mother, and as you all say, family is so important."

Madge's eyes darted in Amelia's direction, and Amelia raised her lips in what she hoped was a smile and not a snarl. If Captain Fitz wanted the wedding in London, it meant the duty of hosting would fall upon her. They certainly could not ask his parents to host, and Amelia was Madge's only family in town.

"I think it's a capital idea!" Winifred exclaimed. "I've never been to a wedding. I've never been to anything at all."

"Now will be your chance." Madge gave Winifred's small hands a squeeze. "I'd like for everyone to join us." She turned to Amelia. "And we would like you and Lord Bainbridge to be our principal bridesmaid and bride groomsman."

"We would be honored." Simon's voice brimmed with pride.

Amelia felt the same pride. Her little sister could be difficult and, being five years younger and an unexpected delight to their parents, a wee bit spoiled. But she was also one of her favorite people on earth. With her two older sisters, Penelope and Sarah, Amelia always felt their authority, and perhaps their censure, but with Madge, a comradery existed that she would always cherish. "I'll talk to the vicar in the morning."

Madge let out a deep breath. "Would you, Amelia?"

Amelia smiled. "Of course. I insist you have the wedding breakfast here."

"Truly?" Madge's eyes glistened with tears.

"Truly."

"And Father and Mother?"

"I will send for them," promised Amelia.

"And Penelope and Sarah?"

"The entire family, if you wish."

"Thank you, Amelia." Madge hugged her tightly. "I'm so glad because I wrote and told them already."

TWO

Dear Lady Agony,
After reading your recent opinion on the marriage
season, I would like your opinion on the words honor *and*
obey. *As you must know, our great lady Queen Victoria*
emphasized the words at her own wedding, illustrating
that, although she is our esteemed monarch, she is also a
modest matron. You have never been afraid to voice your
concern for unwise words. I wonder if you consider these
two of them.
Devotedly,
A Wondering Wordsmith

Dear A Wondering Wordsmith,
Your account of Queen Victoria's wedding vows is
correct. She indeed repeated the aforementioned words
with emphasis. Then again, she is the Queen of England
and can emphasize whatever she likes. It does not
diminish her authority in any way. We will continue to
obey *her regardless of her devotion to her husband, which*
is perhaps the only sense of the word that truly matters.
Yours in Secret,
Lady Agony

"I am not hosting a wedding breakfast for your sister, and that is final." Tabitha emphasized both syllables in *final* with the stomp of her cane on the parquet floor of the breakfast room the next day.

"That's correct, Aunt—you're not." Amelia tipped her chin in challenge. "I am."

Madge had left for Mells only an hour before, and already

Tabitha was making demands. *Let her make demands.* Her breath would be better saved to cool her tea, which had just been poured. Even without her younger sister's brazen admission of informing their family of her plans, Amelia would be hosting her wedding party. She had the space, the resources, and the time. Their parents had none of those, and while Captain Fitz's family might have been fully capable, the reception was the obligation of the bride's parents. Hosting the breakfast would relieve their parents of a good deal of pressure.

Bailey, the footman, pulled out a chair, waiting for Tabitha to be seated, but Tabitha didn't budge from the doorway. Garbed in a blue-green morning dress, she stood tall and proud like a peacock. However, peacocks were not only pretty; they were fierce. They could be aggressive when their territory was invaded, and now might be one of those times.

For if the Scott family was known for anything, it was invasions. When traveling, descending upon a function like a gaggle of geese, they were often met with varying degrees of enthusiasm. Some found it hard to believe—and a little odd—that a family could be as close as they were. But their livelihood had not only made them close; it had made them partners of sorts. They might spar like gladiators during the day, but they always closed the night as a family.

Bailey coughed, and Tabitha's eyelids lowered in his direction. He edged closer to the wall, his fingertips dropping from the back of the chair.

Tabitha returned to Amelia. "You will disobey me then."

"We are mutual friends, Aunt." Amelia reached for her teacup, hoping the action would encourage Tabitha to sit down. "We do not obey or disobey but listen to and respect one another."

"You are not respecting my decision."

"Considering the decision involves my younger sister, perhaps it is not your decision to make?" In the spirit of reconciliation, Amelia allowed the statement to lift in question. It was enough for Tabitha to move to her chair and sit down. Immediately, Bailey served her customary dry toast.

"Your sister is trouble. You know it. I know it. And the *ton*

MURDER IN MATRIMONY

knows it. Can you imagine what sort of mischief she could make at a wedding?" She paused. "Or wedding *breakfast?*" Which was perhaps worse since the Amesburys were organizing it.

Amelia set down her teacup. "It is her own wedding, Aunt. Why would she make mischief on her special day?"

"Mischief follows her wherever she goes, Amelia." She leaned over her plate. "Look what happened at our recent ball. A man was *murdered*." Pointing her long fingers, she tapped out both syllables of the word on the table.

"That was not her fault. In fact, she herself underwent a great deal of suffering. For that alone she deserves to have a wedding breakfast here." Amelia made the last statement with much emotion, wondering why it was that she possessed the greatest empathy when a family member was absent. Truly, Madge should be present to witness her passionate defense.

Tabitha ate her toast in silence, and the seconds stretched together in blessed solitude. Eventually she said, "I suppose your entire family will attend."

"You may be sure of it." Amelia knew her immediate family would not miss Madge's wedding nor would her extended family, including aunts and uncles. It was the bride's prerogative, however, to invite intimate relatives and favored friends since the wedding was intended to be a sending from her paternal home. Amelia would not deny her that. "We will need to make certain accommodations for family members who travel into town. Rooms, of course. Food. Entertainment." She cleared her throat, not wanting to broach a certain subject but knowing she must for arrangements to run smoothly. "There is my uncle Henry, who's always been overly fond of sherry. It might behoove us to remove it from the library during his stay."

"Uncle Henry?" Tabitha sputtered the name like a curse word.

"Aunt Gert—Gertrude—only partakes of wine, however, and that can easily be managed during the dinner hour." Amelia looked to Bailey, who dipped his chin, cataloging the problem for later. "Trust me. You do not want to see her blootered. She has a very loud voice that grows louder still with drink."

Tabitha took her last bite of toast with such force that brittle crumbs scattered to her plate.

"Do not concern yourself, Aunt." Amelia used what she hoped was a reassuring tone. "I can make the necessary arrangements."

Tabitha slowly dabbed her mouth and replaced her napkin before responding. "You can take the sherry out of the library, but more must be done for a wedding party than to hide the liquor. Someone must plan the wedding breakfast, and that someone must be me."

Point taken. Tabitha studied menus as some captains studied maps. If Amelia wanted a first-rate wedding breakfast for her sister, which she did, Tabitha should be the one to plan it. But how to encourage her . . . that was the question. "I would not be averse to you making arrangements."

A familiar smile, the one that brokered deals, flicked across Tabitha's lips. If Tabitha hadn't been born into the aristocracy, she might have made a fine banker. "And I would not be averse to you curbing your guest list."

The statement was akin to checkmate. "Understood. I will stop at cousins, but aunts and uncles must be invited."

"I will tell Jones to lock the liquor cabinet before their arrival."

"A prudent plan." Amelia pushed out her chair. "I will see the vicar this afternoon. Madge will be back in two weeks, and I have much to do before then. Miss Hernandez took her measurements last evening for her dress, and alterations will be completed when she returns. We have not one moment to lose."

"Mr. Cross," Tabitha tutted.

Tabitha accused the Reverend Mr. Cross, whom they met before he became vicar of All Saints on Margaret Street, of popery, but Amelia liked the vicar a good deal. In fact, she liked him so much that she'd told him about her secret occupation as Lady Agony.

It was after church one Sunday when Mr. Cross was telling her about his involvement with the rookies in Wapping. Although he was the vicar at All Saints on Margaret Street, he also conducted services at St. George-in-the-East. Like many men of the cloth, his services were lent out to the poorer parishes of town. But unlike many, he was truly devoted to them. He had since created a society of clergymen committed to helping the needy: the Society for the Greater Good.

One man, or even many, could only do so much, however, and when he told her about a troublesome candlemaker in the borough, she told him her secret occupation and promised to reveal the deplorable working conditions of the candlemaker in her column, which she promptly did the following week. The candlemaker had been sanctioned shortly thereafter, and Mr. Cross was pleased with the outcome. Since then, he and Amelia had become friends of sorts. She knew if she could trust him with her identity, she could trust him with anything. He was only one of four people who knew her secret.

"While you are exchanging niceties with your favorite vicar, I will see to the breakfast." Tabitha sniffed. "To accomplish it by the end of the month would be impossible for anyone who did not have my good connections. As it is, it will take much cajoling on my part, and you know how much I hate cajoling. I'll have to make allowances that I'd rather not."

Amelia had a feeling the word *cajole* meant two different things to them. She'd never seen Tabitha plead for anything a day in her life. Tell, yes. Ask, maybe. Cajole, hardly. "I know you will meet the challenge, Aunt." She gave Tabitha's shoulder a pat as she walked by.

Tabitha shrank from her touch. "Of course I will meet the challenge, Amelia. The point is not *if* but why."

"Goodbye." Amelia hurried out of the breakfast room before debating that question.

Outside, the day was hotter than she liked it. The overcast sky had cleared, and early morning raindrops made the city shine. The air was heavy with a hint of hazelnuts from a nearby costermonger cart in Hyde Park. As she made her way to Margaret Street, a kaleidoscope of scents including bread, ale, and smoke assailed her, and she took in the good and the bad with equal pleasure.

She crossed Oxford Street and the street after, and All Saints on Margaret Street, completed just last year, arose in medieval majesty. She admired the gothic architecture, the inlaid red-and-black stone, and the towering spire that rose 227 feet in the air, higher than the towers of Westminster Abbey. A cloud broke away, and a stream of sunlight brushed the cross that reached the sky. Perhaps it was preordained that Amelia was here, arranging a wedding for her sister.

Or perhaps it was penance for faking illness on Sundays when she was a child.

For it might have been her own wedding she was arranging, she thought gloomily. Simon had admitted to caring for her and then kissed her in a way she couldn't keep from thinking about. Had she been any other woman, he would have felt obligated to propose to her. After all, women and men did not simply kiss for the fun of it. They did so only under the auspice of engagement.

But their relationship had been unique from the start. He'd admitted to being the person who'd told Edgar Amesbury to find a wife who knew neither his name nor fortune. Only then could the woman be trusted to carry out his wishes after his death, a death which came much sooner than anyone thought, including Amelia. When she married him, she knew he was ill but assumed he would improve with treatment. But his disease, which had progressively worsened, grew worse still, and his death, when it came, was quick and shocking. Their adventure had ended before it had begun, and Amelia was left with only the idea of love and the promise of what might have been.

After his death, she clung to her letters from the penny paper. Her childhood friend Grady Armstrong was the editor, and when one of his writers quit, she happily took up the work. It was a way to live without leaving the house, and in her deep mourning period, it was just what she needed. She had her work, she had Winifred, and that was enough.

But now she wasn't so sure.

Simon was on her mind often, so often that she had to remember it was Madge getting married and not herself. She drew her eyes from the spire. Now was not the time for daydreams or speculation. She must look straight ahead if she was to plan a wedding in less than a month.

When she entered the church, Mr. Cross was conversing with a parishioner in hushed tones. Although Amelia knew him to be a calming presence in her life, he was not having the same effect on the fellow parishioner. The man, who loomed over the priest, was obviously having a spiritual crisis, so Amelia paused, respecting their privacy.

She studied the baptistry at her left. It was a rich brown marble, complementing the polychromatic colors of the church, including the patterned floor. William Butterfield, the architect, had reimagined medieval architecture for their age while retaining a strong sense of history. Like many medieval churches, windows were installed above the arcade, allowing light to descend on the sanctuary from above. The result was majestic—heavenly, almost—with the east-end altar bathed in surreal beams of light. Some thought ten years of work had been wasted on a bygone era, but Amelia took the project as proof that anything could be accomplished with the right vision, even her sister's hasty wedding.

Mr. Cross finished his conversation with the parishioner, promising him more time when the day was done, and turned toward the baptistry. Mr. Cross was a middle-aged man with an enthusiastic step that belied his age. Trim with a balding head and two smooth patches of brown hair above each ear, he had eyes that were sympathetic and kind, and upon first meeting him, one would understand he was a good listener. He was quiet but not uninterested, and his words—and tranquility—had the power to ease one's mind.

Today, however, he appeared distracted, perhaps with parishioners' problems or his own daily tasks. His glanced at the sanctuary, then held out his hand. "Lady Amesbury. What a pleasant surprise."

Amelia took his outstretched hand. "I hope I'm not interrupting. I'd like to speak to you about a family matter, if I may."

"Certainly." He motioned in the direction of the vicarage, which was attached to the church. They walked through the vestry in silence, and she noted his robes hanging ready for the week. The office, directly afterwards, was small but, like

Mr. Cross, personable with a shelf of his beloved books and a painting of the Ascension. He was a great lover of literature and bemoaned not having more money for books or time to read them.

"I was thinking about you only this morning." He waited for her to be seated. "And here you are. The good Lord works in mysterious ways."

"Has another situation arisen in Wapping?" Knowing his commitment to workers' rights, she understood he might have another column for her to write under the auspice of Lady Agony. The area had many industrial sites. It was also laden with crime, not to mention destitution and poverty. It was too much for one man, or society, to undertake alone, and she would be happy to lend her services again.

For the first time that day, a brief smile touched his lips. "I am certain many situations have arisen in Wapping since my last visit, and there is one person I would like you to help specifically, but none of that now. You need *my* help." He folded his large hands on the desk. "How may I be of service?"

Amelia felt instantly at ease. With him, she could unload her burdens without judgment or scorn. "It's my sister, Margaret Scott. Captain Fitz has proposed to her, and they are to be married."

"You'd like the wedding performed here." He completed her thought.

"If your schedule allows for it." Despite Mr. Cross's calm demeanor, she squirmed a little in her seat. "You see, Margaret would like the wedding to take place this month, if possible," she added, noting the raise of his eyebrows. "She's not the most patient person, and once she decides on a thing, she follows it through immediately."

He leaned in slightly. "She sounds like someone else I know."

Amelia released a laugh, relieved by his good humor. "We are quite alike. That is true. But Margaret's passionate behavior can be trying for others at times."

"As in the time she broke a man's arm?"

Amelia had commiserated with him about the situation after a church service one Sunday. He'd been a great help to her then, assuring her God would never give her more than she could handle. "Yes, as in that time."

"Not to worry, Lady Amesbury." Mr. Cross leaned back in his chair. "I've handled more trying people than your little sister. All I need is a date, and I will wed your sister and the captain into never-ending happiness." He called to Mr. Dougal, the young curate he'd brought on six months before, who managed his schedule, among other things, while training for a living. He was a round, good-natured man with ginger hair and a ruddy complexion. Inexperienced, he knew little of parish life or patrons. But he greeted everyone as a friend or an opportunity to do good, and Amelia appreciated his attitude even if it was a little naïve. "Dougal, we must prepare for the wedding of Lady Amesbury's sister, which is to take place . . ." He looked to Amelia.

Amelia provided the date.

Mr. Dougal frowned. "That does not give us much time."

Before Amelia could apologize, Mr. Cross came to her rescue. "We have little to plan on our part, Mr. Dougal. However, Lady Amesbury has much to do, so we mustn't keep her."

"Quite true," Mr. Dougal said with new determination. Mr. Cross's attitude had that effect on others. "I'll add it to the parish schedule, and congratulations, Lady Amesbury."

"I do apologize for the short notice," Amelia said after Mr. Dougal had left.

Mr. Cross waved away her concern. "You bring the bride and groom, and I'll do the rest."

"Thank you." Her burdens felt lighter, and she had Mr. Cross to thank. Much was still to be done, in terms of arrangements, but he had not objected to a sudden wedding. Another priest might have questioned the timing or reason. Accommodation, however, was his natural reaction. It wasn't so much whether a thing could be done but how. She believed it was what made him successful at his work in Wapping. Which reminded her of his look of consternation when she'd first arrived. "How is your society work progressing?"

He tapped his fingertips together. "Slowly. Not all are happy to have a man of the cloth interfering with their livelihoods."

Amelia frowned. "How so?"

"That is a long story for another time." He gazed over her shoulder, perhaps to ensure Mr. Dougal was not lingering in the hallway. "What of your blackmailer? Have you had any success in identifying him?"

The blackmailer. Amelia's life had been so upended by her sister that she'd almost forgotten about the person threatening to reveal her identity to all of London. *Almost.* The person had written to the journal twice already, insisting that Amelia report the name of the Mayfair Marauder. If she didn't, the writer promised to give her identity to one and all.

Amelia had endured this sort of harassment once before, months ago. At the time, she was terrified, worrying for herself and her family. But not any longer. She refused to be the victim, so, like many victims, she took justice into her own hands.

"You'll be pleased to know the paper is publishing the letter in its entirety tomorrow." Amelia revealed the information with marked assuredness. "I will not bear the injury of the black-mailer's words alone. When my readers see what has been said, they will commiserate with me, and the person will stop."

Mr. Cross frowned. "I am not certain that is a good idea."

"It is the only idea that will work. I cannot work under fear. You know as well as I do our occupations will not allow for it."

Mr. Cross quirked a brow, perhaps unconvinced. "Still, Lady Amesbury, I worry for your safety. Londoners can be defensive, especially when it comes to objects of wealth. This person wants retribution. Revealing him might cause more pain and anger."

For the first time, Amelia questioned her action, but it was too late. The letter would be included in tomorrow's paper. "What else? Am I to quit writing?"

"No." He smiled his magnanimous smile. "Your work is too important. I want you to continue helping others always. To do that, however, you must exercise caution. People are desperate to know your name, one person in particular." Mr. Cross looked around the room as if that person might be hiding behind the dark green curtains outlining the window behind his desk. "Yours can be a lonely occupation, as can mine. We must be secure in the fact that what we are doing is true and right. Involving your readership will only make *you* feel better. It will not solve the problem."

He was right. Amelia wanted empathy, not resolution. She wanted her readers to see what she endured for their benefit. But the work benefited her too, perhaps more so, for without it, she would have no way to spend her time and creativity. "Of course you're right. You always are." She put a hand over her eyes. "What have I done?"

"What every other blackmailed individual has thought of doing." He stood. "Come now. It will be all right. You have God on your side."

She lifted her fingers from her eyes, doubtful of divine intervention.

He smiled and put a hand on her shoulder. "And you have me."

THREE

Dear Lady Agony,

The Mayfair Marauder terrorized families in Mayfair, breaking into their homes and stealing their most prized heirlooms. Supposedly, the identity of this bandit is known by you, yet you allow the person to go unreprimanded. That decision does not belong to a penny paper authoress but to the Metropolitan Police. If you do not name the bandit at once, I will name you. I have determined your true identity and will unveil it to one and all without warning. Do not doubt it, and do not cross me. If you do, your family will pay the price.

Devotedly,

A Concerned Citizen

Dear Readers,

The above letter was sent to me by a fellow reader, and after fretting over it for nearly a week, I decided the best response was to print it in its entirety. This is not the first time I have been threatened, even by this reader, but I do hope it will be the last. I took up the pen in earnest, doing what I can with the ability and passion I possess. I endeavor to do right with each response, and while you might not always agree with me, I hope you will respect my decisions. When it comes to the one concerning the Mayfair Marauder, I made it with the purest intentions. I will not reverse course.

Yours in Secret,

Lady Agony

The next day, when the paper arrived, Amelia scanned it and tossed it on the stack of afternoon mail. Knowing the letter was forthcoming didn't make it any easier to see in print. She had cringed reading her own words. How could she have been so dense? The response would help no one. In fact, other readers might rally around the author, A Concerned Citizen. They might take the writer's side, agreeing that indeed Amelia should identify the jewel thief in her column.

She wouldn't do it in a hundred years, or even a thousand. Lord Drake was a kind person. Yes, he'd stolen Tabitha's famed diamond brooch, but he'd also returned it. In the meantime, he and Amelia had become very good friends, and she'd no more turn him over to the police than Kitty Hamsted, who was expected at her house any moment. The only person who knew his identity was Simon, and that was because they'd been partners in the investigation. He'd understood why she'd kept his identity secret. Lord Drake's reputation would be ruined if she revealed his thievery in her column. Whether or not the Metropolitan Police would be able to charge him with a crime didn't matter. He would never be welcomed into polite society again.

When the library door opened, she looked up, anticipating a much-needed conversation with Kitty over a cup of tea. What she saw, however, was Simon storming the room with the paper tucked under his armpit. She closed her eyes briefly. Knowing his penchant for overreacting, she hadn't told him about the blackmailer. He had no idea she was being harassed. She opened her eyes and met the fury in his.

He did now.

"Lord Bainbridge to see you, my lady," the butler announced in a winded voice.

"What in God's name were you thinking?" Simon asked.

"That'll be all, Jones," Amelia said. "Thank you."

Jones shut the door.

"Well?" Simon prodded.

"Please calm yourself." Amelia motioned to the chair across from her desk. "I do not need the neighbors overhearing your outburst."

He folded himself into it like a petulant child who had just been told he couldn't have a second dessert. "I am not calm,

Amelia. Imagine opening the papers to find your closest confidante is being blackmailed, and you yourself were unaware of the situation."

Despite his grave tone, her lips turned up in pleasure. "I am your closest confidante?"

He didn't return her smile.

"I would be upset, naturally." *Undone* would have more accurately described it, but she kept that to herself. "I wouldn't be unmanageable, however. I'd realize that my confidant was capable of making his own decisions."

"Even when those decisions involve other loved ones, including dear family friends?" He ran a hand through his black hair. The result was a distracting loose wave covering his forehead. Amelia imagined it looked this way at sea after a strong burst of wind did its work.

She refocused on the topic. "You're right. I should have told you. You've been friends with the Amesburys for years and deserved to know our reputation may be in peril."

"I don't give a damn about anyone's reputation!" He grasped the arms of the chair as if to keep himself from becoming unmoored. "I care about family. I care about *you*."

She knew he did, but it was still nice to be told. There was a time in their relationship when he wouldn't have expressed the notion as vocally—or passionately. Although the circumstances could be better, she saw it as positive progress. "I apologize."

He opened his mouth in surprise, as if ready to contradict her, then closed it. "How many letters have you received from the blackmailer?"

"Three." She pointed at the letter to Lady Agony. "That was the third, and before you ask, it was the most threatening."

He inhaled a sharp breath. "Three letters. The person is determined."

"It would appear so. But I am determined, too. I refuse to have my decision undermined."

"And I refuse to have your safety jeopardized." His words were no louder than a whisper, but their intention was clear. He planned to be her protector, her savior. The problem was

MURDER IN MATRIMONY   21

she didn't need saving. Mr. Cross had made her question the
reason behind her action, but that didn't mean she didn't stand
by the action itself. In fact, it might even work. If it didn't,
she had other avenues of recourse, none of which included
Simon Bainbridge brandishing a shield or sword.

"All we can do is wait and see how the blackmailer reacts."
She wondered if a new letter was being written as they spoke,
if A Concerned Citizen was busily penning a response to her
bold action. To see his own words in print must have been
a great shock. "With any luck, this will be the end of the
blackmail. Sometimes all it takes is someone knowing about
another's bad actions to make them cease. Let us hope that
is the case here."

"And if it's not?" he asked.

"I will not keep it from you. I promise."

The word seemed to appease him, and his shoulders relaxed.

Mr. Jones returned to the door. "I apologize for the inter-
ruption, but Mrs. Hamsted says she is expected. Shall I put
her in the drawing room?"

"No, no. Please bring her in."

Kitty Hamsted entered in a whirl of lavender frills. Her
parasol was lavender as well with a straw-colored handle that
matched her hat. The purple flowers on the brim of her bonnet
made her blue eyes look violet, and Amelia welcomed the happy
sight. The tension in the room was released by her entrance,
and Amelia stood and motioned to her enthusiastically.

Kitty walked to the middle of the room and poised the
parasol at her side in a dashing manner. "You, my friend, are
the talk of the *ton*." She paused. "Lord Bainbridge, excuse me.
Jones did not tell me Lady Amesbury had company."

"Mrs. Hamsted, it's always a pleasure."

Simon and Amelia came away from her desk, joining Kitty
in the seating area.

"Pray tell, why am I the talk of the *ton*?" Amelia asked,
unable to keep the curiosity out of her voice.

"Not you." Kitty adjusted her skirt to avoid a crease before
sitting down. "Lady Agony. Reprinting the letter was a brilliant
idea."

22 MARY WINTERS

Amelia sneaked a peek at Simon, who had developed a light twitch in his jaw. "Not everyone thinks so."

"Not everyone is as brilliant as you are, then." Kitty leaned closer, lowering her voice in a way that made Amelia and Simon lean in, too. "Even Lady Hamsted is reading Lady Agony. Can you imagine it? My mother-in-law. I would have never dreamt it." She clapped. "Bravo."

"Yes, well, Lady Agony might have increased her readership, but Lady Amesbury has increased her chances of retaliation." Simon cleared his throat. "I do not mean to be a killjoy, but Amelia's safety is my utmost concern."

"Of course it is." Dropping her smile, Kitty rushed to agree. "It is mine as well." She turned to Amelia, the skin around her eyes creased with new concern. "Do we believe the black-mailer knows your identity? I did not believe it was the case."

"It is hard to say for certain," said Amelia. "The letters are still coming through the magazine office, so we have no proof there. The blackmailer claims to possess the information but has provided no evidence to support it."

"I worry it's forthcoming." Simon spoke the words into his lap, perhaps not wanting to put the idea into the atmosphere.

"Until we have proof, I see no cause for concern, and fretting will do us no good." Amelia could do nothing about the blackmailer right now, perhaps not ever, but she could do something about her sister's wedding. She could make plans with Kitty, which is why she'd called in the first place. "Let us turn to happier news: Captain Fitz and Madge's wedding."

Kitty clasped her lavender-lace-gloved hands in her lap with excitement. "We have less than two weeks to plan it. What have you done so far?"

"Sent a note to you." Amelia chuckled, and the remainder of the tension in the room seemed to float out of the window. Even Simon joined in the jest with a laugh.

"I confess I've never planned a wedding." Kitty chewed her bottom lip thoughtfully. "Knowing your sister, she will insist on a robust meal, and the captain, well, I imagine his family is of hearty stock. The Scott family . . . will they be coming?"

MURDER IN MATRIMONY 23

"Yes." Amelia could practically see the designs forming in Kitty's pretty head.

"Just imagine, all of them in the same room, celebrating the grand couple." Kitty sighed. "I, for one, cannot wait."

"It might not be as comfortable as you imagine, Kitty," Amelia cautioned. "Lady Tabitha has voiced concerns about the wedding and does not relish the thought of hosting a breakfast."

Kitty frowned. Not wanting a party was a foreign concept to her. "What could she possibly object to?"

"Considering Miss Scott's recent obstacles with the law, her objections might be valid," added Simon.

Despite her mild agreement, Amelia didn't appreciate the criticism. "Madge had nothing to do with the trouble."

"Her argument with Mr. Radcliffe had everything to do with it," Simon continued. "It placed her on the top of the suspect list."

"A suspect list of one," retorted Amelia. "I cannot imagine Madge arguing with anyone on her wedding day." *Except Aunt Cassandra, whom she despises with unparalleled fervor, and Cousin Matthew, her son, who will undoubtedly show up without an invitation.* Amelia pressed her fingers to her temples. *Which is why they must be stopped from attending. But that was a problem for another day.*

"Nor I," Kitty added amenably. The friends never missed an opportunity to lend each other support. "It will be a lovely day for a lovely person."

The proclamation hung in the air, leaving little room for debate, and Amelia felt better, despite Simon's thick dark eyebrows, which peaked too high in question for her taste. The butler's surprise knock on the door came just in time to put any question to rest. "Yes, Jones?"

"The curate is here from the parish office. I wouldn't have interrupted you, but he states it's urgent. He would not be dissuaded."

Kitty and Simon frowned in tandem. Amelia hoped her smile would put them at ease. "I went to see Mr. Cross yesterday. He and I made plans for the ceremony." She turned to Jones.

24 MARY WINTERS

"Please bring Mr. Dougal in. Mrs. Hamsted will be assisting me with the wedding, and any news he has might be informative to all of us."

Amelia welcomed the curate, who appeared distraught in the extreme. His face was splotched with pink patches, as if he'd had a good cry earlier in the day, and his blue eyes, rimmed in red, attested to the fact.

"Mr. Dougal." Amelia stood. "Is something wrong?" She crossed the room without thinking.

"Something is very wrong, my lady." Mr. Dougal shifted from one foot to the other.

"Please, sit down. This is Lord Bainbridge and Mrs. Hamsted. They are helping me with my sister's wedding plans. Anything you have to say might be said in front of them." Amelia motioned to the green leather couch across from Simon and Kitty, and after they exchanged greetings, the vicar's assistant sat down. "Now what is it that has upset you?"

"I come with news." Mr. Dougal paused. "There is no good way to tell you."

Inside, Amelia faltered, but she attempted a brave face for the young curate. He was distressed, and worrying about her reaction would only make him more so. "I find the best way is outright and without delay."

He took a deep breath, summoning his courage. "Mr. Cross has been murdered."

FOUR

Dear Lady Agony,

Do you read the Accidents and Offenses in the dailies? I do, and increasingly, I'm disturbed by their nature. I find myself thinking about them even when I do not wish to, spending nights tossing and turning long after I've shut the paper. What is to be done about London's problems?

Devotedly,

Saddened by News

Dear Saddened by News,

I am a penny paper authoress, not a constable or clerk with answers to why harm comes to others. I do, however, have answers on how to stop harming yourself, and that is to set the daily aside. It is doing you no good to dwell on the crimes and, in fact, is doing you harm. Sometimes we must be the ones to preserve our own health even at the cost of information. As the old Bible story tells us, not all knowledge is good for us.

Yours in Secret,

Lady Agony

Murdered? The Reverend Mr. Cross? Amelia shook her head. It could not be. Mr. Cross was a pillar of the community. He'd begun a Society for the Greater Good. He was helping the poor in Wapping, finding them work and steering them away from a life of crime. No one in the world would want to murder him. "I'm sorry, Mr. Dougal. I don't believe I heard you correctly."

Kitty came to Amelia's side, grasping her hand.

"You heard correctly," Mr. Dougal said. "He's gone."

Amelia could not find the words to respond. Mr. Cross was

not only her priest but her confidant, and she had very few of them in her life. He'd buried Edgar, counseled her in her grief, and encouraged her to start again. When she told him about her column, he was happy, proud even. He admired the work Lady Agony had done to share workers' grievances and hold employers accountable. Dead? He could not be dead. Certainly not murdered.

After a moment, Kitty asked, "What happened?"

"The police believe it was a robbery gone terribly wrong." The worst of his news heard, Mr. Dougal proceeded more quickly. "The poor box was missing, and Mr. Cross was dead on the floor of his office, struck by the clock on his fireplace mantel. The officers believe he confronted the robber and was killed for doing so."

"That cannot be." Amelia heard the words more than said them. "The poor box is in the vestibule. According to your account, Mr. Cross was in the vicarage."

Mr. Dougal looked from Kitty to Simon, his jowls shaking slightly. "It is what the officer said, word for word. I swear it."

Simon gave him a reassuring look. "I believe Lady Amesbury means the theory doesn't make sense. If Mr. Cross was indeed killed because of the poor box, he would have struggled with the thief near the box, not his office." He glanced at Amelia with compassion. "Correct?"

"Yes." Amelia was beginning to find her voice. "If Mr. Cross interrupted a robbery in progress, one would think he would have been found somewhere in the church."

Mr. Dougal nodded, perhaps relieved to clear up the misunderstanding. "I understand your question, but maybe the thief left through the vicarage. Maybe Mr. Cross caught him fleeing."

Amelia agreed it was a possibility. "The police know the time of death?"

Mr. Dougal nodded. "The clock read ten minutes to ten. Mr. Cross lay there until this morning, when I found him, and called for the constable." He choked on the saliva lodged in his throat. "I cannot get the image from my mind. I think it will be there always."

Amelia understood. Death was the most ordinary thing in

MURDER IN MATRIMONY

the world until it entered one's sphere. Then it was extraordinarily cruel and unkind, offensive even. And surely never forgotten. "When was the last time you saw him, before this morning?"

"Yesterday, before I left, around five o'clock. He had a late tea and returned, planning to work into the night." His forehead creased with consternation. "It's why I am here. I almost forgot." He pulled an envelope out of his great coat pocket. The coat was tight and ill-fitting, and the envelope was badly wrinkled. "He asked me to make sure you received this. Not to send it in the post."

On the envelope, Amelia recognized her name in Mr. Cross's excellent penmanship, the loop of the L in Lady distinct in its perfection. Her fingertips lingered over the ink, a message from a friend now gone.

Mr. Dougal stared at the envelope. "I assume it has something to do with your sister's wedding . . ."

Amelia turned it over, slipping a finger under the seal. She glanced up at the curious sets of eyes upon her, then opened it.

She expected a letter, some sort of explanation of what had happened. A priest would portend his own death. He would know what was about to happen and why. Somehow, he would make sense of it for her. But it wasn't a letter; it was a newspaper clipping that appeared to have nothing to do with him. A notice from the Accidents and Offenses column told of a young woman, Rose Rothschild, who had a fatal and lamentable accident, falling from a ladder to her death at the Baker Biscuit Factory. A verdict of accidental death had been given at inquest and the girl's death mourned by the people who loved her.

Amelia turned over the clipping, frustrated. There was nothing of value on the other side. No writing, no address, no secret message. What use was it to her? What was she to do with it? She knew nothing of biscuit factories, let alone the girl. Why had he left it for her? And why had he given it to Mr. Dougal to deliver instead of giving it to her himself? They'd met only yesterday. He could have given it to her then.

"What is it?" Simon finally asked.

"How should I know?" Amelia snapped, frustrated. "I have no idea what it means. Do you?" She directed the question at Mr. Dougal.

Mr. Dougal leaned over to look at the paper clipping. "I do not know the name Rothschild, but the society met at St. George-in-the-East. It might be near the factory. For whatever reason, the church was a favorite of his. The members had no respect for him or what he was trying to accomplish. One week, they put tacks on his kneelers. The next week, he asked to be transferred there." Mr. Dougal shrugged. "He could not be deterred."

Amelia imagined the clipping had something to do with his work in the East End. She returned it to the envelope. Why give it to her though? Perhaps he wanted her to investigate the girl's death. He, like Amelia, was always on the alert for employers with bad behaviors.

It was just like him for his last concern to be for someone else and not himself. The longer she considered the missive, the angrier she felt. She had wanted an explanation of last night's events. What she received was a newspaper clipping that, while sad, was an ordinary occurrence in London. This girl meant nothing to her, and he'd meant so much.

She sat staring at the envelope, willing it to take on a new meaning. For the letters to rearrange themselves into a secret message, one that would make sense of the senseless act of murder. But nothing changed except the sadness she felt, seeping from her heart to the rest of her body. It took hold and began to make her numb to her surroundings.

Simon must have understood, for he interceded in her lapse of conversation. "Did Cross have any unexpected visitors yesterday? Do any conversations stand out as peculiar?"

"He had a busy morning, but that was not unusual. Lady Amesbury and her sister's wedding was at the forefront of his mind. He wanted it to go as smoothly as possible." Mr. Dougal lifted his chin in Amelia's direction. "He said my lady had enough to deal with and to come to him with questions. He called it an opportunity for me to learn." He smiled, his gaze trailing to the window. "He had great faith in me, more faith, perhaps, than I deserve." He sniffed. "I'm not a gifted orator, and I often fumble my words or their meaning. No one wants a preacher who cannot give a decent sermon."

"I'm sure you can," Kitty put in enthusiastically. "I can tell that from talking to you."

"Thank you." He smiled. "But I'm a buffoon in front of a congregation."

Simon gently cleared his throat. "I take it you can recall no specific conversations then."

"No . . ." Mr. Dougal frowned. "There is one thing. It may be nothing, but I did note it. He had an appointment with someone after hours. It was the reason he dined early."

"Do you know whom the appointment was with?" asked Kitty with new enthusiasm.

"I'm afraid not. He didn't say." Mr. Dougal's face was open and honest and reflected exactly what he was thinking. He looked as if he regretted mentioning the occurrence. The room was too eager for details that might be irrelevant. "As I say, it might not be important."

"Or it might be very important," Amelia countered. "It might have been the last appointment Mr. Cross kept."

Mr. Dougal's breath hitched.

"Do you know if the appointment was with a man or a woman?" pressed Amelia.

Mr. Dougal sat silent for a moment, trying to recall the information. "A man," he finally revealed. "He referred to the person as *he*, but as I said, Lady Amesbury, Mr. Cross gave himself to the church wholeheartedly. He met with persons at all hours of the day. If they needed him, he was there. He did not keep usual hours."

The appointment might not have anything to do with Mr. Cross's demise; still, the meeting was too clandestine for Amelia's taste. The curate seemed to know everything that happened in the church, but he had no information on the appointment, the reason, or the man. Those details themselves made the appointment noteworthy, and she determined to find out the man's name inside that office. He might have information about Mr. Cross's last moments on earth.

When no one spoke for several seconds, Simon filled the silence with an appreciative nod. "Thank you for your time, Mr. Dougal. I'm sorry about Mr. Cross, truly sorry."

"You're welcome." Mr. Dougal stood, and the rest of the group followed.

"Yes, thank you," added Amelia. "If you think of anything else that might be of importance, please let me know."

"I will, and I'm sorry for your loss." Mr. Dougal replaced the hat on his large head and left.

When he was gone, they returned to the seating area, and Amelia drifted onto the couch as if in a daze. How could it be that Mr. Cross was gone—murdered? It didn't make sense, yet she must make sense of it. Her mind began considering the facts, starting and stopping several times when she could draw no conclusions. The loss was too overwhelming to comprehend.

Kitty joined her on the couch, placing an arm around her shoulders.

Amelia started, almost forgetting Kitty and Simon were there. "Oh . . . right. Thank you for coming. I think I need a moment. Feel free to see yourselves out."

"I wouldn't leave you in a hundred years." Simon was sitting across from her and leaned closer.

"Me neither," Kitty added. "Not in a thousand. You need a friend, and we are here."

Amelia was moved by their steadfastness. "I know you mean well, and you are both treasures—"

"No." Kitty was insistent. "You just lost a priest and friend. You will not go this alone—not this time. We will help you find out who killed Mr. Cross."

"I did not say—" she began.

"We know you too well." Simon reached for her hand. "You will not sleep until you do."

Amelia had never been as grateful for her friends as she was right now. They knew her mind went immediately to the murder. She needed to understand why Mr. Cross had left her a news clipping and if it had anything to do with his death. If it did, she had been entrusted to solve it.

MURDER IN MATRIMONY 31

"Let us go over what we know." Kitty sat up, placing her hands on her lap. "The police claim his death was a robbery gone awry."

"We know how often the Metropolitan Police are mistaken," Amelia mumbled.

Simon held up a finger. "Still, the poor box was gone, and the time of death was ten minutes to ten. It might have *been* a robbery."

"In Mayfair?" asked Kitty doubtfully.

"We only need look to the Mayfair Marauder to understand that bad things can and do happen in our part of town." Simon was obviously convinced of his logic and tried convincing them with the reasonable tone of his voice. "And what of this newspaper clipping? The timing seems rather significant."

Amelia pulled the clipping from the envelope. "Rose Rothschild. Age eighteen. She fell to her death off a ladder at Baker Biscuits two weeks ago. A sad accident, truly, but one of many cases of factory mishaps. I must be meant to investigate it—or the baker or the girl." She felt overwhelmed by the possibilities. "How am I to know?"

"You believe Mr. Cross wanted you to investigate the accident?" asked Simon.

"What else?" Amelia shrugged. "I do not know the girl personally, and I've never been to Baker Biscuits."

"They have wonderful biscuits," put in Kitty. "They mean to compete with Huntley & Palmers in Reading. They have a new partner with a head for business and money for expansion. They plan to relocate from their current storefront on Mill Street."

Huntley & Palmers was a popular baker located on the busy road from London to Bath. It had started as a small bakery in 1822 and expanded into a large factory that employed much of the town of Reading. Hundreds had relocated to work at the busy plant. Amelia couldn't imagine how a relatively new biscuit maker like Mr. Baker could compete with a company that now had a factory of five thousand square feet.

"Huntley & Palmers is serious competition." Simon tapped his chin, which, despite it being mid-afternoon, was growing dark with whiskers. "But it explains Baker Biscuits' recent advertisements. Perhaps they intend to make a biscuit town of their own right here in London."

"I saw the advertisements, too. Employees are required to work Monday through Saturday, sixty-eight hours a week." Amelia had gathered no small amount of information about factories and conditions. Most of it related to women and children, and she passed on the facts to her readers, who often seemed to have very few specifics of their own. She attempted to keep them as well informed as she could. "It isn't surprising, perhaps, with the long hours, that accidents are the norm. Factory girls are habitually underfed, overworked, and overheated." She exhaled a frustrated breath. "I feel bad about Miss Rothschild, of course. Still, it leaves the problem of Mr. Cross dead."

"And Margaret without an officiant," added Kitty.

Amelia glanced at Kitty. A matrimony beginning with murder was not a good omen.

FIVE

Dear Lady Agony,
Recently, a bride and groom did not attend their own wedding breakfast, instead taking a quick refreshment in private apartments before leaving for the honeymoon. I was surprised until it happened again. Is this to be the new practice? Please let us know your opinion on wedding day deserters.
Devotedly,
Wedding Day Deserters

Dear Wedding Day Deserters,
The practice has not been determined in poor taste, but it should be. I believe it is a dereliction of duties concerning hospitality and home. One attends a wedding to see the happy pair, not their appendages. It's my opinion the pair had better stay for the cake or risk offending the attendees. Besides, who doesn't enjoy cake?
Yours in Secret,
Lady Agony

Simon and Kitty left, and Amelia jotted off a note to Grady Armstrong, her childhood friend and editor of the paper by which she was employed. She asked him to meet her in Hyde Park after his workday with any information on Rose Rothschild and Mr. Cross. She doubted he would have any details on Mr. Cross's murder that Mr. Dougal hadn't given her already (it hadn't even been twenty-four hours), but it was a possibility. Grady always had his ear to the street for news, and crime was of great interest to the readers of the paper.

She slipped on her dowdiest brown linen paletot, which covered the bulk of her dress, in hopes of being discreet. She

34 MARY WINTERS

did not want her meeting with Grady noted, especially with the blackmailer possibly following her movements. The time was unpopular; that was of no concern. She did not worry about one of her set observing her conversation with a penny paper editor. Furthermore, their meeting place was so out of the way that they rarely encountered passersby.

She fetched a matching parasol. She didn't care for the fringes—her usual parasol was strong and sturdy and not brown—but in this instance, they proved beneficial. They provided several more inches of protection for her face.

Checking the looking glass, she was pleased with the effect. Her hair, auburn with a swirl of caramel brown, was disguised by the placement of a straw—and again, brown—bonnet. Her shape, which was curvier than popular taste, was nondescript under the large coat. She might have been any woman traveling anywhere, surely not a penny paper authoress and definitely not a countess.

Parasol in hand, Amelia tiptoed down the stairs, staying close to the wall. But even flat satin shoes were no match for Aunt Tabitha, who heard and called her into the informal drawing room. Tabitha often reviewed household accounts at the long rectangular desk, and today, she held a letter in her hand. She raised it into the air when Amelia crossed the threshold.

"Do you know what this is?" Tabitha asked.

A smart retort almost passed Amelia's lips, but a quick glance at Tabitha's face checked the comment. "I do not."

Tabitha stood, pressing herself up from the desk to her full height. Surrounded by the pretty gold and blue furniture that defined the comfortable space, Tabitha seemed a dark demigod in her long gray gown. Indeed, with the letter before her, she conjured the image of Poseidon wielding his trident over the vast ocean. Poseidon presided over the seas but also storms, and if Tabitha's face was to be trusted, a tempest was brewing ahead.

"This," said Tabitha, her voice all severity, "is a letter from your mother. She wanted to inform me that eight of your uncles will be in attendance, with their wives, except for Aunt Kate,

MURDER IN MATRIMONY   35

who twisted her ankle in a foot race." She slipped on her spectacles, reading from the letter. "Which is a shame since she and Amelia are one in the same and get along the best of all the relatives." She dropped the letter and stared at Amelia.

"Kate *is* my favorite aunt . . ."

Tabitha narrowed her eyes.

"Except you, of course." Amelia smiled.

"I am serious." Tabitha threw down her glasses. "That is fifteen guests for the wedding breakfast, not to mention your father's relatives, who, she states, are 'hoping for a peek' at the house."

Why her mother hadn't written to her, instead of Tabitha, was a mystery—for about half a second. Of course she must know planning a wedding breakfast was beyond Amelia's domestic talents. She was better at walking than planning. Still, she wished her mother would have had the good sense to route the information through her; she could have made it more palatable to Aunt Tabitha. She wasn't certain how, but she would have found a better way than a direct letter.

"If they have appetites like yours and your sister's, the household will need to prepare," continued Tabitha. "I cannot imagine the strain Cook will be under. I must find assistance for her immediately."

"It isn't as if we are an army, Aunt," Amelia said in her most soothing voice. "Just one small family from Somerset."

Tabitha arched a gray eyebrow.

"The house is sufficient, money is abundant, and your connections are plentiful." Amelia smiled brightly. "The wedding is going to be wonderful." *Without Mr. Cross? How could it ever be wonderful without him presiding?* A flicker of sadness erased her smile.

Tabitha spotted it and descended like a bird of prey. "What is the matter?"

"I have bad news, very sad news indeed from the curate. You might have seen him come in earlier?" Amelia recollected the conversation. "Mr. Cross has died. He was murdered in the vicarage last evening. The police believe it was a robber after the poor box."

Tabitha closed her eyes for a moment, and when she reopened them, they looked much gentler, the type of kind blue oases the Amesburys were known for. "I am sorry, Amelia. I know how much you cared for him."

"Thank you, Aunt." Amelia released a breath. "I appreciate that."

"What is to be done for a new officiant?"

"I will see about it tomorrow. There is always the curate." Amelia swallowed. "Or Mr. Penroy." Mr. Penroy was new to the church, too new, in Amelia's opinion. Old vicars she could tolerate, but young priests very rarely. Mr. Cross had harkened to the old church, the Roman church Tabitha would say, but Amelia preferred the old ways over Penroy's fire and brimstone.

"Let us hope it does not come to that," said Tabitha. "Best secure the curate if possible."

"I will try."

"Time is the issue." Tabitha sighed. "All of this might be managed if we had six months instead of two weeks."

"In the meantime, if there is anything I can do to help with the breakfast . . ."

"There is not." Tabitha smoothed her dark dress and sat down. "See to the wedding ceremony—and rid yourself of that brown hat. It's too dreadful, even for you."

Amelia left with a frown. She knew the bonnet was ugly but dreadful? At least it served its purpose of concealing her face. With a blackmailer in her business, she couldn't be too careful. An ugly hat was a small price to pay for anonymity.

A dozen minutes later, she crossed Hyde Park Corner, passing under the Triumphal Arch. Grady was to meet her at their special spot, a bench tucked next to an oversized plane tree, far away from onlookers and pedestrians. It was deep into the park, but she was used to walking and arrived on time, glancing around to make certain no one had followed her.

They hadn't, and perhaps it didn't matter anyway. The black-mailer claimed to know her identity. Whether he or she followed her might be of little consequence. Unless the blackmailer was considering pressuring her friends and acquaintances for the identity of the Mayfair Marauder. Then it would be of grave consequence.

Grady was her oldest and dearest friend. They had grown up together in Somerset, scheming and dreaming and planning their futures. She didn't have any brothers—only sisters—and he had the job, if not by birth, then proximity. When he was nine years old, he began working in the stables at the Feathered Nest, Amelia's family's inn. He fed and watered horses in need of a rest on the route to London. For years, Grady and Amelia had watched travelers come and go, vowing one day to go, too.

They'd made good on their promise, Grady leaving as soon as he had saved enough money and Amelia as soon as Edgar offered for her hand. Life had taken them on different paths and then brought them back together after Edgar's death. Grady needed an author, and Amelia needed a way to spend her time.

And what a way it had turned out to be. In the long days after Edgar's death, she spent her time thinking about her readers' problems and ways to alleviate them. Her life had purpose, and it had meaning. She found her voice in those days, a voice she hadn't known existed. Soon her role as Lady Agony became as important as her role as Lady Amesbury, more so because she was expressing herself in a way she hadn't before.

The last few months, however, had brought the two roles closer together, and she had to wonder if she had essentially written herself into the person she wanted to be: courageous, forthright, bold, even. Or perhaps the recent murders had made her brave. They involved people she cared about, and she realized what was worth fighting for.

A footstep on the dry grass drew her gaze upward, and she noted Grady's approach. She smiled at her oldest friend, and he smiled back. His shoulders were slightly curved, and his oversized coat hung loosely on his frame. As he approached, she saw his fingertips were smudged with ink, as they always were, and he smelled of it too, that and newsprint.

Grady sat down beside her, took off his cap, and swiped at his dingy blond hair before replacing it. "You send for me, and

I drop everything. If you weren't my favorite author, I might protest."

Amelia recognized the weariness in his voice and regretted her request. "I shouldn't have asked you to come after a long day. I should have waited."

"You're not good at waiting. You do not have the patience for it."

"You're correct, I suppose," she agreed. "I don't. But my impatience has often served me well."

He lifted his shaggy eyebrows, not completely believing her.

She moved on to the topic at hand. The sooner they discussed it, the sooner he could go home and get some rest. "What do you know of Mr. Cross's murder? Have you heard anything at the paper?"

"And so begins another investigation before my trousers have had a chance to wrinkle." Grady slapped his thighs. "What does this murder have to do with you, may I ask?"

"Your trousers are already wrinkled, and it has everything to do with me. Mr. Cross left me a news clipping." Amelia took the paper from her reticule. "He asked the curate to give it to me, personally, on the day of his death. I haven't figured out what I am meant to do with it."

Grady glanced at the clipping. "This is the woman you mentioned in your note."

Amelia nodded.

"I don't know anything about her death beyond what's stated here. What I do know is this." Grady ticked off information on his stubby fingertips. "She lived in Wapping, which was a prized area of your vicar's. Her father owns a pub there, where she used to wait tables. She had worked at the biscuit factory only a month when the accident occurred. Nothing unusual about her death. People fall off ladders all the time, and this one went from the ground floor bake room to the second floor packaging room—quite a height, to be sure."

Amelia didn't hear anything in his account that would signal Mr. Cross's involvement, except Wapping. The poor East End district was an area of concern for him. He was appalled by the working conditions the populace suffered, not to mention the crime and filth that filled the streets. Children and adolescents were of particular worry for him. Young girls and boys kept long hours for little pay, and regulations were practically nonexistent. When he'd heard of a candlemaker keeping children until eleven in the evening, only to return at six the next morning, he reached out to Amelia, asking her to address the abuse in her Lady Agony column. She did so immediately, and the factory came under investigation a fortnight later.

Amelia stared at the newspaper clipping. "I've written about several unfair employers in the column. Some of them in Wapping."

"True." He gave her a lopsided grin. "Many bad eggs have been excoriated by your pen."

"Am I to root out a bad egg here?" She let out a frustrated sigh. "If that is what Mr. Cross intended, I will, but not until I find his murderer."

"Perhaps they are connected." Lines appeared between Grady's eyebrows, making him look more serious. To Amelia, he would always be a boy, connected to green grass and Somerset, but work had taken its toll on him, and it showed now in his concern.

"Perhaps, but I have no way of knowing yet." She changed subjects to the other one she needed to discuss with him. "Simon came to me about the blackmailer. He said it was irresponsible to quote the letter in the column. He was not happy with my decision."

Grady snorted. "What does the marquis know about blackmail?"

He knew more than Grady suspected. Simon himself had been blackmailed with information about his sister's relationship with a known gambler. And what had he done in that instance? Almost exactly what Amelia had done. He had refused to bargain with the blackmailer and instead threatened to retaliate.

Recalling this instance made her feel better about her decision, and her shoulders lowered a little. "Nonetheless, I hope our actions come to fruition. Will you let me know the moment you hear something?"

"Of course." He pulled his hat farther down on his forehead. "The blackmailer is the first and last thought of my workday."

"And if details become available regarding Mr. Cross's murder—"

"You will know them immediately," Grady assured her. "The inquest date is surely coming." He stood. "Until then, be safe, Amelia—and patient. Don't go looking for information where there is none."

She stood also. "You be safe as well. As my editor, you are guilty by association. Be extra mindful until we know if the blackmailer has further intentions."

He nodded his agreement and was off, leaving her to stare after his coattails. It was not in her nature to do nothing, but in this instance, waiting was her only option.

The idea never seemed so hateful.

SIX

Dear Lady Agony,
The size of London ensures many beggars and
destitutes. It is impossible to go about one's day without
encountering a man, woman, or child with a hand
stretched out in earnestness or deception. I avoid certain
streets, and they crop up on others. Avoidance is not the
answer. Do you have another?
Devotedly,
Daily Detours

Dear Daily Detours,
You are right. Avoidance is not the answer. The poor
are not problems; they are people. Until the residents of
London recognize it, poverty will reign in our town.
Solutions are not easy, but you might start by looking
into the state of your neighborhood and visiting the poor
in your parish. Much good can be done without being
deceived by professional beggars. Your help will be
appreciated. Be sure of it.
Yours in Secret,
Lady Agony

The following day couldn't arrive soon enough, and Amelia lingered only until mid-morning before striking out for All Saints on Margaret Street. While she had to wait for more information about Mr. Cross's murder, she could not wait to make new arrangements for her sister's wedding. They must be decided immediately if the date was not to change, and Madge was adamant that it mustn't. With the family invited and Aunt Tabitha involved, Amelia was almost as resolute as Madge. To have the ceremony and reception completed fast, functionally, and fashionably was her utmost wish.

Her sister was counting on her; indeed, the entire Scott family was. For that matter, so was Captain Fitz. He had been a comfort to Madge during her recovery, and Amelia did not want to disappoint him. Violence and crime were unfortunately part of life in London, and despite Mr. Cross's death being devastating to her, it was a fact of city life for many. Beggars, professional and otherwise, terrorized the town, and theft—while less frequent in Mayfair—was not unheard of. Large houses did not have the power to make poverty disappear. They could only shelter the people who lived in them from seeing it.

Despite the drab sky, a light mist clinging to everything it touched, the walk to All Saints was refreshing. Several droplets evaded Amelia's trusty parasol, and the wind swirled them up to her cheeks and eyelashes. Amelia enjoyed exercise, and while her morning tea helped with alertness, it didn't awaken her limbs the way a walk did. With each step, her shoulders grew straighter, thrust back with purpose. She might not be able to solve Mr. Cross's murder yet, but she could certainly secure an officiant—and reel in one slightly out of control wedding.

She proceeded inside the church, which was warm and dry and a nice change from the drizzle outdoors. The church had always been a place of refuge for her and others, but now it was hard not to visualize the violence that had occurred next door in the vicarage. Surrounded by solid stone that invoked medieval times, she felt it impossible that Mr. Cross was harmed in this place. Yet anything might be possible if someone was determined enough.

The knowledge brought a quiver up her spine.

"Lady Amesbury, I thought I might see you soon."

The quiver turned into a chill. "Mr. Penroy."

Mr. Penroy was young with shiny brown hair and a sloping nose that always seemed to be pointed downward. His face was smooth, without a single whisker above his thin lips, and his eyes were the color of dirt in need of water after a long drought. "I've learned your sister is to be married at the end of the month?"

"That's correct. Mr. Cross, bless him, was to perform the ceremony." Amelia was unable to mask a new wave of sadness that had overcome her in the church, and she stumbled over his name. "I cannot believe he is gone."

"Though it pains me to say it, I am not completely surprised at his violent end. He was a favorite of the poor and criminal, and I find one is defined by the company one keeps." He sniffed. "I warned him about Wapping. There is no curing what ails some areas."

"But mustn't he try? Wasn't it his duty?" The questions came out too defensively, but she was unable to stop them.

"Our duty is to perform the work of God." The word resounded in the nave.

Feed the hungry, clothe the naked, harbor the harborless. Amelia knew Mr. Penroy wasn't thinking of the corporal works of mercy. He was thinking of his own ambitions, which had nothing to do with the poor or downtrodden. "Have the police shared any information about his death?"

"Only that it must have been a vagrant, perhaps one who followed him from Wapping. The poor box is gone." He shook his head. "Money is the root of much evil."

Easily said by someone who has money.

Still, it raised a question in her mind. If the vagrant lived in Wapping, it would have made more sense for him or her to kill Cross in that area, where crime ran rampant. The deed wouldn't have been as noticed as it was in Mayfair. Then again, the poor box might not suffice in that neighborhood, or perhaps the church didn't keep one. She'd never been to St. George-in-the-East and made a vow to go as soon as time allowed. First, however, she must secure the details of her sister's wedding at this church.

"I pray the police find the criminal and bring him to justice, as I'm sure, do you." She glanced around the nave. "Until then, I'd hoped to speak with the curate. He has the details about my sister's ceremony, which I hope may still proceed."

"It is best you speak to me since I am to be the new vicar."

44 MARY WINTERS

Even though the promotion had come by violent means, Mr. Penroy was pleased with his new position. His lips turned up at the statement in a way they never did.

She forced herself to remain calm. Mr. Penroy was too severe to be a vicar—too everything, for her taste. He had been an assistant priest for a short while, yet he acted as if he had the life experiences to run the church. Certainly he had the will and motivation, but in Amelia's opinion, it took more than willpower to make a positive change. "My sister's wedding—"

"Shall be performed by me," Mr. Penroy finished.

"Oh." Amelia swallowed her disappointment and tried a smile. "Right, of course."

"I understand your sister and Captain Fitz were swift in their decision to marry." He tsked. "So many young people today make promises with little thought of the consequences." He said this as if he wasn't young himself, and the notion was ridiculous to Amelia. "Which is why I'd like to spend some time with the couple before the wedding, if I may. To be certain they are ready to commit to one another."

"My sister is preparing with my family in Somerset. She will not be back until the week of the wedding." She tried to keep the incredulity out of her voice. The idea of Mr. Penroy knowing whether a young couple could commit to one another, the wedding hanging on his word, was absurd.

"A few hours will suffice."

Amelia blinked. A few hours with Penroy would not end in a happy ceremony, but what was she to do? He wasn't exactly asking. He was telling her what must happen for the wedding to take place. *But Madge and Mr. Penroy together for hours of reflection? God help me.* It was truly in the Almighty's hands now. "I will inform her and Captain Fitz of your request."

"Let us make the arrangements while you are here." He stepped toward the vicarage, and she followed. "It will be one less task for the happy couple later, and as you said, she will be in Somerset until the wedding."

One good thing would come of the demand, and that was Amelia's entrance into the vicarage. She could use the

MURDER IN MATRIMONY

opportunity to inspect for clues to Mr. Cross's murder. The Metropolitan Police had decided upon the crime and criminal, and when they did, they forewent other possibilities. But Amelia hadn't. From the start, the location of Mr. Cross's murder hadn't made sense to her. Now she would have a firsthand look at the scene of the crime.

Mr. Dougal stood in the vestibule doorway, staring at nothing. His mind was somewhere else, perhaps on Mr. Cross, and he did not notice their approach. When Mr. Penroy said his name, he jerked his head. "Oh! I am sorry. Excuse me. It's Mrs., or rather, Lady Amesbury."

Amelia greeted him warmly, understanding his earlier statement about fumbling his words. When distraught, it might be easily done by anyone.

Mr. Penroy showed him no similar sympathy. He scowled, his nose seeming to grow longer. "We have no time for woolgathering, Dougal. I need Mr. Cross's schedule. We are behind already."

"Behind?" Mr. Dougal asked.

"Behind, yes." Mr. Penroy's voice was clipped, and the last word came out like a hiss. "We have a funeral and wedding to host, not to mention myriad tasks to complete that Cross deferred in favor of his Society for the Greater Good."

"Right." Mr. Dougal cast a furtive glance in Amelia's direction. "Of course. The schedule. It's in his office. On his desk." He took a step in that direction, and they followed.

Not only was Mr. Cross's office open, but it was in use. Mr. Penroy breezed inside as if he'd used it for two years instead of two days. He'd assumed Mr. Cross's role, and, although Amelia shouldn't, she had to wonder if it was by design.

Mr. Penroy had profited a position from Cross's death, and while Cross's belongings remained intact, a new stiffness permeated the room, a stiffness named Penroy. He owned these things now, possessed them. He perched on Cross's old chair as if he didn't want to soil his trousers, touching the papers in front of him lightly with his fingertips. "I have a great deal to sort out here, in due time. There has been no time to speak of yet. Cross was focused on making a name for himself in the East End and let matters lapse here." He thumbed a few errant papers. "Dougal, where is the calendar?"

Mr. Dougal opened and shut his mouth like a fish. "I suppose it might be, it could be, in the parish."

Mr. Penroy stood up, a stern look on his face, and Amelia had the idea Mr. Dougal was about to be scolded. "One moment, if you please."

Amelia nodded, biting her tongue. She wanted to defend Mr. Dougal, but their absence would give her the opportunity to peruse Mr. Cross's desk. A moment might be all she needed to gain a clue from the night of his death.

When it was silent, she glanced over her shoulder at the door, then back to Mr. Cross's desk. The smattering of papers closest to her concerned the Society for the Greater Good. Seven priests, according to the names on the paperwork, had pledged to help the poor and displaced not only in Wapping but in other poor areas of London. They convened every month at St. George-in-the-East.

A pen, a paperweight, a prayer request for a parishioner. A tin of his favorite treats. Amelia saw nothing of consequence. Her eyes lifted from the desk, to where the clock had once graced the mantel. Now an empty space met her glance. She perused the rest of the fireplace for clues to the altercation. Near the hearth was a statue. She rose and went to it, bending down to examine the nameplate. St. Anthony of Padua, the patron of the poor. It didn't surprise her that he kept it in his office. His work, his passion, involved the poor. She examined the fireplace box, littered with ash, checking the stone for stains, but she saw no blood or other marks that revealed clues to Mr. Cross's murder. If she didn't know the story, she would have assumed the clock fell to the floor and had been taken away for repair. If only that had been the case . . .

"Lady Amesbury, what are you doing?"

She glanced at the door.

The new vicar had returned and was waiting for an answer.

SEVEN

Dear Lady Agony,
* I am sorry you are being blackmailed. One would think a woman who took up an honest cause and defended it with her pen would be praised, not terrorized. But it is always the case, I'm afraid. People have a good deal of morals until a situation affects them. Then all bets are off.*
* Devotedly,*
* People Are Petty*

Dear People Are Petty,
* Thank you for your kind note. I have received many like it and would like to take a moment to thank my readers for their support. People can indeed be petty, but they can also be generous. You are certainly one of the latter.*
* Yours in Secret,*
* Lady Agony*

Amelia had no excuse to give Penroy, so she told him the truth. She was drawn to the empty spot on the mantel, where the clock had once sat. If his frown was any indication, he was dismayed by her curiosity. He stated that the Metropolitan Police had taken it into evidence, which was unfortunate. It was a nice timepiece, and Mr. Cross would have not approved of the waste. On that, he and Amelia agreed. Mr. Cross was considerate and frugal. He once told her he couldn't abide indulging in excess when others had so little. He loved books yet would not spend a farthing on a new one because of their high cost. He and the other priests had so much already. It was one of the reasons he had created the Society for the Greater Good. With the abject poverty in London, a stark

48 MARY WINTERS

contrast to their own lifestyles in Mayfair and other posh parishes, how could they not work toward a solution to the problem? To Mr. Cross, the solution was better wages, better working conditions, better lives for the poor. Amelia wondered what would happen to the society now that Cross was gone. Would they continue his work? She asked Mr. Penroy.

"I could not say." Penroy took a seat at the desk, and she returned to the chair across from him. "I am too occupied with the needs of *this* church. Mr. Cross spread himself thin, too thin, in my opinion. I have been dealing with the daily business of All Saints for some time. It is a new church, and it has not been easy."

She hadn't thought of the situation from Penroy's perspective, and she felt an inkling of empathy for the man. The church was newly built, the members newly installed. Cost and debt alone would take considerable effort. Penroy would be left to manage affairs in Cross's absence. And from the sounds of it, Mr. Cross had been gone a good deal. She would find out how much when she visited the East End church.

Penroy thumbed through the pages of the newly retrieved calendar. "Speaking of business, let us get to the business of your sister's wedding. What date do you suggest before the ceremony?"

Amelia leaned over the desk, hoping for a glimpse into the small notebook. It was brown and battered and something that might have been carried in Cross's jacket pocket. "May I ask if Scotland Yard reviewed this appointment book?"

"Yes, they did." Mr. Penroy removed his hand, and the notebook folded shut automatically. "However, they didn't find anything of use. Cross met with his fair share of thieves and addicts, but rarely did they make appointments, if you understand."

She did. His appointments were restricted to church people and patrons. But what of the man the curate mentioned? Was the after-hours appointment written down? "Did he have any appointments scheduled at the end of the day?"

Mr. Penroy flipped to the date of the murder. "He had the evening marked off, as if he had plans outside the church, but

MURDER IN MATRIMONY 49

Mr. Dougal said he was in the office when he left." He flashed her a peek at the booklet. The evening hours were struck through with an X.

Amelia squinted at the mark. "Mr. Dougal mentioned an evening appointment. Do you know whom he might have met with?"

"I do not. What I do know is that he was preoccupied with the poor in the East End. If he met with someone after hours, it was probably one of them. He'd made quite a name for himself over there. Even the bishop knew of his work, which perhaps isn't surprising since Cross was always asking for more money."

Cross's purpose wasn't fame. Amelia knew it as well as she knew her favorite pen.

However, Mr. Penroy continued before she could argue. "He thought the poor needed his help more than the residents of Mayfair. He met with vagrants at all hours—after long days, long nights, long absences from the church. But the faithful need inspiration, too. Neither can survive without inspiration. People such as yourself need just as much help as the downtrodden."

Amelia felt vaguely insulted.

He smiled. "Now then, let us have the date."

Thirty minutes later, Amelia returned home. She had just entered the morning room when she heard the voice of Grady Armstrong. She frowned, wondering what brought him all the way from Bond Street during the middle of his busy workday. Perhaps he had discovered more information on the Rothschilds or Mr. Cross. Curious, she did not wait for Jones to seat him. She went straight to the entry.

"Mr. Armstrong," Amelia said with a smile. "This is a surprise."

Grady handed Jones his hat, and as he did, she noted the furrow on his brow. Something was wrong. He had forgone his lunch to tell her whatever he was about to share, and from the worry lines on his face, it was not positive news.

"Mr. Armstrong must be famished," Amelia continued smoothly. "Please have tea sent to the library. Tell Cook we have a visitor."

50 MARY WINTERS

"Yes, my lady." Jones nodded and was off.

Grady followed her silently into the library. She glanced backward a few times, only to realize he wouldn't be uttering a syllable until they were in private.

"Goodness, Grady." She shut the door. "We've dealt with our fair share of thieves, murderers, and thugs. No need for you to pull that face on me now."

"This arrived today." He wordlessly retrieved a letter from his inside coat pocket. "I brought it over directly."

Amelia met him in the middle of the room, glancing at the paper. "The blackmailer."

"Yes."

She perused the block letters, so familiar to her eyes now. The handwriting was indistinguishable. The author could be a man a woman or a child. The person had gone to great lengths to disguise his or her penmanship, writing in uppercase letters.

Dear Lady Agony,

You were foolish to publish my letter. If you repeat the mistake, I will make sure you pay the ultimate price. I know your schedule, I know your identity, and I will upset both if you do not act.

Print the name of the Mayfair Marauder without delay. This is the last time I will ask nicely.

Sincerely,

A Concerned Citizen

"It isn't good, Amelia." Grady returned the letter to his coat pocket.

Amelia took a seat on the green leather couch and gestured for him to join her.

He took the chair across from her. "You won't want to hear this, but I think it's time to reveal the name of the Mayfair Marauder."

"I cannot do that."

"What other choice to you have?" he continued steadily. "It's his name or yours, and quite frankly, he did commit a crime. If anyone should pay, it is he."

"You cannot be serious." Amelia shook her head in disbelief. "We've never cowed to readers' outbursts before. Why would we now?"

"This is different." His Adam's apple bobbed in a nervous swallow. "The blackmailer seeks revenge. People like that will not quit until they have it." He leaned closer. "You must protect what is yours, Amelia. Your home, your livelihood. Winifred."

Of the three, the last gave her chills. Winifred and her future must be cared for. Amelia had promised Edgar, and even if she hadn't, Winifred was the person she loved most in this world. She could not have any harm brought to her. But did the blackmailer actually know who she was? To date, she had no evidence to confirm it. The letters were not sent to her home. They were sent to the journal. The person might be vindictive but also harmless.

"I made a promise—"

"I know, and I also know how seriously you take your promises." His brown eyes searched hers with desperation. "But you cannot take a chance. *We* cannot take a chance. I won't allow you to."

Grady did not know the name of the thief. Only she and Simon knew it was Lord Drake. But from the look in his eye, if it was up to him, he would reveal the name straightaway.

"Lord Bainbridge, my lady." Jones barely had the name out of his mouth before Simon joined them in the room. Amelia expected him this afternoon, and his early arrival was not ideal.

"Mr. Armstrong." Simon took a seat next to Amelia on the couch, the leather squeaking as he sat down. "How good to see you—again."

"Lord Bainbridge. Always a pleasure."

"The tea, Jones?" Amelia inquired.

"Will be right in." Jones shut the door behind him.

Simon seemed ready to make another quip about Grady's frequent visits when Grady preempted him with an unlikely remark. "I'm glad you're here." He reached again for his inner coat pocket. "We've just received another letter from the blackmailer."

Amelia stared open-mouthed at Grady. *Of all the churlish*

behaviors. He was trying to force her hand by including Simon in what was effectively their business. Her business, if she was to be completely accurate.

"May I have a look?" asked Simon in a conciliatory tone.

Amelia continued to stare as he read the letter, watching for any reaction.

"The answer is obvious to me." Simon returned the paper to Grady. "She must confess the name of the Mayfair Marauder."

Grady's face slackened with relief. "I told her the very same."

"It is clear that the person knows who she is and will have his revenge," continued Simon. "It's only a matter of time."

"I agree."

"I'm glad we do." Simon looked at Amelia. "When will you reveal the name?"

Amelia calmly smoothed her dress. "Never."

A maid entered with a hefty tea tray. "Here we are!"

The three of them watched her place the tea things on the table. Amelia was grateful for the assortment of sandwiches and cakes, especially considering it wasn't the traditional time for tea. Cook was considerate when it came to male guests, however. She had three sons of her own and knew how hungry men could be at the noon hour.

Perhaps sensing the tension in the room, the maid glanced tentatively at Amelia. "Shall I pour?"

"No, thank you. I'll take it from here."

When the maid was gone, Amelia poured three cups of tea. "Sugar?"

"No." The word was a curse in Simon's mouth.

"I'd like sugar." Grady selected three sandwiches. "And milk, please."

"Milk, Lord Bainbridge?"

"You know I take it black," Simon spat.

"Do I?" Amelia tilted her head. "I'm not good with domestic details."

"You will reveal the name of the thief, Amelia. Grady and I agree it's the right thing to do."

"It is *my* column. It is *my* decision." Never had Amelia felt so passionate or possessive about her work. It was her work alone. Who were these men to tell her how to do it? Of course they cared for her, and she cared for them, but she did not tell them how to do their jobs, and she preferred they offered her the same respect.

"And if the blackmailer comes after you?" Simon set down the tea she offered.

"That is a risk I'm willing to take."

"I am not," said Simon. "I know his identity, and I am willing to reveal it."

"You wouldn't!" Amelia gasped.

"I could and would if it meant preventing harm to you or your family." He was as obstinate in his words as she had been in hers. "Frankly, I'm surprised you wouldn't do the same."

"I would do anything for my family. You know that. But the blackmailer might not even know my identity. When I know for certain, I'll act."

"You'll reveal the name of the Mayfair Marauder, you mean?" Grady clarified.

"I'll act on the best interest of everyone involved," she stated. "Until then, I ask for your patience on the matter. We won't print the letter. Silence at least will pacify the blackmailer."

"For now," answered Grady. "But not forever." He drank his tea.

To Simon's credit, he did not answer. He studied her like a mathematical equation that was just beyond his calculation. He didn't understand her loyalty to Lord Drake; perhaps he was even envious of it. She and Lord Drake were bound by their shared experience and sorrow. They'd both watched their loved ones battle diseases, Lord Drake longer than Amelia. She could only guess how hard it was for him to see his father suffer, enduring the arduous work of watching a person fight an illness that was as cruel as any war. Unless one had been through it, one couldn't imagine the feeling of helplessness. In war, one might retaliate with a gun or knife. But against a disease that took a person from his loved one day by day? It was an invisible enemy fought in the dark.

"Have you any updates on Mr. Cross?" Amelia asked, switching topics.

"Word is the police are combing the East End for a thief or beggar who did the deed." Grady held up his empty cup, and Amelia refilled it. "They suspect one of his connections from Wapping. A lot of bad men live in that area."

"A lot of good, too." Amelia wasn't sure why she felt defensive. Maybe it was because she knew how much it meant to Mr. Cross and how hard he'd worked there. He talked often about the good he was doing and how many were changing their ways. He was convinced that all they needed was someone to care about them, to show interest. He had, and it made a difference.

"Tell that to the altar server who was hit with an orange during one of Mr. Cross's visits." Grady set down his teacup and reached for a piece of Victoria cake. "The congregation was so angry at Mr. Cross for getting in their business, they threw fruit at him during the service."

"Fruit?" Amelia questioned. "That sounds fairly harmless."

"It hit an altar boy, who needed new spectacles." Grady searched the tray for one more piece of cake. "When Cross returned the next week, they threw rocks, and St. George-in-the-East was closed for a day because of a broken window." He settled on one and took a bite.

"Not exactly harmless, if you ask me," put in Simon.

It sounded as if Mr. Cross had overstepped his authority, which was surprising, in a way, considering how mild he was in Mayfair. He rarely said anything that might be considered controversial. He preached about the poor, yes, but the congregation was accustomed to that. They expected it, even. Mr. Cross wanted and needed money for the poor in the East End, and he drew up a collection regularly. Many of the women in the congregation volunteered to help those in need.

Which gave Amelia an idea. She'd been considering how she might gain access to the parishioners of St. George-in-the-East, and now she had it. When the time came, she and Kitty could volunteer. Many women participated in weekly or biweekly prayer meetings. If they approached the women with the idea of helping, they would surely be welcomed.

For now, she returned to Grady's information. The police

MURDER IN MATRIMONY 55

were combing the East End for a vagrant, and she wondered if they'd had any luck. She asked him.

"I'm afraid they don't have any solid suspects yet." Grady dusted sugar from his hands. "Police know of several professional thieves in Wapping, but their whereabouts could be accounted for—in the East End."

"It doesn't make sense to me." Amelia shook her head. "Why would anyone follow Mr. Cross all the way to Mayfair when they could have killed him in Wapping?"

"I think the answer is obvious," said Simon. "The poor box. What could be taken in Wapping that would be worth the same?"

If the purpose was money, more was to be had in Mayfair than any other part of town. Even Penroy thought money was the root of most evil. Mr. Cross might have talked of the abundance in his Mayfair church to the wrong person. If that was the case, the person might have been enticed to follow the priest across town. "Your point is well taken. If you are right, the murderer is someone close to St. George-in-the-East. I will need to visit the parish to determine if that is the case."

Grady put on his hat, which he had tucked between his knees. "Will you go today?"

"I can't." She frowned. "I have a dinner to attend. One of those long, ostentatious events that require several hours of preparation and many petticoats."

"Dreadful." Grady stood, and Amelia did the same. "Where at?"

"My house," Simon ground out.

Amelia gave Simon a playful wink before walking a chuckling Grady to the door.

EIGHT

Dear Lady Agony,

I am new to hosting dinner parties and would like to attempt a French dish. I can testify to its deliciousness, for I tasted it in Paris. The problem arises with my cook, who claims she does not know how to prepare it and will not attempt it. I think her attitude is incorrigible, but I cannot hire outside help. It is beyond my means to do so. What else am I to do?

Devotedly,
A Professed Francophile

Dear Professed Francophile,

Your cook's attitude is not incorrigible; it is absolutely correct. She should not attempt a dish with which she isn't familiar. You are new to hosting, but I can vouch for her rightness. I have attended many parties where a foreign dish is attempted and made inedible by inexperience. Therefore, do not assault your cook. Thank her for helping you avoid a colossal mistake.

Yours in Secret,
Lady Agony

Amelia might have teased Simon about the dinner party, but in truth, she was excited to attend this evening. It was the first gathering the Bainbridges had held since Lady Marielle had come out this season, and Amelia was looking forward to talking to her at length. According to Simon, the family had invited twelve guests, including one of Marielle's suitors, Lord Traber. Amelia had met him at her ball, and he appeared to be a fine gentleman. Time—and Simon—would tell if the couple advanced in their courtship. He was the

MURDER IN MATRIMONY 57

ever-watchful brother, and last time the two were together, it had ended with Simon stalking her gardens for evidence of a clandestine meeting. He found none but was still convinced of their secret retreat.

"Your style is improved, Amelia." Tabitha assessed her olive-colored gown as she descended the stairs. "I wonder if Simon Bainbridge has something to do with your recent choice." She raised a shapely gray eyebrow, but no criticism tinged her voice, and her lips pursed in a half-smile. She'd seemed to come to terms with Amelia and Simon spending time together as of late, even going so far as extending him an open invitation to dinner.

"More likely Kitty Hamsted. I find Lord Bainbridge's style rather plain, don't you?"

"Always clever, but you don't mistake my meaning." Jones helped Tabitha into her cloak, a rich black velvet with Hungarian cord trimming. "I'm pleased with tonight's invitation and cannot help but wonder if you haven't positively influenced Lord Bainbridge as well. I have seen changes in him—and the Bainbridge household—of which I approve."

Amelia shrugged wordlessly into a deep green cape, a shorter article she enjoyed wearing in the summer months. Her instinct was to rush to thank Tabitha, but she resisted. Tonight would be a first for the Bainbridges, and whether she had anything to do with it hardly mattered. Her own need for acceptance shouldn't be the focus. For if she was honest, she still saw herself as an outsider, and no matter how many times she told herself Edgar had chosen her for that reason, it didn't matter. Somewhere deep inside, she wanted to belong to a world she loved so much, a world that she still held at some distance because of the difference.

It was impossible to forget she and Simon were dissimilar in that way, and while he praised her uniqueness, sometimes she worried it would become an obstacle in their burgeoning relationship. At one time, Tabitha had thought it might, and no matter how much Amelia disagreed with her, she respected her opinion too much to dismiss it. Tabitha was a pillar of society and knew its peccadillos as well as Amelia did her daily letters. Still, Amelia felt warmed by her praise, basking in it all the way to the Bainbridges' home in Berkeley Square.

The Bainbridge drawing room was filled with elegant guests who, like Tabitha, appeared pleased to be invited by the illusive duke. Since his wife's death many years ago, Christopher Bainbridge had shut his doors to society only to open them many years later for his daughter's first season. Since Marielle Bainbridge's trouble with suitor George Davies, however, the duke had been much more considerate of her feelings. Indeed, the affair had led to a change in the household, one for the better, according to Simon. They were taking dinner together again, a tradition that had long been forgotten, and repairing the years of neglect one day at a time.

After being welcomed by His Grace, Amelia rushed to meet one guest in particular, Kitty Hamsted, who was dressed in a silk black-and-white gown with double-puffed sleeves and a bow at her waist that emphasized its smallness. At her wrist dangled a matching fan that, when used, drew attention to her periwinkle-blue eyes, the only color on her entire person. The effect was utterly striking.

Kitty invited her into her circle with a gracious smile. "Lady Amesbury, good evening."

"Good evening." Amelia dipped her chin. "Mrs. Hamsted, your dress is beyond compare."

"Isn't it?" said Lady Applegate, whose daughter, Constance, was also in attendance. It was her first season, and she and Marielle had become fast friends. "I hope by standing next to her, her elan will rub off on me." She covered a little snort with a plump hand. "My fashion choices have never been popular."

Amelia bit back a chuckle. Lady Applegate was not the most fashionable woman in the room, and in fact, probably the least, despite going to great lengths with her attire. She wore an expensive yellow gown that was more mustard than golden, and her usually pink cheeks, which were pretty and round, looked sallow. But her eyes were full of life, an aqua blue that made up for her dull complexion.

"Not true," said Kitty generously. "Your parties are very popular."

Kitty was being kind. They were popular, yes, but for their

unusualness. Lady Applegate had gone to the same great lengths with her house, and her yard was a menagerie of statues and fountains that didn't quite make sense. Every year the *ton* looked forward to a new lawn ornament, which she never failed to reveal before her yearly ball. It was very like an accident that one couldn't resist watching unfold.

Lady Applegate flourished a yellow-gloved hand. "It's my husband's family's ancient house. I can lay no claim to its beauty, although I have had a hand in the statuary, which, by the way, has gained a new resident. My husband intends to mention it at dinner."

"I heard yours was one of the homes burgled this spring by the Mayfair Marauder," put in Lady Catherine, who stood next to her. Her voice was nasal, and everything she said had a distasteful tone. "Dreadful business."

"Indeed." Lady Applegate's cheeks puffed with offense, looking less sallow. "We were ransacked by the scoundrel. Just imagine, a thief going through my things!" She put a hand to her ample chest.

The house was not ransacked. One piece of jewelry was taken, albeit an expensive piece. More importantly in Amelia's mind, it was returned. She made a pointed comment to this fact. "I thought the thief returned all the stolen items in a gallant gesture of apology."

"Hardly gallant, in my opinion." Lady Catherine sniffed, which emphasized the pointiness of her nose.

"I think it was incredibly gallant." The blonde curls above Kitty's ears shook with disagreement. "Stealing a jewel is one thing. The payoff is worth the risk. But to return a jewel without discovery? That took courage and selflessness. What obligation did the thief have to do so?"

Lord Applegate, who stood a few steps from his wife, had been listening and now joined the conversation. "Why, he was forced into it by that Lady Agony character. Have you heard of her?"

Kitty murmured a *yes*, and Amelia nodded noncommittally.

"Of course we have," said Lady Catherine. "She's made quite a name for herself."

"Not all good." Lady Applegate harrumphed.

"She ought to reveal his name. Those who have been burgled have a right to know who unlawfully entered their home." Lord Applegate, a heavy-set man with a blustery voice and untrimmed side whiskers, turned to Amelia. "Don't you agree, Lady Amesbury? Your house was one of those robbed. What's your opinion?"

Amelia counted to five before responding. She knew what she *should* say to protect her identity. Yes, the thief should absolutely be revealed. But the reply stuck in her throat, not quite wanting to come out. "I am pleased the jewel was returned. That's what matters to me. Had it not been, I might feel differently."

"Still," Lord Applegate continued, "any concerned citizen would appreciate being forewarned of the culprit. As they say, forewarned is forearmed."

Amelia's heartbeat doubled. Any *concerned citizen*? The blackmailer had signed his name A Concerned Citizen. Could the Applegates be the blackmailers? Was Lord Applegate testing her now?

"True," answered Amelia, studying his reaction while trying to mask her own. "Preparation is key in any crisis."

"Quite so." Lord Applegate looked pleased with her answer, his evening jacket stretching with self-satisfaction. "The authoress has obviously let her popularity go to her head. This is a matter for the Metropolitan Police, not a lady."

"If she is a lady, which I doubt." Lady Catherine slid a glance at Kitty. "I do not know of a peer among us who would give out such extraordinary advice."

Kitty's cheeks flushed with anger. She was not as comfortable as Amelia was with people criticizing her alter ego. "Perhaps not, but perhaps it is that advice which makes her so popular."

"Not for long if she keeps the name of the Mayfair Marauder to herself," Lady Applegate added. "I know of three people who have quit their subscriptions already."

The comment gave Amelia pause. Her dear friend Grady Armstrong relied on subscriptions to the paper. She knew

MURDER IN MATRIMONY 61

keeping the name to herself could affect her readership, and even her identity, but she hadn't thought about what it would mean for the magazine. If angered readers quit their subscriptions, it would affect Grady's profits.

"I do not have to quit because I don't subscribe." Lady Catherine put a hand on Lady Applegate's arm, and they shared a smile.

"You must find it difficult to know the contents of her column without a subscription." Kitty fluttered her long eyelashes, feigning ignorance, and Amelia bit back a chuckle.

"My staff are devoted readers." Lady Catherine dipped her chin. "As you can imagine, all the underclasses are. I pick it up now and again when I am bored."

Lady Applegate nodded in agreement as she did with everything Lady Catherine said. "Regardless, she should reveal the name. I personally will not sleep until she does."

Lord Applegate's barrel-shaped stomach expanded. "Nor I."

"Lady Amesbury." Entering the small group, Marielle Bainbridge affectionately reached for Amelia's hands. "I haven't had the chance to say good evening. How are you?"

Amelia smiled, the trouble with Lady Agony temporarily forgotten. Marielle looked entirely like her brother: black hair, green eyes, a Grecian nose. More striking than her looks was her commanding style, a confidence not usually seen at her young age. Amelia admired her independence and forthrightness. She felt entirely at ease with Marielle. In fact, the entire Bainbridge clan was beginning to feel like family. "Very well, Lady Marielle. And you and Lord Traber?"

"I am fine." Lady Marielle indicated Lord Traber with a toss of her head. "Lord Traber, however, is doing his best to survive a conversation akin to the Spanish Inquisition." She leaned in close. "Can you do something with my brother?"

Amelia followed her gaze to the pair. Simon had Lord Traber in the corner, where the young man was tugging on his cravat. His wheat-colored hair fell forward as he jerked on the collar, and he attempted to smooth it back with his hand. She returned to Marielle, who was frowning. They had grown close the last month, and Amelia hated to see her distressed. "I can try." She gave her what she hoped was an encouraging look. "Excuse me."

As Amelia approached the men, she noted the clipped tone of the words, *duty, honor,* and *loyalty.* Goodness! Was Simon having a conversation with Lord Traber or enlisting him in the Royal Navy? It would take all her charm—and luck—to dissuade him from the topic.

"Good evening, Lord Traber. Lord Bainbridge." Amelia tilted her head closer to Simon, hoping he would notice she was wearing his favorite rose perfume.

He did, inhaling briefly. "Lady Amesbury." He glanced appreciatively at her olive gown, which went well with her skin tone, a smile flickering on his lips.

She took a step closer to him so he could appreciate it further.

"Good evening, Lady Amesbury." Lord Traber took a slow breath as if he'd been treading water for some time and was now on dry land. "Lady Marielle has told me so much about you."

Amelia smiled. "Likewise."

"I feel as if we are friends already." Lord Traber seemed pleased with the new direction of the conversation, at least until Simon flashed a scowl at him. Then he looked young and unsure again, quickly dropping his gaze to the floor.

"Before I forget why I came over here, I noticed a family portrait in the gallery," said Amelia. "It must be new."

Simon was immediately interested. "Did you observe Marielle wore my mother's necklace for the sitting?"

"I did not. Would you mind showing me?" Amelia had noticed but thought this would be the perfect escape for the young Traber.

Simon frowned at Lord Traber.

"Oh, I don't mind. Go ahead." Lord Traber gestured to the door with eagerness. "Please."

Amelia gave Marielle, who was watching, a wink as she followed Simon out the door. Quickly, he turned the corner and walked to the portrait gallery.

"I hate to leave that fellow alone with my sister, but I'd like you to see this," Simon was saying.

MURDER IN MATRIMONY

"They are hardly alone. Gracious, Simon, there are twelve guests in attendance."

"Still, I don't like it."

"Will you like anyone who courts her?" Amelia asked.

He turned around. "Most likely not." He continued walking to the newly hung portrait of Marielle, his father, and himself. Marielle was positioned between them, and at the byzantine neckline of her white gown lay a stunning blue diamond. He flourished a hand at the portrait.

"It's beautiful, Simon. Truly. I am so happy for you and your family."

"I am as well." He took her hand. "And I have you to thank for it."

The Bainbridges had been through a lot: death, betrayal, murder. The turmoil had strained their bond exponentially. How could it not? The aftermath of Lady Bainbridge's passing left them bereft, and instead of leaning on each other for support in the difficult time, they dealt with it in their own separate ways. Isolation added to injury, deepening the divide. When Marielle began to court the once-manager of their stables, George Davies, problems compounded, eventually coming to a head when he was murdered. Thankfully, they resolved them—with a little help from Amelia. But the family had done the work of repairing their relationships. She had simply encouraged them. "It was nothing."

He grasped her other hand. "It was everything." He squeezed them. "You are everything."

It was the first sign of affection since his avowal in the park, and she blushed to know he still meant it. She had no reason to doubt it, but life had a habit of getting in the way of their relationship, and with Madge's wedding and Mr. Cross's murder, she worried there wouldn't be time for them.

For this.

He brushed her cheek with his lips, lingering near her ear to breathe in her perfume. He murmured his appreciation, and his words were quiet and breathy.

She was smiling—and then she wasn't. His lips were upon hers, warm, willing, and passionate. He cupped her face as gently as a summer breeze. Her shoulders relaxed, and she felt herself grow closer to him, his wide chest supporting her. A moan echoed, and she was not sure if it was hers or his. All she knew was that it felt like two puzzle pieces, coming together perfectly, made for this purpose, and she never wanted to be apart again.

Somewhere, it felt like a hundred miles away, a bell rang, the lightest chime floating through their kiss. She pulled back. "Simon, it's the dinner bell."

He pulled her close again. "Let it ring."

NINE

Dear Lady Agony,

Women in crinolines can take no comfort in social outings: no dinner table, ballroom, or box can accommodate ourselves and our families. Walking next to another is almost impossible. And the garden? It must be forgone altogether lest we chop off the heads of our favorite flowers. This does not even touch on the personal damage the crinoline has wreaked. Those casualties are brought up in the paper as commonly as musicals or comedies. What is the solution?

Devotedly,

The Crinoline Conundrum

Dear The Crinoline Conundrum,

I see only one solution, and that is women must stop wearing the cursed undergarment. The hoops of the past century were scorned and ridiculed. So must be done of the crinoline—often and publicly. Just yesterday, I read of a nine-year-old girl whose crinoline caught fire when she stood too near the fireplace. She died before the fires could be extinguished. Was there universal outrage? Was it decried on the front-page news? No. It was quietly mentioned on page six. It is one thing if you, ladies, want to risk health for fashion, but in the name of Jove, do not put your child in this firetrap. I implore you. Stop this insanity at once.

Yours in Secret,

Lady Agony

The dinner party had been a success—or at least the kiss had been. Truly, Amelia couldn't remember anything else, and if she found out the lamb had been overdone and the pudding burned, she would be completely staggered.

What she recalled was Simon's devotion. They were inseparable the rest of the evening, trading bits of conversation and stealing glances whenever they could. It was the respite she needed from weddings and murders, and she awoke the next day feeling refreshed, revitalized, and ready to tackle her problems anew.

It was market day at Petticoat Lane, a street in the East End where it was often said a woman could have her petticoat stolen at one end and sold back to her at the other. Despite the jest, Amelia infinitely preferred petticoats to crinolines. They required half the space—and risk.

Market day was always chaotic, and she had less of a chance of being detected in the crowd than any other day. So as soon as her daily rituals were completed and the family were involved in their own tasks, she stole away to pay a visit to Isaac Jakeman.

Isaac Jakeman owned a jewelry store near Petticoat Lane that operated as a front for his more lucrative endeavor: selling fenced jewels. He'd never mentioned the business himself, of course. She only discovered it when she and Madge went looking for the missing Amesbury diamond several weeks ago. The night had turned dangerous, and Mr. Jakeman had perhaps saved their lives. Since then, they had become acquaintances of sorts. Amelia appreciated having a connection to the East End, and he appreciated having a recommendation to her favorite modiste. Or his wife did, in any case.

Today, the East End street was notoriously chock-full. Known for its variety of leather goods, not to mention clothing and jewelry, the area was crowded with thrifty shoppers. Seedy fencers would replace them tonight, but for now, her driver carefully maneuvered around the clumps of people, looking for a place to stop.

As her carriage slowed, Amelia pulled the brim of her hat lower on her forehead. She'd paired it with a black walking dress she'd worn while in mourning and an oversized paletot that disguised its intricate beading. All her clothes were well made. They were the reason Isaac Jakeman didn't want her frequenting his store. She didn't fit in, and he didn't want his clientele getting nervous. But over the last month, they'd grown closer as associates if not friends. She glanced out the window as her carriage stopped near Wentworth Street. *I like to think of us as friends*. After all, they helped each other out, as friends did, when it was possible, or in Jakeman's case, profitable. Amelia hoped he would be able to shed light on Mr. Cross's murder or the Rothschild girl.

Jakeman might have information on one or both. He would certainly be aware of St. George-in-the-East, the riots in February, and Mr. Cross's volunteer efforts since. He would know how the people of Wapping perceived the new priest.

"Be careful, my lady." Bailey helped her descend the carriage steps. He was a large footman with broad shoulders, and he steadied her with one strong hand. More impressive than his size was his loyalty and respect. He never asked questions and did as he was told, which was true of most domestics. But Amelia was not most employers. She took clandestine walks, ill-advised carriage rides, and hair-raising detours. Nonetheless, he treated the situation as if it was another aboveboard day in Mayfair.

"Thank you, Bailey. I will." She craned her neck, glancing past the corner, to see if Isaac Jakeman's store was open. It was.

"And if you need anything—"

"You'll be three steps behind me." She gave him an appreciative smile.

He smiled back.

It was one of the compromises she'd made before she'd climbed into the carriage. If she wasn't taking Lettie, her lady's maid, or anyone else, he should really follow a few steps behind her—for appearance's sake. After all, it was the only way he could carry her packages if she bought something at the market. They both knew she wasn't going on a shopping excursion; however, Bailey was her ally and confidant. If he wanted to be a stone's throw from her, so be it. She trusted him enough to let him.

Isaac Jakeman was speaking with a customer inside his store. She would have known his hooked nose anywhere, but especially here, where he was bent over a piece of black velvet cloth displaying several loose gemstones. As if feeling her presence, he looked up, his long eyebrows extending past his small brown eyes. He folded the velvet square. The customer, a young man with darting eyes, cast a glance over his shoulder. Seeing her, he buttoned his coat and walked out the door, passing her without a word.

"Lady, you scare away my customers," Mr. Jakeman said after the door shut, but his voice held no malice.

"I don't see why. I am shopping the market, like any other woman."

He chuckled, a warm, full sound. "You are not any woman. Far from it." He lit a cigar and puffed easily on it. "So why are you here?"

Amelia was glad to get down to business and took the chair he proffered. "Mr. Cross was murdered three days ago. It was said he worked with the disadvantaged at St. George-in-the-East."

"The Society for the Greater Good." He blew out a stream of smoke. "I've heard of it."

"You have? Wonderful."

"Not wonderful, Lady. People did not like that priest. He stuck his nose in where it didn't belong, encouraging people he did not know to find their greater calling and some such nonsense." He lifted his eyebrows. "He, like you, should have stayed in Mayfair—where he belonged."

"I resent that. He did a lot of good in these parts, and to be honest, I've had a hand in a few positive results as well." She cleared her throat, feeling slightly embarrassed at her self-praise. She wasn't just being nosy; she cared about the people she inquired after.

"Positive results." He let out a long stream of smoke, reclining into his chair. "You have a funny way of talking."

She wished she could reveal who she really was: Lady Agony. Not some spoiled Mayfair lady of leisure. Then maybe he would realize with whom he was dealing. "Regardless, it sounds as if you might know who wanted him dead."

He lifted his chin at her. "What was he to you?"

"He was my priest." She swallowed. "And I liked him." The truth was she'd really liked him, and that was new. She was a woman of faith but not religion. As a child, she'd sat through

MURDER IN MATRIMONY

church waiting patiently for it to be over. The holy men had seemed as far away from her as heaven itself. But Mr. Cross was different. He cared more about people here on earth, including her.

If anyone had told her she'd reveal her secret pseudonym to only four people, one of them a priest, she would have never believed them. But she and Cross were connected by their mutual concerns, and she'd felt as if she could tell him anything, including her deepest secret. Had he lived, she would have told him about Simon and their blossoming relationship. He would have given her good advice, and as an authoress of advice herself, she knew how precious another's opinion could be.

"All right." He uncrossed his leg and sat up straight. "So you liked Cross. I understand. But even if I knew who hated him, what good could it do you? You are a lady. You have no business knowing such things."

"Maybe not, but I have this." She opened her reticule. "He left me a newspaper clipping. I want to know why and what it means."

He took the paper and read it. "The Rothschild girl. I remember that."

"You do?" Her voice sounded overly eager, and she smoothed her skirt, effecting nonchalance.

"She had a good job with her papa at the Plate & Bottle. What better employer than family, right? But your priest preaches about the ill effects of late nights and the liquor one Sunday, and the girl gets work with Baker Biscuits. Next thing you know, she falls off a ladder and dies." He stubbed out his cigar. "A cautionary tale?" He shrugged. "I don't know. But I do know the priest should have kept to Mayfair, like I said. If he had, the girl might be alive today."

The comment caught her off guard. Was Isaac Jakeman right? Was the clipping meant as a cautionary tale about sticking one's nose in where it didn't belong, as she herself so often did? Was that why Mr. Cross left it for her? Perhaps he himself felt guilt or remorse over his actions. Maybe he wished he wouldn't have gotten involved in a world so different from his own—and wished the same for her.

She twisted in her chair. It could not be. He was active in the East End until the day of his death. It had to mean something else.

"You do not agree?" he prodded.

"In truth, I don't know. I hadn't considered the idea before now." She sighed. "It feels as if I'm missing something. Do you know that feeling?"

"No, I don't. I don't miss nothing."

She gave him a wry smile. "Where is this Plate & Bottle?"

"Nowhere you know, Lady. A public house in the East End is no place for you." He nodded toward the window. "Even with your man outside."

Amelia followed his gaze. Bailey looked away, perhaps embarrassed that he was caught looking in on her. She smiled. "Point taken. Where does the Rothschild family reside then?"

"Above the same pub."

Amelia murmured a sound of displeasure.

Isaac Jakeman held up a finger. "But her mother is devout. A frequent visitor of St. George-in-the-East."

"Are you a member?"

He shook his head. "I only know what goes on there. It is my job to know."

"Hmm, yes." Amelia tucked the newspaper clipping into her reticule. "How did your wife's gown turn out?" She had recommended her modiste when he and his wife attended a large party thrown by a textile manufacturer, and he'd been appreciative of her help.

His small eyes widened with his smile. "She thought it very beautiful. It had puffy sleeves and the, the . . ." He motioned to his stomach. "Big skirt. It was nice. Pretty color, also."

Amelia stood. "Glad to hear it. If she needs anything else, please let me know."

"You are kind to me, and I am kind to you."

She held out her hand. "I enjoy how that works. Don't you?"

He shook it. "Indeed, I do."

TEN

Dear Lady Agony,

So many discuss clothing in this column. I wonder what they think about surplice? It is said the vestment was the reason for the riots at St. George-in-the-East in February. Thousands of parishioners took offense to the priest's wearing of the garment and hooted, hollered, and swore during the service. Some said the rioters should have been banished. Others said the rector should have been removed for disobeying the wishes of his flock. If anyone could imagine a white robe causing so many problems, I believe it is you. What is your opinion?

Devotedly,
Sinners, Saints, and Surplice

Dear Sinners, Saints, and Surplice,

Clothing is not always clothing. It is often an outward sign of our prejudices or values. Such was the case earlier in the year at St. George-in-the-East. The rector wore his vestments in obedience of his orders and was castigated for it by raucous churchgoers. The precedent was disastrous and dangerous. The next time an article of clothing is noticed, I hope readers ask themselves why before reacting. It might not be your fashion sensibilities but something deeper causing your reaction.

Yours in Secret,
Lady Agony

Upon leaving Petticoat Lane, Amelia pointed her driver toward St. George-in-the-East. It was only a mile away, and she hated to risk another outing on what could turn out to be a wasted trip. Besides, it was safer to stop in daylight than nightfall, when rioters might be present. The church, built in the 1700s, was a stalwart of Wapping, an unchanged building in a world full of industrial changes. From the south, she could see the four pepper-pot-shaped turrets as well as the tall western tower. Stone, strong, steadfast—these were the words that came to Amelia's mind as she gazed upon the outward edifice.

Inwardly, though, the church was undergoing a transformation, and Mr. Cross had been part of it. He took up the work where the previous priest had left off, unable to continue due to an illness many thought was caused by constant strain. Some parishioners felt ostracized; others felt seen. Regardless of their feelings, however, Mr. Cross welcomed them unequivocally. He gave help to the poor, offered advice to the downtrodden, and said prayers for everyone.

As Amelia entered the church, she knew he did not regret his time here. No matter what Isaac Jakeman said or how it made sense, she knew it could not be so. Standing in the nave, she *felt* his passion. He cared about this place. He loved this place. It was as strong as the scent of candle smoke that lingered in the air. She didn't have to see it to understand.

The church was quiet now, the morning crowds dispersed. An old woman bent over a back pew, her lips moving silently in prayer. A man, perhaps without a home, closed his eyes in another pew, using it as a makeshift bed. A priest pretended not to see him as he snuffed out the last candles at the altar, walking past him with his eyes cast downward.

"Excuse me?" Amelia said.

The priest smiled. "May I help you?"

Amelia realized he was older than she'd assumed. Yet his face had none of the hard lines of age, and his eyes showed eagerness to assist her. "I hope so. I am Lady Amesbury. I'm here because of Mr. Cross. I attend church at All Saints in Mayfair."

The priest lowered the gold candle snuffer. "Such a tragedy. I could hardly believe the news." He shook his head. "I'm Mr. James, the rector here."

"It's good to meet you."

He extended his arm as if to shake her hand and then

MURDER IN MATRIMONY 73

remembered he still held the candle snuffer. "Walk with me? I need to return this."

Amelia followed his short, energetic steps.

"How long did you know Mr. Cross?" he asked.

"Two years," she answered.

"I knew him only four months." He tucked away the snuffer in an antechamber of the church. "But I enjoyed his company and respected his stalwart commitment. He recruited me for the Society for the Greater Good. I admit I was honored. He did not mind that we served different communities. In fact, he sought out my advice for its difference." He shut the closet door. "Remarkable, if you ask me." He motioned toward an office. "Not everyone values diverse opinions."

"I understand the church is undergoing some changes." Amelia took a seat at a small wooden desk.

"That is a polite way of putting it. People in Wapping don't want religion; they want miracles." He chuckled, taking a seat as well. "Now, how may I help you?"

"It's about a parish family, the Rothschilds? I wonder if you know anything about them."

He leaned forward. "You know Miss Rothschild died in a terrible accident?"

"Yes, I do." Amelia liked how easy the man was to talk to. He didn't put on airs, and he wasn't intimidating. His face was open and inquisitive, and he seemed genuinely interested in talking to her. It was no wonder Mr. Cross recruited him for the society.

"Then you know she fell off a ladder after taking a position to get out of the public house her father owns. Some say the accident was punishment, for putting herself above her family."

"Did her family say that?" Amelia wondered if it was in fact retribution for not staying in her place. She couldn't imagine a family member hurting another in that way but was not naïve. Families came in all shapes and sizes, and she didn't believe every family operated as the Scotts or Amesburys did. It was a known truth that people often hurt the ones closest to them.

His sandy-colored eyebrows peaked with curiosity at the

question. "Her mother was glad she got work outside the neighborhood. She herself has been with the public house since the day her husband opened it many years ago. It's not surprising she wanted a different life for her daughter. She is a virtuous woman who maintains a weekly prayer group even among the late tumult."

"What about Miss Rothschild's father?"

The rector shook his head. "He did not see it quite the same way. He had to hire a girl to wait tables, and she was not as efficient as Rose. A selfish complaint but perhaps a valid one." He clasped his hands in front of himself on the desk. "I have to ask, though, what does any of this have to do with Mr. Cross?"

Amelia didn't know how to answer. In truth, she didn't have the answer herself. Mr. Cross had left her Rose Rothschild's obituary, so her death must be important. But what did it have to do with Mr. Cross or his own murder? It could be a clue or an errant message or nothing at all. Further complicating the matter was Amelia's own secret identity. She couldn't let on that she did investigative work under an alter ego. "I'm not sure what her death has to do with Mr. Cross. I know Miss Rothschild was a recent worry of his. I thought it might be relevant to bringing his murderer to justice."

"I take your point." Mr. James tapped his fingertips together. "But I heard it was a thief after the poor box?"

"That's what's been reported," answered Amelia evenly.

"You believe the reports are wrong?"

"I believe the Metropolitan Police report what they see in front of them. A vicar with a questionable following in the East End and a missing poor box." She shrugged. "It's the easiest answer. I've found, however, that the easiest answer isn't always the correct answer."

"Quite true." His brow lifted in surprise. "But a lady doesn't concern herself with such things . . . does she?"

"Society presumes what young ladies—and rectors—concern themselves with, but we know better."

He smiled, revealing a brightness in his eyes. It was the light of passion and vigor, an enthusiasm for life that hadn't been

MURDER IN MATRIMONY   75

dimmed by difficult experiences or turmoil. Amelia suspected that even when he grew to be an old man, Mr. James would know the precious gift that was life.

She returned the smile. "Do you know where I could find Mrs. Rothschild?"

"As I mentioned, she meets weekly, on Monday, with her prayer group." The smile faded from his face. "The Society for the Greater Good is meeting that night also. We are holding a special assembly. Mr. Cross would want his work to continue, and it must. They cannot win."

"They?" Amelia noted the new determination in his voice, and she understood that while his passion made him eager, it also made him resilient. He believed nothing was beyond his capabilities if he only tried hard enough.

"The evil doers," Mr. James said. "The people who do not want his work to succeed."

"Are there many of them?" Too late, Amelia realized the ignorance of her words and wished she could take them back.

"Observe, and you will see. Factories, docks, pubs, warehouses, brothels. It would be better for business if residents did as they have always done. Work, drink, and prostitute themselves." He leaned forward. "They are many who despised the work Cross did—and the work I do."

The importance and gravity of the priests' work became clearer. She had read about the riots at St. George-in-the-East. Of course she had. At the time, she had a vague understanding of the disagreement. Now she realized a war had been waged against the East End, and the East End had retaliated in kind. It was much deeper than clothes or cassocks. It struck at poverty, depravity, and livelihoods. "I appreciate the work you're doing, and I hope someday, parishioners will as well. Obviously, some, like Mrs. Rothschild, do already."

He acknowledged the statement with a dip of his chin.

"Do you happen to know what time her prayer group convenes?" she continued.

He gave the time. Then his blue eyes crinkled mischievously, and he looked quite young. "Why? Are you in need of prayer, Lady Amesbury?"

"Always," she said with a smile.

"Let us pray now then."

After the prayer, Amelia walked to one of the church exits. She had a plan, and it felt good. On Monday, she would enlist Kitty to attend the meeting with her, and she would talk to Mrs. Rothschild about her daughter's accident. If the discussion supplied new leads, she would follow them. If not, she could put the incident behind her and focus on Cross's murder instead.

The church bells rang out, and she thought the timing was fortuitous, a sign that the inquiry was moving in the right direction. She understood very little of Mr. Cross's connection to the East End before today. Now she understood a good deal. With gratitude, she glanced up at the bells.

"Looking for the Almighty?"

The deep voice startled her out of her reverie, and she recognized it instantly. She scanned the area for Simon.

"I hope you were asking Him for safe passage home, because it's taking all my wherewithal not to pick you up and toss you into my carriage."

She turned around and saw him near the corner of the church. "Such words in front of God and everyone."

He came toward her like a lion released from his cage. "I mean every one of them. You're reckless, careless, hopeless—and irritating as hell. When I lost you on Petticoat Lane, I'd hoped you had returned home, which would have been the prudent thing to do. But I should have known better. I should have known you were capable of more mischief."

"Mischief?" She did not appreciate that he used the same word that Tabitha had used to describe Madge. "You overstate the circumstances. You are standing in front of one of the oldest churches in London. It isn't as if it's a brothel or pub."

"It might as well be. Parishioners riot and loot. They pummel their priests. What might they do to a young woman alone?"

"I am not alone." She pointed across the courtyard to her carriage. "I have Bailey."

"You are alone right now."

Indeed, she suddenly felt quite alone. The bells had stopped, and the city noise faded to a distant clamor. It was only she and Simon in the empty church courtyard. The instant recalled their seclusion last evening in the portrait gallery. Warmth crept into her cheeks as she remembered his mouth upon hers and his hands in unspeakable places. She closed her eyes, willing the memory away, and when she opened them, he was staring at her.

"I see you remember just how dangerous a moment alone can be."

She shook her head in frustration. "With *you*."

"You are never in danger with me." His eyes were sincere, and she regretted her cavalier comment. "I would never allow anything to happen to you, Amelia. It is the reason I want to be with you. Even here—especially here." He pointed to the church. "Why didn't you tell me you were coming?"

"Would have you said yes?" she asked.

"Of course I would have said yes." A small laugh escaped his lips. "Don't you know by now that I can deny you nothing? I would have thought last night proved it to you."

The memory of their kiss by the portrait gallery stirred up mixed emotions. He granted her physical needs, but what of her emotional needs? Did he understand why she was willing to put herself in peril for information on Mr. Cross's murder, and did he support her decision? "I thought you would try to dissuade me from coming. That is why I didn't tell you."

"Dissuade, perhaps. Deny—never." He grasped her hands. "Don't shut me out, Amelia. I know how important this is to you, and if it's important to you, it's important to me."

The empathic tone of his voice testified to its truth, and she returned the pressure of his hands in promise. "Then come with me tonight to the Plate & Bottle after the house is asleep. Mr. Rothschild owns it and, according to Mr. James, bartends. His daughter Rose worked there until she gained employment at Baker Biscuits. We might be able to glean something important about her accident."

"You cannot be seen in an East End tavern." His eyes widened, and the light made them the color of limes. "Think of the gossipmongers. Think of Tabitha."

No, she wouldn't be thinking of Tabitha. Thinking of Tabitha would only dissuade her from her goal. "We won't be dressed as ourselves. We'll be in disguise."

He tilted his head. "This isn't a game of charades, Amelia. This is your life we're talking about."

"And Mr. Cross's life was taken from him. He entrusted me with the information about Miss Rothschild, and you said if it's important to me, it's important to you."

"It *is* important," he admitted. "But you already have the problem of the blackmailer, not to mention your sister's wedding. Can't this wait?"

"You know it can't." She shook her head. "Every moment wasted gives the killer a better chance of getting away with murder."

He dipped his chin in acknowledgment, taking her arm as they crossed the road to her carriage. Bailey was waiting for her and opened the door. After assisting her up the stairs, Simon leaned in. "If you are determined to go, then so am I. Any place, any time. You must know I will be there."

ELEVEN

Dear Lady Agony,
 I was disappointed to read of your being blackmailed.
For shame! Has the dreadful person desisted?
 Devotedly,
 Dreadful Business

Dear Dreadful Business,
 Thank you for your kind words, and thanks to all who
have written letters of generous support. I need not tell
you how much they mean to me, but they do. Very much.
Again, thank you.
 Yours in Secret,
 Lady Agony

The evening crept by at a lethargic pace. Aunt Tabitha droned on about the wedding breakfast for an hour, and that only covered the topic of the three-tier cake and almond icing. Then it was on to meat: pork, lamb, and fowl. By the time they discussed wine, Amelia had drunk two glasses of her own.

In Amelia's opinion, which Tabitha did not share, the wedding should be a simple, happy send-off like the one she and Edgar enjoyed. People went to too much extravagance today. Heartfelt congratulations were all one really needed to celebrate the joyous day.

"Heartfelt congratulations—and ten joints of meat." Tabitha had tsked. "Really, Amelia, thank goodness I am planning the meal."

Eventually, Amelia escaped the conversation and put on her costume. She checked her reflection in the glass. She really did like herself with blonde hair. Tabitha was right; she was better at disguises than déjeuner. She enjoyed playacting as much as she had as a child at the Feathered Nest, where they put on weekly skits. Tonight, she was a gin enthusiast by the name of Polly, who liked nothing better than a tipple after a hard day of selling flowers. With her experience, she would slip into the Plate & Bottle without notice. But would Simon? That was the question.

As she stole down the servants' staircase, she wondered what he would be wearing. If he gave them away with a ridiculous top hat or silk cravat, she would be supremely unhappy. His kid gloves would be a tell of his wealth and finery. She should know. Isaac Jakeman had found her out by the same means. But she knew better now. No detail was too small to escape a criminal's notice. Underestimating them was a mistake she couldn't afford to repeat.

Amelia looked left and right. Few pedestrians dotted the area, and those she scanned easily. A man, a man, a man, a woman. She frowned. It wasn't like Simon to be late. Where was he?

"You make a fetching blonde, but I must admit, I prefer brunettes."

She spun around, facing Simon—who did not look like Simon at all but a pirate. His black hair was mussed, as if he was just thrown from a ship, and he wore an ordinary white shirt, open at his tan throat, and breeches with a tear at the knee.

She swallowed. Concentration was going to be harder than she thought. "Is that so? I rather like being a blonde."

"I hired a cab." He tipped his chin. "There, at the corner."

"A wise move." After they entered the cab, however, Amelia wondered how wise she was to enlist Simon in her latest plan to gather more information about the Rothschild family. Isolation sat between them like a loaded gun. They'd been alone together before, but always as themselves. These people they had created, these facades, had somehow done away with the decorum they had to follow. She was left with the shape of his throat, the swoop of his hair, and the cut of his breeches.

"I discovered the Plate & Bottle has been in operation for over a decade." Simon fastened his shirt cuffs, which were a bit too white to look well used. "Meals were once served there, but now it's a drinking establishment, well known by locals. It should provide a good mix of patrons."

"Good. Good." Amelia repeated the word because her mind was blank.

"Good?" Simon pressed. "Not, 'Where did you get the information?' or 'Who did you interview?' or 'Why did you not wait for me?'"

"Where did you get the information?"

He smiled, and she came undone a little. "I thought you'd never ask. I found it out by my valet. He's a bit of a roughneck, if you recall. I found him outside a gaming hall, selling oranges, and I hired him immediately. He knows all the seedy places in town. I don't know why I didn't think to inquire before."

"Did he know the Rothschilds?"

"He knew of Mr. Rothschild, the proprietor. Not personally, of course, but he said the man bartends most nights." He paused and then continued. "He thought well of him, though. I got that impression."

"Did he mention his wife?"

Simon shook his head.

"Rose?"

"No one else."

"Oh." Amelia let out a disappointed breath.

He frowned. "But still, the father. Open a decade."

"Yes, good work."

He preened in his seat. "Do you like my costume?"

"Very much."

"I imagine you are surprised I could pull it off." He had a look of smug satisfaction. "It is convincing?"

"Quite. You look like a pirate."

He leaned in, and she could swear she smelled salt water. "A pirate, Amelia?"

Amelia looked into his sea-green eyes, sighing at the sound of her name in his mouth. She'd dreamed of sailing away with a pirate since she was a little girl, and gazing into his rugged visage was perhaps the closest she'd ever been to achieving it. She swallowed, nodding silently.

"Forgive me." He raised his dark eyebrows into a crafty look. "I forgot how much you like pirates."

He was teasing her, but with one more moment in the cab, she would have shown him just how much she liked them. As it was, the driver announced their arrival near the Plate & Bottle, and she refocused on the gray East End street outside and their task at hand.

Despite the late hour, the street was crowded with people. A man flung open the door to the pub, narrowly missing a woman who sat near the entrance, waiting for her husband to get his fill. Seeing it was not him but another man, she dropped her eyes again, focusing on a fissure in the pavement. Simon walked past her and opened the door.

Amelia ignored her as well, but it was harder, she guessed, because she knew how much most women depended on men for their livelihood. Flower sellers, matchbook makers, serving classes, and even governesses could and did make money. But livelihoods were more than money. They were houses, businesses, and property that wives could not hold. If it seemed foolish to Amelia that a wife should wait outside a bar for a husband, she was wrong. It might be the only way a man returned home in the evening to pay the rent that supplied the roof over her head.

The single-room pub was dim, and Amelia was thankful for the bleak cover. A mirror above the bar reflected an oil lamp on a worn piano, and she and Simon sat down at a corner table, basking in its obscurity. Although dim, the pub was friendly, with casual conversation and laughter mingling. Patrons celebrated the end of the day with pints of ale gently sloshing out of their glasses as they roamed from bar to table.

Simon fetched them two pints, and Amelia took a small sip. Simon took a larger one and wiped his mouth with the back of his hand. She gleaned the hint and took a deeper drink, not displeased with the taste of it. Her wig was making her warm, and she was grateful for the cold ale.

The man at the next table chuckled and said, "Tough day, luv?"

"Indeed, it was," she answered in a thick Somerset accent.

MURDER IN MATRIMONY   83

"What day in't a hard one," Simon added convincingly. "But I ain't complaining. It could be worse. Look at Cross. Just killed this week."

"I reckon he went to hell just like the rest of us will." The man added in a low voice, "If the world has any justice at all, that is, and I ain't saying it does." He tipped his chin toward the bar. "Rothschild was a happy man once. Cross should have stayed out of his business."

"The old vicar got what he deserved." Simon took a long drink of his ale.

"Maybe. Maybe not. I ain't saying either way. I'm only saying a man, priest or no, should mind his own business."

Amelia thought the notion was ironic coming from someone who was speaking freely about someone's business with strangers. "I say he did get what he deserved. Little Rose might be alive today if it weren't for him."

"Some might say you're right." The man emptied his glass of ale. "And others might say she was dead anyway."

Simon leaned a large elbow onto the table, his head dipping. "What do you mean?"

"Milly Hines?"

"Who?" Simon asked.

The man's craggy face grew bored. "Mrs. Rothschild's friend who worked here."

"Right, Mrs. Hines." Amelia nodded evenly. She hoped she sounded like she knew whom she was talking about even though she hadn't heard the name before. "How many years ago was that now?"

"Oh Lord. Three years, I suppose? Knifed down after her shift by drunkards. Lost the use of her leg after that, then lost her husband, too. She relies on the charity of others now." The man shook his head. "No wonder Mrs. Rothschild turned devout. If I weren't who I was, I might too." He stood to get another pint of ale.

Simon and Amelia shared a look of surprise. *Mrs. Rothschild had a friend who was hurt at the pub.* After a long night of serving, the woman suffered an attack that changed the trajectory of her life. It was no wonder that Mr. Cross encouraged people to find other places of employment. Factories were dangerous but perhaps not as dangerous as the streets of East End London. It was hard to comprehend which one was worse, or if the two were even comparable.

The detail had Amelia doubting everything, including her ability to discern life outside of Mayfair. For all she knew, she was investigating the wrong pub, the wrong church, and the wrong people. She took a swig of ale.

"Careful. You'll get tipsy."

"I hope I do. This case has boggled me from start to finish. What I want to know is why Mr. Cross was murdered and by whom. Not all *this*." She indicated their surroundings.

"Mr. Cross was all *this*," said Simon. "This was his work."

Amelia didn't think she could feel any lower, but she did. Mr. Cross was his work, and his work was the East End. She knew that better than anyone, yet Simon had been the one to say it aloud. Every string she pulled unraveled another spool of thread she'd rather let alone. She had Miss Rothschild's death to investigate as well as Mr. Cross's. Now there was the damage done to Mrs. Hines.

Amelia took another drink.

"Chin up, Amelia." Simon swigged his ale. "You'll get this sorted out in that pretty head of yours. You always do."

She slid him a doubtful look, and he tweaked her cheek.

A broad-backed man with stubby fingers began to finger the keys of a broken pianoforte, the ale in his glass quivering as he steadily progressed. Despite the piano being out of tune, the sound was tinny and bright, and several patrons cheered him on.

When he got the notes to his liking, he cleared his throat and began to sing, "Come to the garden, Maud. For the black bat night has flown. Come to the garden, Maud. I am here at the gate alone. I am here at the gate alone." The song was not targeted at the imaginary Maud from Tennyson's poem but a real woman to his left, at whom he was lovingly batting his eyelashes. Whoever she was seemed to enjoy the attention and moved closer to the instrument with every refrain. Her actions garnered several whoops from the crowd, and she curtsied politely before joining him on the bench. When he was finished, she praised the performance with a kiss on his cheek, and he pretended to swoon. Then they both took turns at the pianoforte, their hands flying across the keys in a raucous polka.

A few chairs slid backward, and Amelia was surprised to find hers sliding back also. Behind her stood Simon, his hand proffered as if he was in a fine Mayfair ballroom. But when they began to dance, they acted as they never had in Mayfair. Perhaps it was the disguises, or perhaps it was the pub, or perhaps it was their own neglected desires. Whatever it was, no one would have recognized the couple by the swing of their hips or the laughter on their lips or the way their bodies met, warm and perspiring at the end of the song. Simon held her that way for a long moment, her chest heaving from the exercise and her mind buzzing from the ale or the turns or both. Then he kissed her, not the soft warm caresses she was used to. But a hot, short kiss that left her wondering who this pirate was—and how she had ever lived this long without him.

TWELVE

Dear Lady Agony,
   A new bonnet with false gemstones is gaining popularity. At first, I thought it surprising and a bit garish, but now I'm not so sure. It might be pretty. What is your opinion on the hat?
   Devotedly,
   Shiny and New

Dear Shiny and New,
   Personally, I have no use for a hat with false gemstones. I agree with the adage "Beauty unadorned is adorned the most." Simplicity can do no wrong; false gemstones, however, can do a good deal. My advice is to keep your distance from the new bonnet.
   Yours in Secret,
   Lady Agony

The next day, Amelia jotted off a note to Isaac Jakeman, inquiring about Milly Hines. Then she dove into readers' letters. She sorted them into piles: relationship advice, household advice, health advice, and social advice. Some days she wore many hats—and wrote about many hats— but topics of regularity were getting easier to respond to. For instance, the more times she told women to forget obsessing about men, the easier it became. Other topics, like household chores, remained a mystery to her. She understood their necessity, yes. She, like most people, did not enjoy living in disarray. But the extent of questions on how and how often baffled her. As long as the house looked reasonably presentable, what did it matter? More important to her were the people inside the household. If they were as well taken care of as the chores,

MURDER IN MATRIMONY

lives would be happier indeed—but perhaps letters to her less frequent.

When Jones told her Lord Drake was waiting in the drawing room, she was surprised to find it was already late morning. She had been answering letters for hours. She stretched as she stood from her desk, noticing her hands were dotted with ink. She wiped them off the best she could and then went up the flight of stairs, where Lord Drake stood at the window of her drawing room with some sort of magazine tucked under his arm.

Lord Drake turned around, and she noted he was dressed impeccably, as always. He wore a bright yellow waistcoat that showed off the cut of his well-tailored frock coat and cream-colored cravat. But his brown eyes were lined with concern, and his infamous dimple was nowhere to be seen. "Lord Drake."

"I apologize for the odd hour, Lady Amesbury. Thank you for agreeing to see me." His tone was tense, and he swallowed nervously. "I need to talk to you."

"Of course. Please, sit down."

Lord Drake sat on the chintz chair across from her, looking very unlike the notorious rake he was known to be. Amelia knew his reputation primarily kept the hungry mamas at bay, for his real interest was for a man in Cornwall. Lord Drake's father was ill, and Lord Drake was the sole heir to a prestigious dukedom that was centuries old, not to mention a residence in Cornwall that was famed for its size and history. However, Amelia knew how costly the entailment was and the lengths to which Lord Drake had gone to keep his dying father comfortable in their home. He had resorted to stealing jewelry from the wealthy in Mayfair with the idea of dismantling and selling it. She had found out his identity mere weeks ago when he had taken—and returned—the famed Amesbury diamond. Since then, they'd become fast friends.

"My crime has been discovered." Lord Drake spread the magazine onto his lap, pointing to a column in the left-hand corner. "This person says my identity is known with some certainty by a Lady Agony, and she must reveal my name immediately." He shook his head. "Do you know this Lady Agony? I must admit I'm out of touch with London gossip."

This was the difficult part of her job, lying to people she cared about. *Not lying*, she rationalized. *Just not telling the entire truth*. Of course Lord Drake was out of touch with London gossip. He'd spent most of his time in Cornwall with his ill father. It wouldn't take him long, however, to make the connection if he stayed in Mayfair. She knew his identity; Lady Agony knew his identity. With consideration, he might surmise they were one in the same person. "I do know of Lady Agony, yes. I follow her letters."

"And does she know who I am?" asked Lord Drake.

"She purports to." Amelia pointed to the paper on his lap. "May I?"

"Certainly."

She scanned the column, then flipped to the freshly printed front cover of an admired woman's domestic magazine. It was wildly popular for its editor, who was the gold standard of advice on domestic details, which is why Amelia was stunned to see a response to A Concerned Citizen in the column. Amelia would think the author was too busy with household hints to respond to crime. However, the authoress seemed quite invested and even agreed with A Concerned Citizen. Certainly, if a thief's name is known, it should be given to the Metropolitan Police. Any law-abiding citizen would agree, which suggested Lady Agony herself was not law abiding. *Insulting!* The authoress demanded Lady Agony reveal the name immediately. Anything else was an obstruction of the law.

Lord Drake wagged a finger at the paper. "It seems to me they are trying to force her hand, even going so far as to suggest her interference with justice. I do not want any ill will to come to this woman. If she indeed knows my secret, she deserves my thanks for keeping it."

Amelia smiled. The longer she knew Lord Drake, the more she liked him. His first thought wasn't for his crime or subsequent punishment but for a stranger. "If this person knew your or Lady Agony's identity, would they not take their complaints to the Metropolitan Police themselves?"

His brow puckered. "I take your point."

"Certainly, you do." She shut the magazine. "All columns

of this nature are known for their sensationalism. They need subscribers, and one way to lure them is with grandiose statements such as this."

"Still, A Concerned Citizen seeks revenge. In my experience, revenge is a dangerous motivator."

It was Amelia's experience as well. People didn't think or act rationally when their feelings had been hurt or their security had been threatened. The latter had been the case with A Concerned Citizen. In Amelia's opinion, the person was upset at Mayfair homes being entered without permission. Little did they know that Lord Drake, as one of the most eligible bachelors this season, had been extended an invitation to every home he'd thieved.

"Which is why I must turn myself in to the Metropolitan Police." Lord Drake took a deep breath, and the next words came out in a quick, steady stream of air. "It is the right thing to do, so do not try to dissuade me. I stole the items. I must pay for my crimes. It is the only solution."

"What of your ill father? He cannot manage alone." Amelia tossed the magazine aside. "Turning yourself in is not the solution."

"There is no other. I thought on it all morning, and this is the only answer that causes harm to no one but myself."

"It causes harm to your father, and you cannot allow that, and neither can I. I have a different plan. What if we find out who A Concerned Citizen is?" Lord Drake opened his mouth, as if to interrupt, and she continued more quickly. "As you stated, the person wants revenge, and it does no one in town any good to have a spiteful person such as that making threats. I could reach out to the person. Make certain whoever it is feels less anxious. It might prevent future violence."

"You would do that?" he asked.

"Of course I would." Amelia felt his surprise. Very few people in the upper echelons did something without gaining something in return. "As a victim of the thefts myself, I have an advantage that you don't. I can allow the person to voice their frustrations and empathize with them." Saying the words aloud revealed an idea. A Concerned Citizen might be concerned

90   MARY WINTERS

because they themselves had been a victim of the thefts. If so, their motive for revenge was clear. Amelia expressed the idea to Lord Drake.

"It's a reasonable idea, and one with limited possibilities. I committed five thefts this season. If what you propose is true, the letter writer has to be someone from those five families. Oh!" Lord Drake's brown eyes grew as round as two cups of coffee. "What of Lady Tabitha?" He put his hand to his mouth, half covering a gasp. "She's known for her unwillingness to compromise."

That was a nice way of putting it. Tabitha had a strong sense of justice that imbued all aspects of her life. She would not abide wrongness; it simply would not do. But spitefulness wasn't in her nature. Amelia couldn't reconcile the vengeful spirit of the letter writer with the aunt she knew and loved.

Furthermore, Tabitha would never threaten the Amesbury reputation by naming Amelia as Lady Agony, which, she supposed, could point to why the threats had come to nil. The threat itself may be enough for Amelia to stop writing under the pseudonym. Still, the idea was unfathomable. "I do not believe it is her, but living in the same house, I can easily confirm the fact. I'll check her name off the list first and foremost. Then we can move on to the other possibilities, which include . . ."

Lord Drake ticked off the thefts on one hand. "Lord and Lady Applegate, Lord and Lady Hamsted, Mr. Timmons, and his neighbors, Mr. and Mrs. Heigh."

"Lord Applegate said something the other night at Lord Bainbridge's dinner party that might be of interest." Amelia thought back to the moment in the drawing room before dinner. "He was discussing the thefts and used the words 'concerned citizen.' It may be nothing, but it may be he is the concerned citizen who wrote this letter."

"It is worth checking into." Lord Drake buttoned his coat and stood. "After you make certain it is not Lady Tabitha, that is. I would rather jump in the Thames than have it be her."

"You and me both," Amelia muttered.

After he left, she walked to Aunt Tabitha's study, which amounted to an antechamber connected to her bedroom. After a late breakfast, Tabitha either wrote letters at her exquisite mahogany writing desk or took a short nap. Amelia paused, listening for the tell-tale scratch of her pen. It always reminded Amelia of a painter's knife on a canvas. Hearing nothing, Amelia continued to her bedroom door. A soft snore greeted her ear. Tabitha was indeed napping.

Amelia took a breath and returned to the study, placing a hand on the door handle. She checked the hall for servants, but there were none to be seen, their morning chores being finished hours ago. She turned the knob and pushed open the door, ducking inside the room.

Despite being in her own house, Amelia felt her chest began to heave. She felt like a sinner in church, trespassing on hallowed ground. The mahogany desk was as stunning as she remembered, and she felt a pang of jealousy bolt through her chest. Whereas some women loved beautiful gowns, shoes, and jewels, Amelia loved large desks, broad pen strokes, and lined linen paper. She laid a hand on the wood grain. *Gorgeous.*

Determined not to dally, Amelia opened the lid. Six dovetail drawers were shut neatly, unlike her own desk drawers, which were half open with to-do lists, reminders, and penny postage stamps, not to mention the occasional ribbon from Winifred's hair or a chocolate wrapper from her favorite bonbon. Amelia opened the first and second drawers, finding staff allowances and Christmas gift ideas. *Gracious! It's only Summer.* The third contained menus. The fourth and fifth drawers held household expenses, indoor and outdoor respectively. Running a home was work, and Amelia respected the time and effort Tabitha gave to the family.

She quickly opened the last drawer and, finding nothing of interest, turned to the large panel beneath the writing area. Ivory paper and the sweet smell of roses greeted her. She inhaled deeply. Nothing to smell here but flowers and paper and . . . was that a calling card? Amelia shuffled the paper to one side for a better look. Her hand started to sweat the moment she touched the card. *Thomas Huxbey, Superintendent of Scotland Yard.* What was Tabitha doing with the calling card of a superintendent?

Anxiously, Amelia glanced about the room, looking for copies of penny papers, convinced she would find them stuffed into a corner. What greeted her was a towering Ming vase, a chair and reading lamp, and a small table with a portrait of Tabitha's dear brothers. Amelia shook her head. Her imagination was running amuck, and she tried to rein it in. The only time she'd seen a penny paper in the house was when Winifred's friend Bee lifted it from the servants in her house. *Although* . . . Amelia tapped her chin. Tabitha did seem to know the goings-on in the column. She'd mentioned the trouble between Lady Agony and a few male readers not that long ago. Was it possible that she was A Concerned Citizen?

Movement from the adjoining bedroom prevented further consideration. Amelia quickly shut the desk and ducked out of the room, continuing to her own bedroom on the same floor. She needed space—and time—to think this through. When the door was shut, she proceeded to the bed and sat down, perplexed. She stared at the birds etched in the canopy bedstead. *Sing to me the answers if you please.* Silence assured her they were not real, no matter the lengths the artist went to make them appear lifelike. She would have to find answers all on her own.

She pondered the likelihood of Tabitha knowing her secret pseudonym. Letters came and went from the house all day every day. She met with the editor of a popular penny paper, Grady Armstrong, quite frequently, sometimes in her house, but most times in the nearby park. And despite being a countess, Amelia was no lady, not in the aristocratic sense. Tabitha had tutored and mentored and lectured, but try as she might, Amelia still didn't fit in. Eccentric advice such as that in the column was not only possible but probable from a woman like Amelia.

Amelia put her hands over her face. The evidence was more damning than she ever considered. The question was no longer if Tabitha knew she was Lady Agony but if the entire household knew. She should have been more careful. She should have been more discreet. She shouldn't have begun writing in the first place.

No.

She stood.

Writing was her passion. Readers were her people. She did good work, and she would continue even if her name was given to one and all. The vehemence with which she believed this shocked her, and her chest filled with air and something else. The work had come to matter that much, so much that it couldn't be separated from who she was—who she'd always wanted to be. She was just a girl from Somerset, a rural community with rural ideas, and writing freed her from them. On the page, she could be anyone. An aunt, a wife, a mother. The person you would turn to in a calamity if that person existed in your life. She wanted to continue to be that person, and come hell or high water—or Aunt Tabitha—she would not give up.

THIRTEEN

Dear Lady Agony,
    I am in need of a new handkerchief. What is the most popular design? So many styles abound. I cannot decide which I like best.
    Devotedly,
    Handkerchief Heyday

Dear Handkerchief Heyday,
    It is indeed the heyday of the handkerchief, with options for every man, woman, and child. Colored embroidery is a great favorite right now. Scarlet thread on white cloth is popular with not only handkerchiefs but cuffs and collars. I recommend you try it for elegant results.
    Yours in Secret,
    Lady Agony

A melia had been on edge all day and decided it was because she'd worked through her morning walk. So out she went to relieve her anxieties. The noise of the city was salve for her soul, and she absorbed its energy through the pores of her skin. The energy turned into thinking, and she realized she held more facts to the mystery of A Concerned Citizen than anyone else, which should make it easier to unravel. She couldn't assume Tabitha was the blackmailer because she had the superintendent's business card in her desk. Instead, she would find out what business Tabitha had with the superintendent.

One possibility was Tabitha's friend, Lady Sutherland. When Madge was suspected of murder, Lady Sutherland contacted an acquaintance at Scotland Yard. It was how they'd found out about Detective Collings's resentment for Edgar. The card might have been obtained then.

Only, Amelia didn't recognize the name. During the ordeal, she and Tabitha had shared every nugget of information with each other in hopes of clearing Madge's—and by association, the Amesburys'—name. One would think that if Aunt Tabitha had the name of a superintendent, she might have mentioned it during the investigation.

She would ask Tabitha about the contact at the Yard, casually, of course, but quickly. After ensuring Tabitha was not A Concerned Citizen, she would move on to more viable possibilities. Lord Drake would not have to turn himself in to the police to solve the problem after she solved it for them.

Behind her, the sun broke free from dense clouds, its rays stretching toward the quiet grasses that lay beyond bustling Hyde Park Corner. She paused to watch the park go from hazy to light green, her breath catching at the sight of the wide-open space unfurling before her. She wasn't so far removed from Somerset that she couldn't appreciate green grass and room to roam. The wind, which was surprisingly gusty this afternoon, scattered plane tree leaves into the air, and the scene reminded her of her childhood and those long afternoons that made up her days.

Back then, she and her sisters enjoyed the activities nature provided them: walks, horse races, picnics. One of her favorite pastimes included long walks to their favorite swimming hole. Her mother never failed to bring lemonade and fancy cakes, and her father always remembered his violin. Far from the eyes of town, Madge would accompany him with a voice that would make morning larks jealous. Afterwards, she would be the first to jump into the pond, soaking Penelope and whomever else dangled their feet into the water's edge. Amelia looked forward to the excuse to jump in after her, splashing her in kind. After several reciprocal splashes, they would climb out of the water and sun themselves on a warm blanket, dozing while their mother read poetry by Shelley or Byron or psalms from the Bible. Amelia thought nothing in her imagination, even heaven itself, could equal those happy days with her family.

The sound of horses' hooves interrupted her reverie, and she wheeled around to see a hansom cab boring down on her. For a moment, she thought the horses were spooked, out of control, but then she saw the whip of the driver high in the air. The cab was moving so fast that she could not make out his face, which was hidden by the low position of his bowler hat.

"Look out!" cried a man on the street.

Only then was Amelia shaken out of her trance. She stumbled backward, the cab narrowly missing her. The person inside the cab turned to glance backward, their face half covered by a handkerchief or cloth. As the cab made a corner, however, the gusty wind caught the cloth, tearing it from the person's grasp. The white fabric twisted in the air before floating down, down to the street, where it stopped moving and started again. Amelia spun to race after it.

"Miss." Someone touched her arm. "Are you all right?" It was the man who had hollered out the warning. His face was craggy with deep wrinkles, and his concerned eyes scanned her for harm.

"Yes, thank you." She glanced at the cloth bouncing along the road. "I have to see about that handkerchief." Then she was racing down Piccadilly, determined to fetch the cloth. Had it not been so white or the street so dirty, she might have lost track of it a few times on her chase. As it was, however, she was able to keep eyes on it as she followed it from Piccadilly to Down Street, where it caught on a wrought-iron post. She heaved a breath as she reached for the cloth, which was indeed a handkerchief, albeit one with a smudge from the post.

She took several small breaths, the magnitude of the event now catching up with her. As she glanced at the material, she noticed her hands were shaking. She pressed the cloth against her chest, forcing herself to take deeper breaths. Never had she been so close to physical peril. Never had she been taken so unaware.

After a particularly deep breath, she looked down, noting the hankie was fine linen, something she might see a man or woman carrying in Belgravia or Mayfair. The embroidery at the corners depicted a man in a fishing boat in various states of catching a fish. The stitching was fine and white and different than the darker colors most men carried. It surely belonged to a woman. Still, she could also understand how it would appeal to a man as well.

Her stomach rumbled, and she told herself she was shaking because of hunger, not distress. She tucked the handkerchief safely away in her pocket and began walking home. A strong cup of tea and a sweet piece of cake always made her feel better. It was late, and she was disoriented. She'd been wool-gathering when the phantom cab came out of nowhere.

Except she knew what she'd seen: a person watching her from a hidden position. Had their intent been to scare her, they had achieved their objective. The blackmailer was the first person to come to mind.

But the blackmailer's identity was anyone's guess.

When she returned home, she went straight to the drawing room and loaded a plate with two scones and a tartlet as large as her fist—then stared at it. Even Cook's fresh raspberry jam wasn't appealing. She brushed at a few stray crumbs and sipped her tea. It was only her nerves. They would go away with enough tea.

"There is a sight I don't see every day." Tabitha pointed her cane. "A full plate of food in front of you. What is the matter?"

"I don't seem to be hungry."

Tabitha stared at her for a moment, then walked over and put a hand on Amelia's forehead. "No temperature." She selected the chair next to her. "Are you ill?"

"No." Amelia picked up her fork and poked at her scone with serious effort. "Might a woman not be hungry?"

"A woman, yes." Tabitha glanced up from her freshly poured tea. "You, no."

Amelia took a bite and regretted it. She washed the scone down with a sip of tea and changed the subject. Now was as good a time as any to quiz Tabitha on the card she found in her study. "Have you heard from Lady Sutherland lately? How has she been?"

Tabitha stared at her with interested blue eyes. "Lady Sutherland?"

98 MARY WINTERS

"After her help with Madge, I never had the opportunity to inquire."

"She was a good deal of help." Tabitha added sugar to her tea. "If not for her, I would have never known about Collings's hatred for our dear Edgar."

"We owe Lady Sutherland our eternal gratitude for the information." Amelia meant every word, and her chin tipped with earnestness as she said them. When Madge was being investigated after the death of Mr. Radcliffe, Lady Sutherland talked to a person at Scotland Yard who told her a great deal about the vindictive Detective Collings. Collings had been in the Royal Navy with Edgar before taking a position with Scotland Yard, and they both applied for a promotion. Edgar received the commendation, and Collings was convinced he did so because of his family's title, but it wasn't the case. At the time, Edgar's older brother was alive and was in line to inherit the earldom. Edgar never planned on being anything but a retired seaman from the Royal Navy. Collings eventually quit and took up a government position at Scotland Yard. When the Amesburys' ballroom was the site of a murder, he saw his chance to enact revenge, attempting to involve Madge in the process.

But Tabitha and Amelia had put a stop to his plans. Amelia wished there was some way to put a stop to his career. "Collings was a menace to us and greater society. He should not be under the employ of Scotland Yard, in my opinion."

"Mine as well." Tabitha stirred her tea gently, as she had taught Amelia to do, without disturbing the teacup. "Which is why I spoke to his superior."

Amelia sat up straighter. "Who?"

"Thomas Huxbey, Superintendent of Scotland Yard."

Ah!

"I met him in person last week." Tabitha put down her spoon. "An admirable man, my age and not a day younger. Smart and, if I may say, in ridiculously good health. Doesn't look a day over sixty."

"Good health, hmm?" Amelia felt the corners of her mouth flick upward. She'd never heard Tabitha compliment a man in the two-plus years they'd lived together. Something about the way Tabitha revealed the detail told Amelia her aunt admired him exceedingly.

Tabitha lowered her lids enough to indicate her impatience. "If I may continue . . . he promised me that Collings would be dealt with, and a man such as he does not go back on his word."

"Do you mean Collings will be released from his position at Scotland Yard?"

"I mean exactly that." Tabitha sipped her tea.

"*Gracious.*" Amelia was glad to see him go. Furthermore, she was glad Aunt Tabitha had a reason for having the superintendent's card in her desk drawer. She was not A Concerned Citizen, not that Amelia really thought she ever was. Still, Amelia could move on to her next suspect with confidence.

"If my suspicions are correct, and they usually are, our spiteful Detective Collings has left the force already," said Tabitha. "Just in time for the arrival of your relatives."

Amelia smiled despite her upset stomach.

"Do you know I've had a letter from one of your aunts?"

Amelia closed her eyes briefly, shaking her head.

"It is from Henrietta, but 'please call me Hen.'" Tabitha put her teacup down with a plunk. "As if she doesn't have a last name at all. Hen requires a carriage for her and her four sons, whom she describes as strapping. She understands cousins haven't been invited, but since her husband cannot attend, she'd like to be allowed an exception. *Four* men instead of one."

"I'm sorry, Tabitha. Hen is a lovely woman. Fertile, but lovely." Amelia tried to don a serious face, but it was impossible. "I can find a cab for her and the boys if you'd like."

"A cab is the least of my problems. Forty-five, Amelia. Forty-five." She emphasized the number. "That is the current head count for the wedding breakfast. I'm going to have to order more mutton—unless their eating habits resemble yours this afternoon."

Amelia looked down at her still-full plate. After hearing about her family and enjoying a chuckle, she felt a little of her appetite return. She tried another bite of her scone, knowing full well that her family and extended family were big eaters, drinkers, and talkers. They enjoyed gathering, and when a gathering included food—which it usually did—the festivities seemed to go on for hours. In fact, Amelia remembered a time when her cousins stayed so long that her mother made breakfast for them before they left.

"I'm afraid they all enjoy food a good deal." Amelia reached for the jam. "I would go ahead and order an extra joint of mutton after all."

FOURTEEN

Dear Lady Agony,
I cannot get a single flower to bloom in our dreadful weather. Please recommend one that will not succumb to disease, drought, or my lack of gardening skills. Any advice will be appreciated.
Devotedly,
Brown Thumb

Dear Brown Thumb,
Our weather presents certain challenges to be sure, but I believe I have the perfect flower for you: the chrysanthemum. Few if any plants are so accommodating. For large, colorful blooms, make sure you allow no more than three buds on the stem. Keep watered, especially in warm weather, and fertilize three times a week. That is all one must do to keep the pretty plant alive. Let me know if you succeed.
Yours in Secret,
Lady Agony

The next day, Simon and his sister, Marielle Bainbridge, collected Amelia for Lady Applegate's garden soiree, which was to include the unveiling of her latest statuary. At the Bainbridge dinner party, she had promised that the piece would eclipse even her best works. Amelia wasn't sure what Lady Applegate considered her best work, but if she had to guess, the newest lawn ornament would be large and garish and supremely fun to look at.

But Amelia wouldn't be only looking at lawn ornaments. She planned to see if Lady Applegate showed any signs of guilt after Amelia's near miss with a hansom cab yesterday. She would also be looking at her linens for a handkerchief such as the one that was left behind on Down Street.

She hadn't had the opportunity to tell Simon about the ordeal yet and perhaps never would if he and his sister kept arguing the way they were. He'd barely acknowledged her as she climbed into the carriage, pausing only a moment to smile at her before returning to one of his favorite subjects as of late: Lord Traber—Marielle's romantic interest. He was moving too fast for Simon's liking, but the end of the season was approaching, and they'd been courting for a month. If Lord Traber didn't propose this season, he surely would next.

"I simply do not understand why he suggested taking you when he knew very well that I was going myself." Simon pulled at his collar. "Applegate put me on the spot at dinner the other night, and the entire table heard my affirmation—despite my wholehearted desire not to go."

"Perhaps you should have stayed home." Marielle tilted her chin, and it looked almost as square as Simon's. Her black hair was the same, and her emerald eyes mirrored his.

"Perhaps you are right. Perhaps we should turn the carriage around."

"You wouldn't," exclaimed Marielle.

"I would." Simon's black eyelashes created a smoky haze over his green eyes, and the siblings stared at each other like two tigers deciding which one would scratch first.

Tired of their sparring, Amelia announced, "I was almost killed yesterday. By a hansom cab. On a walk."

That got their attention.

"Amelia." Simon reached across the carriage for her gloved hands.

Marielle asked, "Are you all right?"

"I'm fine, as you can see, but it rattled me." Amelia sighed. "I was a hair's breadth from the carriage wheel, and the driver didn't even bother to stop."

Simon turned her hands over, as if examining them for physical harm, then squeezed. "The driver should be arrested. To encroach upon a lady and not even stop. It's deplorable."

MURDER IN MATRIMONY

"Reckless and unconscionable," agreed Marielle. "People operate under a perpetual rush. I hardly walk anywhere these days."

"You would do well to follow my sister's example." Simon frowned. "This town is no place for pedestrians."

Actually, London was the perfect place for pedestrians—if they watched where they were going. Amelia loved her morning walks on London's streets. She would no more quit them than quit her letters. Here was life in its most intimate setting. Houses came to life with activity; vendors materialized from invisible alleys; carts rolled out with colorful goods. She learned more about people in that precious hour than all the parties this season. She would dodge a hundred cabs before she gave it up.

The Bainbridge carriage halted in front of the Applegates' home. As soon as the footman put down the stairs, Marielle was off to find Lord Traber. Simon and Amelia followed at a slower pace.

Simon paused on their approach to the lawn. "Are you certain you are fine?"

"I am, but there is more to this story than I could mention in front of Lady Marielle." Amelia quickly relayed the specifics as well as her suspicions about Lord and Lady Applegate. It was possible the incident was an accident, but it was also possible that the incident was arranged by the blackmailer as a warning.

"If that is true, one of the Applegates could be your black-mailer," he surmised.

"Yes." Spotting a new twitch in his jaw, she added, "Which is why we must remain calm and use this outing to our advantage. With everyone outside in the garden, we might have a chance to peer into a writing desk or catch a glance at the sewing basket. We might find material that matches the handkerchief."

"If we do, rest assured I'll box Lord Applegate's ears for terrorizing you the way he did yesterday."

"You'll do nothing of the sort." Her voice relayed her growing exasperation. Simon was rational when it came to all subjects—except her. His chivalry was growing irksome. "You'll tell me straightaway, and we'll formulate a plan. Lord Drake came to me yesterday about turning himself in."

"Not a bad idea," said Simon smugly.

"It *is* a bad idea." Why were men so quick to act? Couldn't they comprehend the far-reaching consequences of their actions? "Lord Drake returned the items. No good will come of him being arrested, only harm. He has a father who is quite ill. His beloved home in Cornwall will fall to ruin or be dismantled for firewood without Lord Drake. There is no one to care for it for him."

He blinked. "He has an estate in Cornwall?"

"Yes, he does." *Utterly oblivious.* "Promise me you won't discuss the question with Lord Applegate?"

"Fine," grumbled Simon. "I promise." They continued walking, and Amelia noted how guarded he was, as if another hansom cab might bowl into them at any moment. "How long do you think we'll be here?"

"I suppose that depends on the size of the statue."

He didn't exactly smile, but his lips suggested a grin, and that was all it took for her heart to do that thing it did when they were together. It had become so frequent that she couldn't imagine it ever disappearing. In fact, she couldn't imagine a life without Simon. They'd grown closer, and their relationship was more serious, allowing her to imagine a new life, one with him by her side.

They reached the lawn, and smack in the middle of the newly disturbed grass was a towering object covered with tenting material gathered at the middle and bottom. It was over eight feet tall and three feet wide and completely out of place in the small ornamental garden.

"Good God," Simon muttered.

"Or gods." Amelia squinted at the object. "Or muses. It has to be more than one of them under there."

"Lady Amesbury. Lord Bainbridge." Lady Applegate rushed to greet them, her bosom heaving as she padded over in too-tight moss-green slippers. She was dressed to match her garden today, and a repeating hydrangea pattern covered two thirds

MURDER IN MATRIMONY   105

of her skirt, which was so wide Amelia had to take a step backward to allow room for it.

"Good afternoon, Lady Applegate," Amelia said. "What a perfect day to unveil your new statue." She motioned to the cloudless sky.

"I simply could not wait until next season." She smiled at the covered object. "When you see it, you will understand."

"And why would you neglect us the pleasure of seeing it *this* season?" said Simon, and Lady Applegate tittered at the compliment. "When your husband suggested the idea at my dinner party the other evening, I promised myself not to miss it."

Lady Applegate's cheeks flushed, and she looked as pleased as one of the blush-colored roses in her garden. "It won't be long now. As soon as everyone is here, we will undrape it. Then we will enjoy cake and champagne to celebrate the artist, who, by the way, took the train in from Sheffield to be here."

"My." Amelia could think of nothing else to say. Nonchalantly, she was looking for signs of guilt or distress: biting a lip, darting a glance, avoiding a conversation. Yet she detected none of those. If Lady Applegate had been the one in the hansom cab, she was a very good actress.

Lady Applegate excused herself to greet another guest, and Amelia scanned the grounds for Lord Applegate. She found him talking to Oliver Hamsted, Kitty's husband, of all people. Kitty was unable to attend, for she was helping her neighbor decorate a nursery for a new baby, and the crib was arriving today. Amelia scrunched up her nose, turning to Simon. "I wonder how Mr. Hamsted was persuaded to attend. I cannot imagine he's interested in statuary."

"Perhaps at the dinner party, as I was." Simon tipped his chin at a cluster of people by a Statue of David fountain. "I see quite a few of my guests here."

They approached Oliver, and Lord Applegate gave them a hasty welcome. He was on his way to check on the artist. He lowered his voice. "You know these types. Very erratic with a tendency to fly away at a moment's notice, not unlike the birds I study. They are uneasy creatures but worthwhile all the same." He considered himself an amateur ornithologist and admired birds as much as his wife admired statues. Several fountains in the garden attested to his favorite hobby. "Help yourself to a drink."

Amelia watched him walk into the house, waving a footman toward them as he did.

"How were you persuaded to attend, Hamsted? My party?" Simon asked Oliver.

"No," Oliver explained. "My mother. She insisted I come in her place. A headache." He took off his glasses, cleaning off a fingerprint. He replaced them on his narrow nose. "Now I have one as well after hearing Lord Applegate talk about his wife's highly anticipated statue. The man must be deaf and blind."

"Blind for certain." Simon raised an eyebrow at the draped figure in the middle of the garden. A footman passed with a tray of drinks, and Simon selected a lemonade for Amelia. "What do you think is underneath there?"

Amelia took the glass. "A mermaid?"

Oliver raised a finger. "An octopus."

"I hope whatever it is, it will be holding a carafe of whiskey." Simon refused a second glass of lemonade from the footman. "It certainly would make the spectacle more tolerable."

Amelia sipped at her lemonade, knowing it would be impossible to investigate until the creature was unveiled. Then, when the cake and champagne were served and everyone was distracted, she would make an excuse of having to visit the water closet. Once inside the house, she would search for any suggestion of Lord or Lady Applegate being the blackmailer. If she could get a glance at their penmanship, on a note or letter, she might be able to identify similarities, if not the author altogether.

Trudging behind Lord Applegate was a small man with a tall hat who took a fleeting glance at the house before they walked to the center of the garden. Lord Applegate introduced him as the artist, and he started when they clapped. Lord Applegate asked him to say a few words before revealing his creation, then shoved him in the direction of the draped figure.

"Uh . . . good afternoon. Thank you to the Applegates for

MURDER IN MATRIMONY   107

inviting me to this event." He blinked at the crowd. "I'm rather accustomed to my studio and clay and those sorts of things, but it's nice to join real people once in a while." He smiled, and a few partygoers chuckled. "This marble statue was inspired by Lady Applegate's fondness for parties. She is bold and creative and never afraid to take chances." The artist, not used to making speeches, swallowed, warming to the subject. "I wanted to imbue that same zeal in her request, and I believe I have accomplished that." He put his hand on the drape. "Ladies and gentlemen, I present you with Dionysus, the ultimate host of festivities."

At that, he unveiled a large statue of the robed god of wine and fertility. In one hand, Dionysus held a pine-cone staff and in the other, a drinking cup. Around his head was an ivy wreath, and behind him was a branch covered in grapevines. In truth, it was a nice representation of the Roman god. Amelia glanced at the other statues. She just wasn't certain it should be placed next to a Christian representation of an angel.

"Not holding a carafe of whiskey, but still a drinking glass," Amelia said to Simon.

"If only it was filled with a beverage." He smirked.

Lady Applegate was pleased with the unveiling and clapped her hands rapidly. She congratulated the artist with a glass of champagne, then made a toast. As soon as the cake came out, Amelia and Simon knew now was their chance. It was time to slip inside and find out if either of the Applegates was Lady Agony's blackmailer.

FIFTEEN

Dear Lady Agony,
   I understand love letters are to be returned or destroyed, but I have a special collection I am reluctant to part with. The author himself is dead, so no apprehension exists there, and my husband passed away many years ago. The only concern is for my children. I am unsure how they will respond to them when I am gone.
   Devotedly,
   Love Letters of Long Ago

Dear Love Letters of Long Ago,
   It is impossible to know what your children will feel upon finding them. They might feel surprised, joyful, or disappointed. The better question might be: How much do you care? Try to weigh your answer against the pleasure the letters bring you. Then make your decision.
   Yours in Secret,
   Lady Agony

Once inside Lady Applegate's morning room, Amelia realized how out of place Simon was and how unhelpful he may be. He certainly wasn't the stealthy accomplice Kitty was. With her small stature and quick movements, Kitty could slip in and out of places that Amelia wouldn't deign to go—in between fence posts, behind bookshelves, up garden trellises. To be honest, Amelia's backside was a little too curvy to attempt such feats.

Inside the small mint and white room, Simon looked like a gorilla—large, hairy, and all thumbs. His shoulders were a dark square upon the light wall, and black whiskers darkened his chin despite it being only three o'clock in the afternoon. When

MURDER IN MATRIMONY   109

he took a step forward, a small pink vase on a table shook, and Amelia quelled the urge to tell him not to break anything. Instead, she asked him to mind the door. If he wasn't moving, their location might remain secure.

"What do you mean 'mind the door'? I'm not a buffoon, Amelia."

Your words, not mine.

"If we both search, we will finish twice as quickly," he continued. "Let me do something."

"Fine," she agreed. "You take the shelves. I'll take the desk."

He grunted an approval, and she made her way to the small oak secretaire, which provided writing space and a shelf. Noting a stack of stationery, Amelia opened the glass cabinet. The paper was ivory and contained Lady Applegate's initials. Not familiar. She moved to a second smaller pile. It contained a crest, which Amelia assumed belonged to the Applegates. Unremarkable. She scanned envelopes, postage stamps, and sealing wax but found no connections to the blackmailer.

"*Psst.*"

Amelia looked up. Even his whispers were loud.

Simon had the drawer open of a small whatnot. Similar to Lady Applegate's garden, it overflowed with bric-a-brac. The shelves contained tiny crystal figurines, picture frames, miniature spoons, and what appeared to be a medal from some government office. He held up a magazine.

Amelia squinted at the title for a better look. It was the same magazine Lord Drake had brought to her attention yesterday.

Simon flicked the paper. "She reads the magazine. She might be the blackmailer."

"Look for Lady Agony's columns. If she reads one magazine, she may read the other." She opened a drawer and found a note that read: *Garden fountain?* Lady Applegate was obviously contemplating a new piece for her garden, and Amelia's first question was where would she place it? Ignoring the question, she stared at the penmanship of the note. It wasn't much to go on, but Amelia saw no similarities to the blackmailer. It was true that the blackmailer tried to disguise his or her writing by using print instead of cursive. Still, Amelia felt as if she would recognize it when she saw it. Perhaps she was giving herself too much credit.

She continued to a lower, deeper drawer. There, she found menus, obviously written by the housekeeper. The penmanship was wholly different than the note about the garden fountain. She sifted through receipts, written by any number of merchants. Then, in the farthest corner, she noted a slim stack of letters with a ribbon around them. *Success!* She reached for them, slowly untying the gold ribbon. Her hand shook a little at the idea of facing the blackmailer's handwriting. Instead, she saw love letters to Lady Applegate from a long-ago romance. The handwriting belonged to a man, so it was no use to her, but the sentiment behind the words was tenable, and Amelia felt herself release a little sigh. She was thoroughly touched by the words and feeling behind them.

"What is it?" asked Simon.

She smiled. "Old love letters."

"I have nothing of value here either."

So romantic. She frowned, retying the bow that secured the stack of letters, and put them back in the drawer. When she did, she noted an appointment book. Upon opening it, she noticed it contained the addresses of Lady Applegate's friends. They were printed—and nothing like the print of the blackmailer. She flipped several pages just to be sure.

"It's not her," Amelia said aloud. Simon came closer, and she flashed him the appointment book. "I am certain."

"We still have Lord Applegate to investigate." Simon nodded toward the door. "We should check his study while everyone is outside."

She agreed and replaced the appointment book, shutting the drawer.

Simon opened the door and peeked around the corner. He signaled her to follow, and she hoped he knew where he was going. One wrong turn would cost them another ten minutes in the house, for it was a large property with lots of clutter—in other words, obstacles—for them to navigate. At one point, Amelia almost tripped over what she could only assume was meant to be a door stopper. It was a cast-iron cheetah as big as a log. It sent her sailing into Simon's solid back, and they both shared a chuckle when they were safely inside the study.

At least Amelia hoped it was the study. Dark velvet curtains didn't allow much light to enter through the double windows behind the desk. But it smelled of cigars and something else, a lighter floral fragrance that was less masculine. Probably a bouquet of flowers Lady Applegate had brought in from her garden. She could have sworn she detected the scent of lilies.

"So stealthy, Amelia," Simon jested. "Luckily I caught you before the entire house was alerted to our location."

She swatted his arm. "You did not see the size of that cheetah. It was as high as my knee."

"One might think it bit you by your reaction." A rustling noise came from behind the tufted couch, putting an end to their banter, and Simon slid her behind him. "Is someone there?"

Silence was his answer.

He turned around to Amelia, holding a finger to his lips.

She nodded, willing her heart to stop thudding. If they were found by a member of society, they would need to explain their presence, not to mention their solitariness. It wouldn't take long for word to spread about their indiscretion at a party the size of the Applegates'.

Quickly, he strode to the couch and peered over it.

Even in the low light, Amelia could see his face transform into a thousand emotions: surprise, angst, then anger.

"You!" he spat.

"Good afternoon, brother." Marielle stood and dusted off her dress, spotting Amelia. "Oh, Lady Amesbury."

"*Lady Marielle?*" Amelia was so surprised that she could think of nothing else to say.

Simon pointed a finger at Lord Traber. "What in the hell are you doing in here alone with my sister?"

Lord Traber popped up from the floor, his cravat untied. His Adam's apple bobbed nervously as he swallowed, searching for something to say. "I . . . which is to say, we . . . were . . ." He looked to Marielle.

Marielle nodded encouragingly, but Lord Traber didn't continue.

"Looking for that book, I imagine," Amelia provided. "A field guide to birding in Surrey Hills." She turned to Simon. "Lord Traber is traveling there in a few weeks, and Lord Applegate is a great enthusiast. They spoke of it earlier."

"Oh yes!" Lord Traber quickly agreed. "I am going to Surrey Hills."

"And Lord Applegate loves birds," Marielle added.

Both statements were true. It was why Amelia put the two together off the top of her head. Lord Applegate's narrow bookshelf was filled with several books. She just hoped one of them was on birding since he proclaimed to be an amateur ornithologist.

"Birds, hmm." Simon's voice was as sharp as the blade of a knife. "I don't care if he writes for Baedekers! You are not to be alone with my sister—ever."

"They are not alone," tried Amelia. "After all, we are here."

Simon pointed a finger at Lord Traber's chest. "I imagine it's rather hard to find a book behind the sofa, in the dark."

"We hid, naturally, when we heard a sound," Marielle explained. "I did not expect it to be you. Which reminds me—what are you doing in here?" She lowered her wide eyelids at Simon.

He matched the fierce glare. "*I* am the one asking the questions."

"Checking on you, of course." Amelia ignored both of them, walking over to the heavy drape and yanking it open several inches. "There. Now we can see well enough to find that book." But she wasn't looking at the bookshelf; she was looking down at the desk, which was directly in front of the window. Unlike his wife's desk, it was neat and clear of clutter. Perhaps this was his refuge from his wife's ever-expanding menagerie.

Now that Amelia could see properly, she noted that the room was austere when compared with the rest of the house. A table, bookshelf, sofa, chair, and desk—simple. She tried the center drawer, but it was locked.

"If I liked you any better, Traber, I'd force you into an engagement, here and now." Simon returned his gaze to the young man. "As it is, however, I'd like an apology and your word that you will never engage my sister alone again."

"I . . . uh . . ." Lord Traber's voice was no louder than a mumble.

"I need your word, Traber."

"Come now, Lord Bainbridge." Amelia tried another drawer. "Be reasonable. No harm ever came from reading a book."

"Dash it all!" Simon exclaimed. "No one was reading a book."

"Keep your voice down." Amelia found a ledger of accounts. "Ah ha."

"Lady Amesbury. Are you, is that—"

"It seems Traber has forgotten how to speak altogether." Simon crossed his arms, and the black fabric stretched taut at his shoulders. "I believe I asked you for an apology and your word to never see my sister again."

Amelia glanced up.

Marielle crossed her arms, looking only a little less fierce. "And I believe you are behaving like a brute. We *will* be seeing each other—frequently. There is nothing you can do about it."

Amelia went back to the ledger. The argument was coming to a climax; she needed to find an example of Lord Applegate's penmanship fast.

"Oh really?" challenged Simon.

"Really," Marielle repeated.

Amelia used her fingertips as a guide, scanning line after line of letters and numbers. Despite being in print, the blackmailer's letters included a curl in the letter "z" that made it distinct. If she could find the letter in the ledger, she might be able to make an instant match. Harrods . . . Tattersalls . . . John Timms . . . Thomas Ziegler. "Success!" No curl was found in the letter "z." She shut the ledger, and when she did, she noted three pairs of eyes on her.

She returned the ledger to its place and casually strolled over to the bookshelf. "*The Birds of Europe.*" She pulled out the book. "I thought I recognized the tome. It is sure to be indispensable, Lord Traber, if Lord Applegate agrees to lend it to you."

"I'll ask him right now." Lord Traber nervously took the book when she offered it. "Thank you."

Amelia smiled. "You're welcome."

"I know what this is, Amelia," said Simon. "It is your poor attempt to conceal this man's vile actions against my sister, and I will have you and everyone in this room know that I am aware of it. This book is a prop like any in your vaudeville acts. If I didn't know better, I'd declare you a conjurer, pulling it from a well-disguised hat."

Amelia raised an eyebrow. "Not a hat, a bookshelf." She opened the door to the study, checking the hallway for signs of activity. Seeing none, she tossed a look over her shoulder. "Though as for that, books are rather magical."

Without a retort, Simon threw up his hands and followed, his sister and Lord Traber trailing behind him.

SIXTEEN

Dear Lady Agony,

So many young women are ignorant of the art of the handkerchief. Could you give them a refresher on the ways one can employ it if the need arises?

Devotedly,

Handle Your Handkerchief

Dear Handle Your Handkerchief,

When conversation affords no entrance, a handkerchief speaks what words cannot. Commit these to your memory like the lines of your favorite prayer, ladies. They might just be your salvation.

Drawing the handkerchief across your cheek means I love you.

Drawing the handkerchief across your eyes means I am sorry.

Drawing the handkerchief across your lips means I desire your acquaintance.

Drawing the handkerchief over the shoulder means Please follow me.

Drawing the handkerchief through your hands means I loathe you.

Yours in Secret,

Lady Agony

That evening, Amelia was in the library, enjoying a well-earned spot of brandy. The soiree had been trying from start to finish. It had begun with an oversized statue of Dionysus and ended with a makeshift defense of Lord Traber and Lady Marielle being alone together in Lord Applegate's study. Whether or not Simon bought it was of little consequence. They were released from any wrongdoing by the excuse, and while Simon did not like his sister's suitor any better after the incident, he did not mention it again.

She had the good sense to remind him that had they wanted to, Marielle and Lord Traber might have begun their own line of questioning. Simon and Amelia had also entered the study alone, and Amelia actively sought out writing materials on Lord Applegate's desk while opening the curtain. If the situation had been any less tenuous, *they* might have been the ones under scrutiny.

For the moment, Amelia forgot all that, sipping the brandy and briefly closing her eyes. Her life was a maelstrom of issues right now: her sister's wedding, the impending visit of her extended family, the blackmailer, and Mr. Cross's murderer. But surrounded by books, with a spot of brandy, she could forget all that and pretend her most pressing issue was fiction or nonfiction.

Amelia had no sooner picked up a book than she heard a familiar tap at her window. *Isaac Jakeman.* She set down the novel and went to the curtain, pushing it back discreetly. A hooked nose was the first feature she recognized, and as he drew closer to the window, the second was his small eyes, intelligent and missing nothing. His lips curled into a smile as she stepped to the side to allow him entrance.

"You received my note on Mrs. Hines." She didn't wait for an answer but went immediately to the library door and locked it. "Brandy?"

"Please." Isaac Jakeman waited by the decanter.

She was not stingy with the pour, and Jakeman took the snifter appreciatively.

He drank, then examined the color of the brandy. "It is good."

"Thank you for coming." She gestured to a chair before taking one herself. "I wrote when I heard of Mrs. Hines's attack behind the Plate & Bottle. I was surprised you had not mentioned it."

Isaac shook his head almost imperceptibly. "You call me, I tell you everything I know since the beginning of time. Is that how this works, Lady?"

MURDER IN MATRIMONY 117

She'd obviously offended him. "Not at all. I just thought you might have mentioned her, but perhaps you don't know her?"

He drank deeply before answering. "I've met her. I didn't know her. She was a friend of Mrs. Rothschild and worked in the dining room before they closed it. Now they serve only liquor. Though, Mrs. Rothschild still bakes her biscuits because no one can do without them."

"Who committed the crime against her?" Amelia puzzled over the information. "I never heard about it in the papers."

"You think every East End crime is reported in your Mayfair papers?" He tsked. "Lady, you don't know much about anything."

She bristled at the criticism, probably because it was true. But it wasn't for lack of trying. As Lady Agony, she assisted readers from every area of the city. She tried to educate herself on the many ways of living outside her small circle. When readers had problems beyond her scope, she did everything she could to learn about them so that she could assist them better in the future. "Help me understand then. I want to know."

He put down his glass. "Look, I like you. You think you want to help. But what you actually want is to find justice for your high-born priest. That is all. What happened to Mrs. Hines or Miss Rothschild?" He waved away the idea in the air. "You do not really care about those women."

"Yes, I do!" Amelia was just as surprised as Isaac Jakeman at the forcefulness of her answer, and her quiet repetition was admission of it. "Yes, I do."

"Why?" He took out a cigar and tapped it on the table. "Because they are tangled up with your priest?"

"Because an attack on a woman should not be commonplace. In the East End or the West." Amelia felt a passion ignited that until now had lain dormant. "It should not be ordinary; it should be extraordinary. In the papers, it is reported that *A woman was killed*, as if she did the killing herself. The culprit remains unnamed. No more obfuscation. No more silence." She shook her head. "I must know who harmed these two women."

Isaac lifted his long, arched eyebrows. "I did not know you felt this way."

"Nor did I."

"Your priest felt the same way." He tapped his cigar again. "Maybe you are more like him than you know."

She felt the words like the wing of an angel. Even in death, Mr. Cross was teaching her what it meant to care, to love. It was easy to love thy neighbor. It was a little harder to love a stranger from the wrong end of town. She cared about Mr. Cross because he had been good to her, but she hadn't really understood why she should care about these two women. He had taught her why, yet she still had much to learn. She promised herself she would be open to more lessons. "Do you know why Mrs. Hines was attacked?"

"For your sake, Lady, I wish I did." He sniffed his cigar, then replaced it in his pocket, leaning forward. "What I do know is this: if the priest was to blame, I would happily say so. However, he came to the East End only after the old priest became ill in February. Mrs. Hines was attacked long before that."

It was a question of simple math. Mr. Cross might have encouraged Miss Rothschild to leave the public house, and one of his reasons might have been the previous attack on Mrs. Hines. He did not serve St. George-in-the-East, however, at the time of her attack. "As far as you know, it was a case of her being in the wrong place at the wrong time."

"Yes, and that's as far as anyone will know unless the attacker comes forward, and that will not happen in my lifetime." He crossed one leg over the other. "You give me your sad story. Now let me give you mine. My dear wife, Francine, you know how much she enjoys the fashion. I bought her a new horse at Tattersalls, and she requires a habit for riding."

"You need a tailor." She stood and went to her desk. "I have the best."

"I do not doubt it."

Amelia scratched out an introduction. "Reticules are a nuisance when riding. Hussain will ensure she has pockets in her skirt." She walked the paper over to him.

"She wishes to ride in Hyde Park, at the fashionable hour."

MURDER IN MATRIMONY 119

A question lurked behind Isaac Jakeman's pewter-colored eyes, and she went about answering it immediately.

"And why wouldn't she? If I see her, I will greet her warmly."

"I do not like her to go. On the East Side, we are respected. We are known. Here?" He shrugged. "I cannot protect her."

"I understand." She held out the paper. "You do not want her feelings hurt." After he took it, she crossed her arms. "But I'll let you in on a little secret. Women get their feelings hurt all the time. I do. She will. Anyone who feels deeply, which is most women I know, opens themselves up to discomfort. It might make us sad in the moment, but it also makes us strong." She caught his eye. "Stronger than you think."

He held her gaze for a moment, and at that moment, she saw so much more than a fence. She saw a man who was caught between two worlds, a man who did not belong to either, a man who would throw over both for the love of his wife.

He folded the paper into his pocket. "Thank you."

"Of course." She dug into the folds of her dress, retrieving the square of fabric left behind after her run-in at Hyde Park Corner. "I have one more question, if I may. Have you ever seen a handkerchief like this before?"

She handed him the handkerchief, and he turned it over, examining all four corners carefully. "This comes from your end of town, not mine. We do not have time for busywork." He gestured to the intricate stitching. "If they have the patience or skill, our women make matchsticks or lace." He gave it back to her. "This is from your Mayfair ballrooms, as if someone dropped it on purpose so that you might follow."

If a woman wanted to be introduced to a man and had no recourse to do so, she might accidentally drop her handkerchief so that he would pick it up, thus ensuring a meeting. Someone could have, in fact, dropped the handkerchief with the intention of her picking it up. But why? That question was harder to answer. Perhaps they wanted to prove they knew she was Lady Agony, or maybe they wanted her to return it, forcing an introduction. If it did belong to someone in Mayfair, it supported her supposition that the blackmailer was indeed one of the victims of the Mayfair Marauder.

"I see the wheels are turning, so I will let them turn and take my leave." He stood, returning his bowler hat to his head. "Good luck with your priest."

"Thank you, and good luck with your riding habit—I mean your wife's riding habit."

He was still chuckling as he disappeared behind the curtain.

After he left, Amelia revisited her brandy, laying the problem aside for the time being. Instead, she considered her family's upcoming visit. Despite the complications—and Aunt Tabitha's complaints—she was looking forward to seeing her relatives. The West End might know how to host a soiree, but the Scotts knew how to have a good time. She found it was always the case with people who cared for one another. They didn't need expensive food or clothes to enjoy themselves. Being with each other was always enough.

Her sister was expected to return to London next week. Their parents planned to join her and Captain Fitz. Then the excitement would begin. Her extended family would arrive and, with them, a general energy and chaos that wouldn't subside until they left. Tabitha would despise it. Winifred would love it. And Amelia was determined to cherish every second of it, for it wasn't every day that one's baby sister got married— even if it was by Mr. Penroy. She wrinkled her nose. *No matter.* She promised to enjoy herself. A priest, a murderer, or a blackmailer had little power against the force that was the Scott family.

SEVENTEEN

Dear Lady Agony,
Is it ever acceptable to eavesdrop? My friend believes it is never appropriate, while I say a situation might warrant it. What do you say?
Devotedly,
Dallying in Doorways

Dear Dallying in Doorways,
Eavesdropping is acceptable if the motive is pure and the situation dire. Both conditions must be met, however, for the behavior to be excused. Otherwise, it is in bad taste and should be avoided at all costs—even information—and you, dear readers, know how well I enjoy staying informed.
Yours in Secret,
Lady Agony

The next evening, Kitty arrived on Amelia's doorstep in a plain gray dress, ready to make the trek to St. George-in-the-East. When Amelia inquired on her fashion choice, she explained she made it on purpose. It was a dress that showed she was serious about volunteer work. Amelia said she didn't believe it mattered what they wore if they were there to help.

"Oh, no." Kitty shook her head, which was free of the curls that usually appeared at her cheeks and behind her ears. "It does matter. I've done volunteer work, and you must appear conscientious."

Amelia frowned, confused.

"Let me put it this way. In a West End drawing room, the nicest dressed woman is liked the best, correct?"

"Yes . . ." It did seem that way to Amelia. The women with the finest clothes were always the most popular.

"In volunteer groups, the opposite is true. Women in dour clothes are most respected. They've denied themselves and given everything to God—or at least the church. It's an outward sign of their commitment."

Amelia glanced down at her brown dress. "Is mine sufficiently dour?"

"Oh yes," Kitty said a little too enthusiastically. "Most of your clothes are plain. You have nothing to worry about."

Amelia sniffed, but what Kitty said was true. She didn't care much for fashion, and her clothes were more practical than pretty, with a few exceptions. She had an emerald-green gown that was exactly the color of Simon's eyes and a jet-black riding habit that displayed her curves reasonably well. These two articles she could recall with pride and pleasure. The other items in her closet were a vague collection of cloth suitable to her station.

Regardless, Amelia would fit in, and that's what was most important. Her focus now was on St. George-in-the-East and the prayer meeting Mrs. Rothschild organized. More than ever, women were getting involved with charity and reform work, and the work didn't only benefit the recipients. Women were learning how to motivate, plan, allocate, and put words into action. What started as a prayer group often transformed into a group that enacted real change. Many women were committed to helping the poor, feeding the hungry, and housing orphaned children. They could be proud of the achievements they, as a whole, were making.

When Amelia and Kitty arrived at Cannon Street Road, two priests were at the door of the adjacent rectory. Amelia wondered if they could be members of the Society for the Greater Good; Mr. James had mentioned them getting together today. The prayer meeting did not start for a quarter-hour, and she and Kitty might overhear something of value. She asked Kitty.

"Overhear?" Kitty repeated. "You mean eavesdrop." She retied the black bow on her bonnet, which could not completely conceal her prettiness. Her cheeks were still as round as apples and just as pink, if not pinker, against the black bow. "I'm willing." The footman opened the carriage door, and she added, "As long as I am not doomed for all eternity for spying on holy men."

"Not likely." Amelia followed her out of the carriage. "In fact, we might be nominated for sainthood if we solve Mr. Cross's murder."

"That is taking it too far."

Amelia tipped her chin to an open window on the ground floor of the three-story brick building. From it wafted a collection of men's voices. Some were quiet and old; others were young and energetic. It had to be a society meeting. "There, in that room. We can seek cover behind the bush."

Kitty agreed, and Amelia led the way, thankful for their plain gowns. They were free of the frills and multiple petticoats that would have marked their approach. She crouched close to the wall, and Kitty followed her example. When they neared the occupied room, Amelia took a step closer to the overgrown shrubbery, concealing their location. From what she could gather from snippets of conversation, it was the end of the meeting. The men were discussing the next one and where to conduct it.

"I refuse to plan another, acting as if all is well." While not shouting, the man's voice was terse. "One priest is dead. Who is to say one of us won't be next if the group continues? I ask what good is it to society if their priest is killed?"

"Point taken, Thompson, but we cannot be cowed into submission." Amelia recognized the voice of Mr. James. "There is work to be done, in Wapping especially."

"Work while they throw rocks?" Mr. Thompson chuckled harshly. "That's what they did to Cross."

"And still he persevered," added another voice.

"Until they killed him," Mr. Thompson retorted.

Silence ensued, and Amelia grasped the enormity of their task. Wapping was a poor district with many problems of drunkenness, prostitution, and gambling. It would be hard for anyone to solve them, especially priests who were sometimes ignorant to the way people lived. Amelia had learned it was easy to be charitable when one had the money, easy to be hospitable when one had a home, and easy to be pious when one had the time. But many Wapping residents had none of these. Their actions and reactions were often physical ones because those were the powers they possessed.

"We cannot just quit." The voice belonged to Mr. James, who sounded slightly defeated in the light of the cold, hard truth.

A beat passed, and then another priest answered. "Let us meet at All Saints then. We will be safe there."

Amelia covered her mouth before she could gasp audibly. It was Mr. Penroy. *What is he doing here?* Penroy had minimalized Mr. Cross's work to Amelia's face. He cared nothing about it. As far as he was concerned, Mr. Cross was trying to make a name for himself in the hope that he would be noticed by the bishop or others in the upper echelons of the church. Anyone who spent time in Wapping, however, must realize the enormity of Mr. Cross's task. Had he desired fame or popularity, he could have obtained it by an easier undertaking.

"Safe?" Mr. Thompson repeated incredulously. "It is where Cross was killed."

"Under normal circumstances, it is very safe, and I will make certain of our safety the day of our meeting. We can put the question of the society to rest once and for all." A few priests murmured their acquiescence, and they agreed on a date. "It is settled, then. James, more tea?"

The thought of Penroy presiding over Mr. Cross's most sacred group made Amelia feel ill. He had told her what he thought of the poor. How could he manage a society he didn't care about? Maybe he didn't mean to manage it at all. Maybe he meant to bury it with the body of Mr. Cross.

Amelia shuddered, and Kitty touched her arm. Kitty knew what was going through her mind and gave her a sympathetic look. Amelia dipped her chin, indicating that she was all right, and they trailed back the way they had come, entering one of the side doors of the church.

Once inside, Amelia said, "It cannot be true. Penroy has

had nothing to do with the society." The church was dim and quiet, and the words, like a prayer, dissipated into the towering space.

"He does now." Kitty sighed. "The group agreed on the next meeting."

"He's officious. That is all. They could not help but agree with him."

Kitty inclined her head. "Are those the women in the prayer group?"

Amelia followed her gaze, noting three women gathered near the entry of the church. They were dressed very simply, and their actions were almost identical. They moved quickly, like butterflies, wanting to complete the most work in the shortest amount of time. They each had items for sorting or perhaps donating, and one woman held a basket. "It must be. I wonder which one is Mrs. Rothschild?"

"Let us find out."

Amelia and Kitty introduced themselves as friends of All Saints on Margaret Street, Mr. Cross's home parish. They had come to help his passion project in any way they could. Never having been to the East End parish before, they thought it was a good place to start.

The women accepted them with kindness and zeal.

"Bless you!" exclaimed a woman of middle age with an excitement that transformed her face. "How good of you to come all the way to St. George-in-the-East."

"Mr. Cross's goodness has no boundaries." Another woman raised her hands, clasped in prayer, toward heaven. "Even now."

"*Especially* now." The woman holding the covered basket on one arm reached out her other to pat the woman's shoulder. "Welcome. We are happy you are here."

"Thank you." Amelia was encouraged and even overwhelmed by their hospitality. What good women these were. If they were indicative of the rest of the parish, it was no wonder why Mr. Cross advocated for them.

"Come." The woman with the basket led the way to a small gathering place, where a table and six chairs stood. The table was scattered with pamphlets, and she quickly straightened and placed them in a pile. "Our numbers are small today. Many are still working, so we are grateful for your addition. Sit, and we will begin with a prayer."

After the prayer, the women introduced themselves. The middle-aged woman was Mrs. Evans, the other was Mrs. Lewis, and the one with the basket was Mrs. Rothschild. She unfolded the cloth covering the basket, and the delicious scent of fresh bread filled the area. Amelia strained for a peek into the carrier. It wasn't bread but biscuits. She had never smelled a scent like it, a mixture of savory and sweet and something else.

"I must say, those smell delicious, Mrs. Rothschild." The compliment came automatically from Amelia's lips, and Kitty, also curious, chimed in as well.

"I've never smelled anything so pleasant."

Mrs. Rothschild had a plain face, worn even, but her eyes glittered faintly at the praise. "Please, take one."

Knowing how poor these women were, Amelia did not want to indulge, but Mrs. Rothschild insisted, and both she and Kitty took a biscuit.

It was unlike any biscuit Amelia had tasted. It was not hard or dry but soft and sweet, resembling a miniature cake. She heard Kitty murmur her appreciation and understood it wasn't only she who thought the food extraordinary. "Mrs. Rothschild, these are incomparable." She stared at the last bite in her hand, regretting it was all that was left. "Truly." She popped it in her mouth. "I have never tasted a biscuit this delicious."

"They are just biscuits," said Mrs. Rothschild modestly. She had long eyelashes, and they were noticeable as she closed her eyes briefly.

"*Just biscuits!*" Kitty exclaimed. "No, they are not just biscuits. I have had just biscuits, and these are anything but. They are . . . I do not know what they are, but they are heavenly."

The other women smiled at Kitty's high praise, and Mrs. Lewis looked upward. "Heaven sent. That is our dear Mrs. Rothschild."

Amelia imagined Mrs. Lewis praised God for all the good things in her life and dismissed the bad. Despite her well-worn dress and gloveless hands, she considered her graces abundant. Her gratitude was more telling than any piece of clothing.

MURDER IN MATRIMONY

127

Embarrassed by the attention, Mrs. Rothschild dismissed the subject by asking them about their acquaintance with Mr. Cross. "Did you know him well?"

"Very well," Amelia said, sobering. "He had become a dear friend of mine. Perhaps I didn't realize how dear until he was gone."

Mrs. Evans murmured her agreement. "All who met him felt that way. All considered him a friend."

"Everyone at St. George-in-the-East?" Kitty pressed.

Amelia was glad for the question. Caught up in the hospitality and food, she'd temporarily dismissed why they'd come in the first place. If possible, she wanted to glean information about not only Rose Rothschild but Mr. Cross as well.

"Not everyone," admitted Mrs. Lewis. She shook her head. "I'm sure you read about the riots in February. Our parish isn't what yours is."

"I didn't mean to insinuate . . ." Kitty let the sentence trail off, perhaps not wanting to insult the women.

"It's all right. It's true," continued Mrs. Lewis. Her face was as placid as a pond at midnight, honest and unaffected. "Our parishioners didn't always appreciate Mr. Cross. The drinkers. The gamblers. The businessmen. They sought to throw him out for arguing against their trades."

"That is unfortunate," Amelia empathized. "I imagine the drinking establishments in the area did not want their customers transformed."

Mrs. Rothschild bristled. She wore a dress that had grown too large for her, perhaps in her grief, and the mantle fell over her wrist. "Their care is money, naturally. It is how they survive. Without customers, they have no business. They rail against the factories, but my Rose made a decent living at the factory." From beneath the collar of her dress, she pulled out a gold filigree cross necklace. "She even bought me this."

"Beautiful." Amelia admired the delicate necklace, surprised by the quality of the token. Rose Rothschild must have made a sufficient living indeed to purchase the jewelry for her mother.

"But the men who own pubs and gin palaces rely on alcohol to keep their families fed." Mrs. Rothschild tucked the necklace back under her collar as if it was too precious for display. "The demand is high in this neighborhood."

Amelia nodded in understanding. "A conundrum to be sure, for businessmen have to eat as well."

"Mrs. Rothschild knows the problem firsthand," said Mrs. Lewis. "Her husband owns the public house. Has for many years."

"I atone for it by doing work here," Mrs. Rothschild was quick to add.

"Most people need to make a living. It is nothing to be atoned for." Amelia smiled gently.

"I have much to atone for, Lady Amesbury." Mrs. Rothschild was resolute, like a sinner determined to make reparations for past sins. "My friend was attacked after working in our pub. She lost the use of her leg, and when she did, her husband left her. She had no children, and her parents are long dead. Now she survives on the charity of others, doing laundry when she is able. I shall never forget it, and I shall never forgive myself."

Mrs. Lewis put a hand on hers. "Oh, Louisa."

The physical contact was no comfort to Mrs. Rothschild. She kept her gaze on the cross at the front of the church, determined to do what she must to make amends with God.

Obviously, Mrs. Rothschild felt an enormous amount of guilt for the accident. It could have been the reason she was so devout. It also might have accounted for her wish to see her daughter gainfully employed somewhere else besides the public house. Having her daughter die must have only compounded her woes. Grief could make one a bit unhinged. Amelia understood that not only from her own grief but also from the vast number of letters she received on the subject. The church was Mrs. Rothschild's respite, and Amelia imagined she would be willing to do whatever was necessary to apprehend Mr. Cross's murderer.

But was Amelia willing to add to her burdens with her own? As she stared at the mother, so strong yet so fragile, she wasn't as sure as when she first entered the church.

EIGHTEEN

Dear Lady Agony,
Recently, a visitor of mine was accosted by a beggar at
King's Cross Station. He had no more descended the
platform than encountered the trouble. How am I to rave
about our palaces and architecture when this behavior
runs rampant? More must be done to secure our great
city. I know not how, but I believe parliament must play a
larger role.
Devotedly,
Distressing Scenario

Dear Distressing Scenario,
The greatness in England does not lie in our palaces or
architecture but in our hospitals, infirmaries, and
orphanages. It manifests itself in the people who support
them. For what good does stone do me? Give me the
living heart of a generous person. That is what makes me
feel great. As to parliament helping, you would have a
better chance of sprouting wings and flying.
Yours in Secret,
Lady Agony

Mrs. Rothschild put the empty biscuit basket in the middle of the table, and the women in her prayer group added their contributions. They had made socks, gloves, hats, and scarves for a local charity that assisted orphans. Despite having little themselves, they gave of their time wholeheartedly, each item tenderly made. Amelia and Kitty had nothing to add, so they committed to a monetary donation.

The women were grateful for their commitment, so grateful

that an observer would think the money was going to the women themselves and not an organization. Mrs. Lewis thanked God for their spontaneous appearance at tonight's meeting, and Mrs. Rothschild quickly wrote down the name of the charity on two separate pieces of paper, one for Amelia and one for Kitty.

"Our dear Mr. Cross is surely smiling down on you." Mrs. Rothschild slid the paper to Amelia. "The orphanage was one of his passion projects. He contributed to it just days before his death."

Amelia saw an opportunity to investigate and took it. "Where did you see him. Here?"

She nodded, and a little wrinkle appeared between her eyebrows, making them appear sharper. "Our conversation was a particular one. He wanted to introduce me to someone, a person who he thought might be able to help me."

An idea struck Amelia, and her heartbeat doubled. If true, her presence was truly serendipitous. "He did? Did he say whom?"

"No . . . yes, a woman." A faint smile flittered across her lips. "It is not much, but it is all I have. He referenced the person as a *she*."

Mr. Cross said he wanted Amelia to help someone in Wapping. It could have been Mrs. Rothschild. "Did he say why he wanted you to meet her?"

"He didn't suggest a *meeting*; he suggested a *letter*. It was all rather secretive." She frowned. "Very unlike Mr. Cross, but he was certain this person could get to the bottom of my problem."

Amelia and Kitty shared a knowing look. The person he meant was Lady Agony. Amelia was exactly where she needed to be. All she needed to do was figure out why.

Mrs. Evans interjected with a plump finger. "Perhaps that is due to the nature of your problem. A woman might know how better to help than a man."

"What problem?" Kitty asked.

"Twice my oven has started a fire. My husband blamed the flue, but I wonder if some person is responsible. Mr. Rothschild

MURDER IN MATRIMONY

claims my goal is to shut down his pub, but I assure you it is not. I like to eat as much as everyone else, and the business puts food on our table." She checked her rising anger, which grew as vocal as a nagging child. She continued more calmly. "When my husband rejected the idea, I mentioned it to Mr. Cross, and he was quite concerned for our safety. I worry if it happens again, I might not be in time to stop it."

"What you are suggesting is sabotage." Amelia couldn't keep the astonishment out of her voice. On top of all that had happened to this woman—a friend maimed, a daughter killed—someone was trying to harm her or her business.

"Perhaps not purposefully," Mrs. Rothschild was quick to add. "Perhaps it was a malfunction."

"But it must be on purpose. Once might be an accident, but twice?" Amelia shook her head. "It cannot be unless it is something relating to mechanics, as your husband suggests."

"Mr. Rothschild blames the church for preaching against alcohol." The sympathy in Mrs. Lewis's eyes was palpable, her voice full of concern for her friend. "He said they wouldn't be happy until the doors are closed for good."

If Mr. Rothschild thought Cross was trying to put an end to his business, he might retaliate to save the pub. So might any of the business owners affected by his preaching. But Mr. Rothschild had an additional reason: his daughter's employment elsewhere and her subsequent death. But could he and would he kill his wife's beloved priest?

"He even blamed poor Louisa." Mrs. Evan crossed her arms over her chest, making her feelings known about the allegation. The idea that Mrs. Rothschild could burn down her own business was absurd to her, but not completely to Amelia.

"He was just angry." The excuse shot out of Mrs. Rothschild's mouth quicker than Amelia expected. Mrs. Rothschild thought the public house was an evil, but perhaps a necessary one. After all, it provided their livelihood as well as their household above it. She wouldn't start it on fire. At least, Amelia didn't believe so, and Mr. Cross must not have either if he wanted her to write to Lady Agony. He must have wanted Amelia to investigate the fires, and that's what she intended to do.

"Of course he was angry." Mrs. Lewis reached over and patted Mrs. Rothschild's hand. "Anybody would be, and we must not blame him for assuming the worst when the worst is what he's come to expect."

"When did the fires occur?" asked Amelia.

Mrs. Rothschild took a moment before answering. "The first fire occurred immediately after Rose's accident. I remember because I was in a fog, and I assumed I had done something without being aware of it. Those first days were unmemorable, a string of mornings and evenings and sleepless nights. The second fire, however, happened two weeks ago, and I was alert and ready for the evening crowd. Something sparked in the stove unnaturally, not like any wood or coal."

Kitty frowned. "Were the contents of the fire examined?"

"They were doused and shoveled out and the flue cleaned." Mrs. Rothschild sighed. "Despite my concerns, my husband went on serving liquor and apologizing for the absence of biscuits in the basket."

Mrs. Evans harrumphed. "Drunkards don't appreciate them anyway."

"Do you know of anyone who might have tampered with your stove?" Amelia asked. "Anyone who might have had a vendetta against the business?"

Mrs. Rothschild shook her head. "The neighborhood depends on it. We have no garden parties, Lady Amesbury. No drawing rooms to play cards in. Everyone comes. None complain—except when we shut our doors at the end of the night. Why should anyone set fire to it?"

It was a fair question, and one Amelia didn't easily dismiss. By all accounts, including Amelia's firsthand, Mrs. Rothschild was right. The neighborhood needed the pub. It was the place they congregated and relaxed and forgot. Other drinking holes existed, certainly. A gin house was not too far from the location, for Amelia and Simon had spotted it on their return trip to Mayfair. But a shiny gin palace was not the same as a public house.

"Mrs. Hines certainly had reason to despise it." Kitty's comment was met with surprise and perhaps annoyance, but

MURDER IN MATRIMONY 133

Amelia thought hers was an astute observation. The attack at the pub had not only taken a limb but her way of life. Furthermore, it was a source of angst for Mrs. Rothschild. If they were still friends, Mrs. Hines might have felt adamant about the pub closing so it could wreak no more havoc in people's lives, including her friend's.

Amelia came to Kitty's defense. "What Mrs. Hamsted says is true. Mrs. Hines has every reason to despise the pub. Do you still share a friendship with her?"

"We are on friendly terms." Mrs. Rothschild's answer was tentative and perhaps betrayed its untruth. "I call on her once a month. I bring her items of use and would bring her more, but she refuses my *charity*. What is charity between friends?" She shook her head. "Regardless of any possible motivations, she does not have the strength to start a fire."

Amelia glanced at Mrs. Lewis and Mrs. Evans, who nodded in agreement. "She cannot move ten feet without a stick or chair for assistance."

"Besides, she hasn't been back to the pub since the accident." Mrs. Rothschild sniffed. "It is probably as my husband said, the flue and nothing more. It is an old stove—ancient."

Amelia wasn't convinced it was the flue. Mr. Cross had wanted Lady Agony to get involved for a reason. Was this it? Was it the same reason he had sent her the news of Rose Rothschild's accidental death? Obviously, he thought he'd have time to explain, but he hadn't. He'd been struck down before he could finish much of the work he had started. With any luck, she'd be able to complete this task for him. "Enough doubt must have existed for you to raise the question with Mr. Cross."

"It was a concern at the time, and I voiced my concerns too often. I should have kept them to myself, for it only added to the strain on his time." Mrs. Rothschild laced her fingers together. "Mr. Cross is gone, and whoever he wanted me to write to is no longer an option. My only prayer is for the arsonist, if one exists, not to act again."

"From your mouth to God's ears," said Mrs. Lewis.

The comment put an end to other possible questions, and

134 MARY WINTERS

Kitty and Amelia thanked the women for their hospitality. They invited them to return any time, and a return trip was a possibility. Knowing Mrs. Rothschild could be harmed weighed heavily on Amelia's mind. If something should happen to her or the pub, she would blame herself. Mr. Cross was counting on her to help stop the violence in the East End. But this was one instance that might be beyond her capability. She could give bank notes; she could give advice; but could she give the community a resolution? She stared at the church, looking for an answer, as the carriage began to roll away.

NINETEEN

Dear Lady Agony,

I wonder how many male readers continue to correspond in this space since the trouble with No Wife of Mine. If I recall, the letter caused quite an uproar. The gentleman, who was a bachelor, proclaimed he would rather see his wife's head on a stake before allowing her to pen such responses. Thus, he surmised you must not be married. You responded that his implied violence against women was shameful, and several men vowed to never read your advice again. Tell me the truth: Do you mind their absence?

Devotedly,
Mad Men Make Mischief

Dear Mad Men Make Mischief,

Of course I mind. I never want to offend half of the population. However, since my correspondents sign their letters, as I do, with a pseudonym, I have no idea if they're really gone. For example, are you a Mad Man Making Mischief? That is for you to know and none of us to find out. Indeed, we work better together when we mutually respect each other's identity.

Yours in Secret,
Lady Agony

In Kitty's carriage, Amelia considered the information they'd gleaned at St. George-in-the-East. First and perhaps most important was the oven fires at the Plate & Bottle. Mr. Cross must have believed they were intentionally set for him to suggest Mrs. Rothschild write to Lady Agony. He had mentioned her helping someone in Wapping the morning of his death; it had to have been Mrs. Rothschild. If something happened to him, she would have the name in the newspaper clipping, and from there, she would be able to discern the problem.

If all that was true, he knew he was in danger the day he died, which meant his death wasn't a random act of violence but murder. She had always known its certainty, but now, she had proof.

The truth hung unchallenged in the carriage. Finally, a piece of evidence among the scattered possibilities in her brain. Knowing he might be harmed, Mr. Cross gave the clipping to the curate. If the worst happened to him, Amelia would be able to discern the message. If not, he would be able to explain it himself upon their next meeting.

"You never believed it was a thief after the poor box, and now you know you were right." Kitty opened her reticule, which was plain and gray like her dress. She glanced up and smiled. "Well done."

"We cannot celebrate yet, I'm afraid," Amelia cautioned. "I do not know how the Rothschilds' trouble connects to Mr. Cross's."

"Maybe it doesn't." Kitty continued the search in her reticule. "You won't know for certain until you have all the information." She sniffed. "I hate switching handbags. I always forget something."

"A hankie?" Amelia opened her bag and saw the folded white handkerchief she meant to show Kitty earlier. "I almost forgot. I was accosted on my walk yesterday, and this fell out of the cab that almost ran me over."

"Truly?" Kitty put a hand to her chest. "Why did you not tell me until now?"

"I meant to, but I had Lady Applegate's party to attend and then the prayer meeting. I suppose it slipped my mind."

"Only you could allow a near-death experience to slip your mind. Gracious, Amelia. You might be more careful."

"I'm sorry." Amelia was chastened by Kitty's raised voice. She hated for Kitty to think her careless. "Would you look at it?"

"Of course." Kitty held out her hand.

MURDER IN MATRIMONY   137

Amelia gave her the cloth.

Kitty unfolded the square, and her breath hitched. "Where did you get this?"

"As I told you . . ." Amelia was confused. She had never seen Kitty's jaw set in such a way. "It was dropped by a person in a cab which nearly ran me over."

"In a hansom?" Kitty pressed.

"Indeed, but why are you acting this way?"

"I know whose handkerchief this is." Kitty's voice was barely above a whisper.

Amelia understood Kitty was good with fabric, but this was outstanding. "Whose?"

"Lady Hamsted."

"Are you certain?"

Kitty did not waver. "Positive."

Amelia was stunned by the revelation. It couldn't be so, yet it must be. Kitty knew her mother-in-law intimately. She recognized the cloth beyond a shadow of a doubt. No matter how improbable, the discovery made sense with her theory. The blackmailer had to be a person whose house had been burgled, and Lady Hamsted's house was indeed one the Mayfair Marauder had broken into.

Amelia closed her eyes, the truth seeping in like a cold, damp cloth. Her skin began to prickle, and she felt ill. Lady Hamsted's beloved ruby had been stolen, and she wanted vengeance. Despite the jewel being returned, she was vindictive enough to hold a grudge. Nothing but public humiliation would satisfy her. She would want the thief revealed to all of Mayfair.

What was even more terrifying, however, was that this spiteful human being knew she was Lady Agony. She must know, for she waited in hiding for Amelia's daily walk, disguised in a cab. There was no other reason for her to take a hansom; she had a carriage at her disposal. Furthermore, the blackmailer threatened to upend her schedule. This must have been the threat she meant. Finally, she was missing from Lady Applegate's garden party, forcing Oliver to go in her stead. She must have wanted to avoid seeing her after the near accident. It all added up to Lady Hamsted being the blackmailer.

138   MARY WINTERS

Kitty must have come to the realization at the same time, for a small cry escaped her lips. "This means—it cannot be!"

"It is true. Lady Hamsted knows I am Lady Agony." Amelia thought back to the theft at the Hamsteds' house. "Only think of it. The day the ruby was taken, six people were present, six people concerned with its return: you, Oliver, Simon, the Hamsteds, and me. No one else at the musical was aware of its theft. With only six choices, Lady Hamsted could easily narrow it down to the two women in the group. Lady Agony is obviously a woman, some of the advice perhaps beyond the reach of a man. She knows you like a daughter and believes you are too good to dissemble. But me? She does not know me well, and what she does know proves I am an outsider. Just the sort of woman who could pen such a column."

"What of Lady Tabitha?" asked Kitty, her voice agitated. "Lady Hamsted wouldn't want to be in her bad favor. She is the doyenne of high society, and if anyone was to speak ill of you, she would be the first to come to your defense."

"Which is perhaps why Lady Hamsted has gone to some length to disguise herself." Amelia tapped her chin. "The handwriting. The hansom cab."

"She really ought not to have been so careless as to drop her handkerchief, then. She never imagined you'd find it, I am sure, and even if you did, I would be the only person who could identify it." Kitty clenched her fists in her lap. "Though as for that, she wouldn't assume you shared your secret identity with me. She has no close friendships like ours. Her friends are limited to those who call between the hours of one and three. As if we would limit ourselves to such restrictions!"

"No, we wouldn't, and I'm sorry for her. Everyone should have a friend as dear as you." Amelia smiled, endeared to Kitty by her response. They were as close as two people could be. They did not keep calling hours, and they certainly didn't keep secrets. She had been the first person to reach out to Amelia when she moved to Mayfair. When Edgar was ill, she forced Amelia to rest, taking her place at his bedside. As Winifred grew older, and Amelia had concerns, Kitty listened to them as any mother might, despite not being a mother herself. And when a letter arrived for Lady Agony with which Amelia needed help, she was at her side, asking what she could do. Now, in what might prove to be Amelia's last act as an agony authoress, Kitty was here.

Again.

"One thing is certain." Amelia considered the positives of obtaining the information. "The day was so blustery that she cannot imagine I saw, let alone found, the handkerchief. That gives us a slight advantage of surprise."

"Still, what are we going to *do*?"

"I confess I don't know." Amelia was at a loss. Any suggestion that came to her she immediately dismissed. The only way to save herself was to print Lord Drake's name, and she refused to do that. She could confront Lady Hamsted herself, but that would only confirm her identity. No solution seemed viable. Any she considered would hurt someone she loved.

They sat that way for several moments, the carriage bumping along the London streets, echoing the difficulties forming in Amelia's head. If Lord Drake came forward, his reputation would be tarnished forever, and he had enough problems with his ill father and crumbling Cornwall estate. She could imagine the angst he would face if he was known to be the thief who terrorized Mayfair this summer. A way must exist to fix this, satisfactory to all parties involved, but for the life of her, she could not come to a single conclusion.

Then she noted a small twitch on Kitty's lips which eventually rose to a smile. "What? What is it?"

"I have it. I have the solution."

Amelia waited.

"We shall tell Oliver you are Lady Agony." Kitty revealed the idea with excitement.

"What? Kitty, no." Amelia couldn't comprehend why Kitty would think such an idea was viable or helpful. In fact, it would only compound the problem. If Oliver knew she was Lady Agony, he would never allow them to spend time together. As it was, he was suspicious when Kitty was injured in her company. Once, he'd asked her outright if she was two people: one a countess and one a harbinger of hazard. She had laughed off the accusation, but he hadn't realized then how close he had been to the truth. Now Kitty wanted to tell him. *Gracious no!*

"We must. It is the only way. If he knows of the problem, he will be able to speak of it to his mother. Imagine." Kitty spread out her hands as if to calm the noise in Amelia's head. "There is no one in the world Lady Hamsted loves as much as her son. If he asked her to, she would forget the entire debacle."

"Think of it, Kitty." Amelia couldn't keep the dismay out of her voice. "We would never be able to go out again for the sake of a letter. Oliver already thinks me reckless. Now he will have a reason."

She held up a single finger. "Precisely. Oliver is not an unfeeling man. He is reasonable and just. If he sees the objective to our outings, he will be more agreeable, not less."

"Love makes you blind." Amelia shook her head. "He will put an end to them forever."

"He won't. I wouldn't suggest it if he would." She touched Amelia's chin, which had dipped low, and lifted it. "Trust me. He believes women's voices are valuable and has done much in terms of his own research to interject them. He is not one of these tyrants who believes women should stay in their place. He might even be pleased with the news."

Amelia agreed he was amiable as far as women's independence was concerned, but where that independence involved Kitty, she wasn't as certain. He could imagine no harm coming to her, and harm was possible, albeit unlikely, when they set off to find the truth of a letter. But would he ban their friendship if he knew her true identity?

It was a question they would soon find the answer to when they joined him in the drawing room. There he sat staring at *The Times*, his glasses sliding down the bridge of his nose, hardly noting their arrival, except to say, "Can you believe this, darling? A prospectus has appeared for The United Kingdom Telegraph Company. Its object is to convey messages at a low and uniform rate no matter the distance. Remarkable." When Kitty didn't answer, he looked up from the paper and started. "Lady Amesbury. I didn't expect you for a visit." He folded his paper. "I apologize."

"Good afternoon," replied Amelia. "No apology necessary."

Looking from Amelia to Kitty, Oliver took off his spectacles, placing them on top of the newspaper. He was observant to a fault, the consummate scholar, and suspected trouble at once. "I trust nothing is the matter?"

"To come to the point, we need to speak with you on a topic of grave importance." Kitty sat on the settee. "If now is a good time."

"Why, of course it is. Any time. You know that, dearest." He joined her on the settee, searching her face for clues.

"It has to do with Lady Amesbury." Kitty indicated her direction.

Amelia nodded solemnly from the striped, high-backed chair.

"Most things of grave concern involve Lady Amesbury." He smiled but dropped the smile immediately when he saw Kitty's reaction. "Is it that bad?"

"The thing itself isn't bad at all." Kitty swallowed as if trying to find a way to make the information sound palatable. "The problem arises as it relates to your mother."

"My *mother*?" Oliver was truly perplexed, his eyebrows forming peaks at the fringe of his shaggy brown hair.

"Perhaps I had better explain it," started Amelia. "There is no easy way to say it, Kitty."

"Say what?" he begged. "Please, come out with it."

"I write under the pseudonym of Lady Agony. I have authored the column for two years."

"*You're* Lady Agony?" Oliver blinked.

"Yes."

He sat silently for a moment, then looked to Kitty for confirmation. She nodded, and he contemplated the information. A smile began to reach across his face until it changed his entire visage from perplexed scholar to amused friend. "I don't mind telling you that I admire Lady Agony's letters. They're smart, and I appreciate nothing better than good writing."

Amelia felt herself smiling, too. "Thank you, Oliver. That means a good deal coming from you."

"Why didn't you tell me before?" he asked.

"The fewer people who know my identity, the better," Amelia

142 MARY WINTERS

explained. "It's the nature of the column, I'm afraid. I thought to tell you eventually."

"Your mother, however, has found out the truth." Kitty frowned.

"Really? I cannot imagine how."

"It is a long story," Kitty warned.

"I am good with long stories," said Oliver, settling in next to her.

Kitty proceeded to relay the information. She told him a clue was first dropped when the ruby necklace was stolen, and bent on revenge, Lady Hamsted had followed Lady Agony's column anxiously for the reveal. When none came, and Lady Agony told readers she would be keeping the Mayfair Marauder's identity a secret, she determined to find out Lady Agony's identity. It was easy enough to do when she began with those who knew the people involved in finding the stolen ruby. Only six people knew of its removal from the house, seven including Detective Collings. If Lady Agony knew the identity of the thief, she certainly knew about the theft of the ruby. It had to be Amelia. She was the only woman who fit the description.

"There is one other," said Oliver.

"Who?" Kitty and Amelia asked in unison.

"First." He tossed his shaggy hair, which perpetually dipped below his eyebrows. "You know who stole the jewels in Mayfair?"

"Yes," said Amelia.

He nodded, but did not ask for a name. "And you know for certain it is my mother's handkerchief, Kitty?"

"Quite certain," Kitty answered.

He considered the problem.

At least, Amelia thought that's what he was doing. His brown eyes bounced from her to Kitty to the newspaper to the bookshelf.

"Oliver?" Kitty pressed.

Oliver stood abruptly. "I have figured it out, although as the rightful authoress, Lady Amesbury, you may not be satisfied with the solution. I assure you, however, only one way to solve the problem exists, and I have it."

MURDER IN MATRIMONY 143

"Do not keep us in suspense, Oliver," Kitty chastised. "Tell us!"

"I must inform my mother I am Lady Agony." Oliver stuck out his chest a little as he pronounced the pseudonym.

Amelia looked at Kitty, and Kitty looked at Amelia. Amelia placed her hand over her mouth to cover a laugh.

"Of all the worst times to tell a joke, Oliver." Kitty was incensed. "Humor doesn't become you."

Oliver drew back as if physically hurt by her words. "It is not a jest. I am serious."

Amelia cleared her throat. "Perhaps if you could elaborate on how you could be . . . Lady Agony, it might help us understand." She was having a hard time saying the words, let alone believing the idea, and Kitty crossed her arms, completely unconvinced.

"I'm surprised you haven't come to it already." Baffled by their reactions, Oliver proceeded to explain his reasoning like a teacher to a pupil. "I read. I research. I write. I've learned under the best historians. It would be the most natural activity in the world for me to conduct research under the guise of Lady Agony. I might need to form an opinion about a topic, for instance, the upper crust's response to crime in London."

Amelia warmed to the idea.

Kitty loosened her arms across her chest.

"What is unbelievable is that Lady Agony is purported to be a woman, and I am a man." He dismissed the idea with the wave of his hand. "Any person conducting research on social issues might proclaim the very same. Everyone knows women are more trusted than men in this area."

Kitty lifted a blonde eyebrow. "It's true. I do not know of an author in a domestic magazine who isn't a woman."

"My mother finds me singular in most ways. She will not find the idea unusual in the least, and I am the only one in the party of six whom she loves with the heart of a mother." Here he turned to Amelia with earnestness. "I am truly sorry for the way she has behaved toward you. The ruby means much to her, but it is no excuse. She has the jewel in her possession. For her to accost you in such a way is deplorable, and I make no justification for it." He tilted his head. "Please forgive her on my behalf."

"Absolutely." Amelia's voice was thick with emotion. "For you to do this . . ." She swallowed. "To assume an identity you do not own and perhaps do not wish to is a grand gesture, heroic even." She stood and took his hand. "I can only thank you, yet how insufficient those words are at expressing my gratitude."

"I am not heroic." He shook her hand. "I am happy to do it, as a friend and scholar. I want your work to continue."

"Truly?" she asked.

"Why, yes." He smiled a lopsided smile. "Diverse ideas are required in any field. I do not see why domestic papers should be any different."

"You are *my* hero, Oliver!" Kitty stood and flung her arms around him. Oliver's cheeks pinkened at her overt affection.

Amelia didn't try to hide her smile. The longer she looked upon the adoring couple, the wider it became. Perhaps Kitty had been right all along. Perhaps Oliver was too good for words.

TWENTY

Dear Lady Agony,
Do you believe friends can be trusted with secrets? I
don't want to burden my friend, yet I am becoming
desperate. I know you will tell me true.
Devotedly,
Secret to Share or Keep

Dear Secret to Share or Keep,
If your friend is a true friend, he or she can most
certainly be trusted with a secret. To whom are we to
unburden ourselves if not our friends? Friends make life
tolerable. So, too, will your life be when you share your
secret. Do so, and feel better soon.
Yours in Secret,
Lady Agony

Two nights later, Amelia, Simon, Kitty, and Oliver assembled in the Hamsted dining room to discuss Oliver's progress. The meal was finished, and they had sent the footmen away so that they might talk in private. The men refrained from smoking, but all enjoyed a glass of port to celebrate the good news Oliver hinted at. The sunlight had disappeared an hour ago, and candlelight filled the room, illuminating the dark burgundy liquid in their glasses. The image brought to Amelia's mind the idea of autumn and the end of the season. Soon, many Londoners would retire to their country houses and take up grouse hunting. Amelia, however, would remain in town, and she wished for nothing else. The thought of perusing shop windows at Christmas and smelling chestnuts roasted by costermongers was her ideal holiday.

Simon's eyes flicked to the closed doors and returned to the company around the mahogany table. "So tell us, Hamsted, was your conversation successful?"

Oliver winked at Kitty, who returned the gesture with a smile, before answering. "Completely successful. I have the pleasure of informing you that my mother accepted my admission whole-heartedly. She even went as far as to say she found Lady Agony's column so enjoyable that she was not surprised it was written by a man. The breadth of topics was evidence of it, and only I, with my eye for detail, could have penned such nuanced pieces."

Amelia rolled her eyes. "Indeed."

"It sounds like something she would say." Kitty chuckled.

Oliver preened. "What can I say? I am a genius as far as she is concerned."

Lady Hamsted had many faults, but not appreciating her son wasn't one of them. She praised him in private and in public and probably in her sleep.

"How did you explain your knowledge of her being the blackmailer?" asked Amelia.

"When you told me she wrote the letters to you in uppercase, I came to the idea." He leaned back in his chair, crossing a leg over his knee. "She writes the letter "z" in a distinct way, as you said, with a curl. When I confronted her, I asked her to write the word *zebra* on a piece of paper. She thought it was one of my clever word games and agreed immediately. I saw the curl, and I remarked on it. Then I said old habits die hard even when one tries to change—or disguise—them. I would recognize her letter "z" anywhere and had recognized it lately in her letters to Lady Agony."

"Brilliant," Amelia said. "A claim she could not doubt."

"Or refute. If I had read the letters with my own eyes, then I must be Lady Agony."

Hearing him say it still brought a smile to Amelia's lips.

"Did she try to force you to name the Mayfair Marauder?" asked Simon.

"At first." Oliver uncrossed his leg and came closer to the table. "She is still sore about the ruby, although she said what really bothered her was the thief entering her bedroom." He frowned. "It seems she's had trouble sleeping in there since the theft. I feel bad about that, certainly, but it is no excuse for doing what she did."

Herself suffering from many a sleepless night, Amelia understood how a lack of sleep could affect a person's wellbeing. When the problem became chronic, it occupied more of a person's mind than a person without the affliction might believe. Not only that, but it led to general unease that, in this instance, Lady Hamsted blamed on the thief. It did not excuse her letters, but it did add perspective to them.

"Once I told her I am conducting research on London thieves and could not name my source, she quit the topic. She thanked me for forcing the thief to return her jewel at once. She might have guessed Lady Agony had a personal interest in the outcome, she said." He grinned at Amelia. "If only she knew how right she had been."

"And it is thanks to you that she did not." Simon held up his glass of port. "To Mr. Hamsted, a dear friend, renowned scholar—and intrepid deviant!"

Kitty and Amelia joined in the toast, and Oliver colored only slightly at Simon's praise. When Kitty continued extolling his bravery, however, he quickly switched topics off himself. "How are the plans coming for your sister's wedding?"

"Tolerably." Amelia set down her glass. "If only I could come to a conclusion about Mr. Cross's murderer, I would feel more at ease. The idea that someone murdered him so near his own church is abhorrent to me. The person must be caught before the wedding."

Simon frowned. "You and Kitty learned of no new prospects at your meeting at St. George-in-the-East?"

"A *prayer* meeting," Kitty quickly added when Oliver gave her a quizzical glance. After she and Amelia told him about her secret pseudonym, Kitty had admitted to accompanying Amelia on some of her tasks. Oliver was actually relieved at knowing the reason behind some of Kitty's excursions. Before this knowledge, he was left to guess at the cause of a tear in her dress or a leaf in her hair. Still, he made both Kitty and Amelia promise that they would include him if future tasks included physical danger, which they promptly did.

"The only prospect it illuminated was a possible arsonist at the Plate & Bottle." Amelia recollected the information with dread and unease. If the person acted again, who was to say he wouldn't be successful this time?

"Excuse me?" said Simon. "I must have missed some part of the story."

Amelia explained that the oven at the Plate & Bottle had started on fire twice. After the second fire, Mr. Cross suggested that Mrs. Rothschild write to someone about the problem, and that someone had to be Lady Agony. The morning of his death, he'd told Amelia he wanted her to help someone in Wapping, and it must be Mrs. Rothschild.

Kitty sat up straighter. "It is possible Mr. Cross knew more about the arsonist than he realized."

The room went quiet as they collectively considered the idea. Something about Kitty's words hit upon a memory, and Amelia recalled her conversation at the vicarage with Mr. Cross. The topic had been Madge and Captain Fitz and their upcoming nuptials. Then she recalled her subsequent conversation with Penroy, also about the engaged couple. Prominent in her mind was the empty space on the mantel, where the clock had once stood. Like Cross, it was gone, and in its place a hole that could never be filled.

Which brought to mind the fireplace.

That's it!

"When I met with Mr. Penroy, in Cross's office the day after his murder, I noted ashes in the fireplace."

"Go on," Oliver prodded.

"When Kitty mentioned the arsonist, I immediately thought of fire. There would be no reason to light a fire on the unseasonably warm day."

Oliver tilted his head inquisitively. "You believe a fire was set on purpose? Like the ones at the Plate & Bottle?"

Amelia nodded. "Yes, perhaps to destroy something of value. Perhaps a piece of evidence Mr. Cross found, as Kitty said, about the arsonist."

"Think back." Simon leaned closer. "Might we be able to decipher the contents of the fire if we were to return to the vicarage?"

MURDER IN MATRIMONY 149

Amelia closed her eyes for a moment, but nothing came. "I cannot say. All I remember is the empty place on the mantel and the ash in the fireplace."

"It would not hurt to revisit it," said Kitty. "Even a small fragment might be enough to determine the contents."

"All of us?" Oliver's face was as bright as a new coin.

Amelia didn't have the heart to tell him Kitty suggested the idea for herself and Amelia. He genuinely seemed excited at the prospect of helping with the investigation, and she wasn't sure why she was surprised by his reaction. He was a scholar, a researcher. He was naturally curious about many subjects, and Cross's murder was now one of them. "I don't see why not. We might be able to make a pretense of preparing for the wedding."

"I've found," said Oliver eagerly, "that the more people involved in a process, the more chaotic it becomes. Chaos may create an opportunity to examine the contents of the fireplace without supervision."

Kitty beamed at her husband with pride.

"If you are occupied with Penroy, as you must be, it will afford me the opportunity to examine the fireplace." A brown lock of hair fell across Oliver's eye, and he swept it back. "I am very good with delicate materials, Lady Amesbury. I study them with gloves at the library. You can trust me to retrieve any evidence without causing it harm."

"Of course I do," Amelia assured him. "You are the most qualified of all of us to figure out the contents." She meant every word; however, she did worry about his clumsiness. He could be physically awkward when it came to parties or events. But in a task that involved document retrieval? He would surely be capable.

"Then we have a plan." Kitty couldn't contain her excitement and clasped her hands together. "Oliver and I will fetch you and Lord Bainbridge tomorrow, and to the vicarage we shall go."

"Do wait until after breakfast," said Amelia. "I promised Winifred a game of jacks."

Oliver crossed his arms. "You certainly live a double life, Lady Amesbury. Countess, mother, authoress. How do you keep it up?"

She looked at the sympathetic eyes returning her glance. "With a great deal of help from my friends."

TWENTY-ONE

Dear Lady Agony,
  I've heard three whistlers in as many days, carrying on like birds in a tree. Please inform your readers that whistling in public is in bad taste. Many seem to have forgotten entirely.
  Devotedly,
  Annoyed Listener

Dear Annoyed Listener,
  I like nothing better than to whistle a tune. However, I keep the noise to myself due to the annoyance it causes others. I remind readers, as you ask, to do the same.
  Yours in Secret,
  Lady Agony

The next morning, Amelia hurried to meet Lord Drake in Hyde Park to share with him the good news. Last evening, she'd sent a note to him, hoping to alleviate his worries at her first opportunity. He had readily agreed to the meeting, no doubt fearing the worst. He would be grateful to learn that the blackmailer had ceased her attempts and was giving up the plan to out the Mayfair Marauder.

With a little help from her son.

Amelia smiled to herself as she entered the gate at Hyde Park Crossing. When she considered Oliver's actions, they still amused her. Who but Oliver Hamsted would have no qualms about claiming the pen name of Lady Agony? She shook her head. She could have told him about her secret work much earlier; he might have been a helpful collaborator. Yet she and Kitty had great fun keeping it from him. All the wild excuses they'd made up for the sake of a letter came to mind, and she wondered if he was now recalling them too. Perhaps never again would she and Kitty be able to slip out the servants' door without him noticing. Then again, he could be terribly obtuse when he was in the middle of writing a book or researching an article. They might still pass by undetected.

Amelia wasn't surprised to see Lord Drake waiting on a park bench even though she was fifteen minutes early. He stood when he saw her approach. He was dressed impeccably, despite the early hour, in a dark brown overcoat, light blue cravat, and matching powder-blue gloves. But the plum shadows under his eyes conveyed his distress and lack of sleep, and the scar near his lip deepened with his frown as he inquired about her request for a meeting. "I take it you do not have good news."

"On the contrary, I have very good news." Amelia smiled. "The blackmailer is no longer a threat. I have it on good authority from her son that she will cease the subterfuge immediately."

"*Her* son." His brown eyes widened. "It is a woman?"

Amelia nodded. "Lady Hamsted."

"The ruby." Lord Drake stood still, thinking, then slowly nodded. "I heard her rail about its theft long after it was returned. I assumed it was braggadocio over its value."

"I cannot say I'm completely surprised." Amelia took a step toward the path, and he followed. She didn't want their conversation remarked by anyone. "An occurrence happened with her daughter-in-law Kitty Hamsted, who is my dear friend, that opened my eyes to her true nature."

"Is that how you found her out?" he asked. "Because of your friendship?"

"I am quite close to the family." Amelia sidestepped a stray branch. "I started with our list of victims, as we discussed at my house. After I ruled out Aunt Tabitha, I sought out the Applegates. But it was Kitty Hamsted who guessed it was her mother-in-law." It wasn't a lie. Kitty had recognized the handkerchief. "Her son, Oliver, was able to confirm it. Once he confronted her, it was easy to convince her to stop. He said if he'd been able to discover she was the blackmailer, it would be possible for others to as well. Once she realized her name, not just the thief's, would be involved in the scandal, she dropped the idea immediately. She did not want the Hamsted name associated with the gossip papers."

They were now at the statue of Achilles and stopped. Towering thirty-six feet in the air, it made a grandiose statement, if not a controversial one, for although a fig leaf covered the hero's nether regions, it did not cloak them completely. As the city's first nude statue since antiquity, it was often noticed and much remarked upon. The dedication to Arthur Duke of Wellington for his efforts in the Peninsular and Napoleonic Wars made little difference to the indignant who thought nudity should be rejected at all costs. Amelia thought such effrontery was not only disrespectful to the sculptor but childish. She couldn't imagine spending so much time on a piece of art only to have it disparaged by petty people.

Lord Drake turned to Amelia. "It would appear my secret is safe once again thanks to you."

"It's the least I could do for a friend," she reassured him.

"I am grateful for your friendship."

"And I yours," said Amelia. "You will be at my sister's wedding?"

"I would not miss it." He, too, was smiling now. "She, like myself, is lucky to count you as a confidante. After the trouble with Radcliffe, I was certain she would be run out of London. I might have known better with you on her side. Not only that, but she is to be married to a fine man. They have my heartiest congratulations."

"Captain Fitz *is* a fine man, and I am very happy for them." She looked in the direction of the exit. "In fact, I should be getting back. Arrangements have been consuming every spare moment."

"I can imagine, especially with so little time to make them." Lord Drake started to say something, stopped, and began again. "By the by, I read Lady Agony's column after we met last time. I have to say that I find it wonderfully refreshing."

"Oh?" Amelia wasn't sure how to reply.

"She encourages independent thinking. We could use more of that in the world." His eyes met hers. "As for the thefts, she

MURDER IN MATRIMONY 153

treated the return of the jewels as recompense enough for the crimes, entirely excusing the behavior. But you know this—having read her column."

"Indeed, I do." She had a hard time looking away, for his eyes were filled with questions she could not answer.

"If I met her, I would shake her hand and thank her for her generosity."

"I'm certain she would like that," Amelia said non-committedly.

"I must let you get back to your wedding plans, and I have a dozen things to do before I am done with the day." He fastened the single button on his coat. "Goodbye, Lady Amesbury." He stuck out his hand.

She took it, and he pressed it heartily.

"Thank you for your generosity. I shan't forget it."

After he walked away, she turned in the opposite direction. He was an intelligent man. He clearly guessed she was Lady Agony. But he wouldn't press her for the information in a hundred years, nor would she press him for confirmation about his relationship in Cornwall. People didn't need to know every-thing to be great friends. Sometimes it was the knowledge that there was more beyond the surface of a person that garnered admiration and respect. She looked forward to learning more about Lord Drake over time.

Right now, wedding plans loomed large in her mind, not to mention the investigation into Mr. Cross's murder. It wouldn't be long, and her friends would arrive to put the plan to examine the fireplace in motion.

What awaited her, however, when she arrived home was not wedding schedules or friends but Winifred on the steps with her jacks. She hadn't seen Winifred play the game in a long time, calling it "babyish" last time her friend Beatrice Gray was over. But now she sat by herself, as if in deep thought, offhandedly bouncing the ball.

Winifred is growing up, Amelia thought as she gazed upon the beautiful girl who was as close as any daughter. Amelia suspected the game was a pretense for what Winifred really wished to do today: discuss Amelia's family. She'd overheard

154 MARY WINTERS

Aunt Tabitha talking about the arrival of various interesting family members and had several questions for her already.

"Good morning, Winifred."

"You're back!" Winifred scooted over, and Amelia joined her on the step.

"Have you been waiting long?" asked Amelia.

"No, but I have been waiting to ask you about the Feathered Nest."

Amelia flourished a hand. "Ask away."

"I can't imagine meeting new strangers every night of the week," continued Winifred. "It must have been thrilling, much more thrilling than your life now."

Amelia smiled. "When put that way, it does sound thrilling, but I assure you, it was not. Everyone I met got to leave while I had to stay."

"But your family." Winifred tossed the rubber ball and picked up jacks in groups of three. "They sound extraordinarily interesting. I do not care what Aunt Tabitha said to Mrs. Tipping. I hope they all come, including Aunt Gertrude."

A sputter of laughter rose to Amelia's lips. "Aunt Gertrude is a wonderful person, I assure you. She is . . . different than Aunt Tabitha in that they have not been raised in the same manner or households. But they are of similar age and authority. They might even get on quite well."

Winifred fumbled her jacks and set down the ball. "I, for one, cannot wait until they arrive."

"Nor I." She noted the sparkle in Winifred's Amesbury-blue eyes.

Winifred's dimple showed. "If they are as good as Madge, I know it will be a fine wedding."

Amelia pretended to clean out her ears. "Madge good? Are you certain we're speaking about the same person?"

Winifred laughed. "She *is* good, very good to me." A little furrow crept up on her brow. "I am surprised she's getting married, though. She seemed to enjoy managing the stables at the Feathered Nest too much to ever leave it."

Amelia was taken aback by the comment. "She enjoyed it very much, but I suppose love changes people, in a way."

MURDER IN MATRIMONY 155

"Even Madge?" Winifred shrugged. "If you say so."

The point bothered Amelia more than she cared to admit. At one time, Amelia would have completely agreed with Winifred, but that was a time before Captain Fitz. Now that they were engaged, Amelia understood her desires had changed. The same change had occurred in Amelia when Simon had entered her life. Her love did not lessen; it grew. Madge didn't love her life in Somerset any less; she loved Captain Fitz more. At least she hoped that was the case.

"Speaking of the wedding, I am going to the church to make final arrangements. The Hamsteds will be here any minute."

Winifred stood up. "Is Mrs. Hamsted arranging the flowers? If so, I'd like tiny pink roses for the braid at my crown."

"Tiny pink roses it will be then." Amelia tried to muss Winifred's hair, but the girl was too quick.

"Don't forget," Winifred instructed as they parted at the steps.

"Never." The promise was easily kept as Kitty's driver approached the next moment and Amelia entered the carriage. After greeting Oliver and Simon, Amelia told Kitty of Winifred's wishes, and she promptly agreed, adding that Winifred looked best in pink.

"I, myself, am wearing yellow, but that is only because it is my last chance to don my chiffon before the change in seasons."

Oliver grasped her gloved hand. "I love your yellow chiffon."

"I know you do," Kitty answered with a quiet giggle.

Simon looked at Amelia and rolled his eyes. She would have done the same if she didn't find their admiration for each other a little bit adorable.

"What are you wearing?" Kitty asked Amelia.

"Madge prefers light blue, and all her bridesmaid sisters will be wearing it. I confess I've been too preoccupied to think much of her selection."

"Really, Amelia." Kitty censured her with a look. "Fashion waits for no one—even murderers. The day will come, and you will be unprepared."

"I assure you it will be fine." Amelia enjoyed a nice dress as much as any woman, but it was hardly the time to discuss

156   MARY WINTERS

fashion. All Saints on Margaret Street was in view, and she dropped the subject. "Now, remember the plan. Lord Bainbridge and I will keep Penroy busy. Kitty will keep watch on the curate in the nave. And you will slip into the vicarage and examine the contents of the fireplace. Are we all agreed?"

Three heads nodded back at her.

"If I am in danger of detection, please give a whistle." Seeing their surprised looks, Oliver continued, "Any tune is fine to alert me. I do not require more than a few notes."

"What of a cough?" asked Simon.

Oliver shook his head. "Anyone might cough accidentally."

"I am not an excellent whistler." Simon sniffed.

The footman opened the door, and Amelia whispered, "For heaven's sake, I'll whistle for Lord Bainbridge. If you are in danger, Mr. Hamsted, you will know it. I'll make certain."

Amelia took the footman's hand and descended the newly placed steps. The church was quiet, a respite amid the bustling streets. Morning service was finished, and only a few stray beams of sunlight hung in the church. It was hard to imagine a murder had been committed so near this place of peace. Yet it had and against one of its foremost members. She still couldn't reconcile herself to it.

Mr. Penroy was talking to the curate but immediately dropped the conversation when he saw the group enter. Although he smiled briefly, his brown eyes remained as dull as dust on hard-to-reach furniture, and the effect was one of judgment and pride. "Lady Amesbury, I must owe the pleasure of such a visit to the nuptials of your sister."

"Good day, Mr. Penroy. Indeed, you do." Amelia motioned to her friends. "This is Lord Bainbridge, and he and I are principal bridesmaid and groomsman, and Mrs. Hamsted is assisting with the flowers. We thought to all come at once so as not to disrupt you more than necessary."

"Come any time." The words were welcoming, but Mr. Penroy's stance was not. He hadn't made a move in their direction, and they were forced to approach him. "Mr. Dougal would be pleased to assist you."

Mr. Dougal appeared to have enough to keep him busy, for

MURDER IN MATRIMONY

157

despite it being early afternoon, his forehead was wet with perspiration, and his shirt collar clung to his thick neck. Yet he nodded cheerfully, his fair complexion, which was prone to flush, giving him an air of willingness. "Certainly, I would."

"I wonder, Mr. Dougal, if you might give us a tour of the church—for reference purposes." Kitty smiled her prettiest smile. "I wish to be as helpful as I'm able the day of the wedding, and I have been inside this masterpiece only once."

"I would be honored." No one was immune from Kitty's charms, and the curate displayed a full set of large teeth. "Let us begin at the beginning." Whatever Mr. Dougal and Mr. Penroy had been speaking of was left off entirely for the sake of the tour, and Kitty and Oliver trailed behind him as he walked toward the altar.

Penroy followed the group with his eyes. "Mr. Dougal is enthusiastic about his work. I will say that for him."

"Mr. Cross esteemed him very much," Amelia put in. It was always this way with her and Mr. Penroy. She felt the need to counter every word he said with another.

"Mr. Cross esteemed many people, which perhaps said more about himself than the persons in his regard." He turned his face from the group, and despite being young, it was a collection of hard lines.

Sensing the difficulty, Simon switched topics. "I confess I am unfamiliar with weddings, being party to none until now. Maybe you can enlighten me."

"I understand." Penroy nodded. "The ceremony can be intimidating, frightening even, for ones not accustomed to participating in the ritual."

"Intimidating, yes," Simon repeated, but Amelia hardly imagined he was intimidated by church rituals. It would behoove Penroy to believe so, however. Nothing pleased the young priest more than explaining protocal.

"And your own wedding, Lady Amesbury? How familiar are you with weddings in town?"

"Not at all," answered Amelia. "My own wedding was an informal affair in Mells, but it was no less meaningful or happy. My groom was ill and did not want to wait, so he obtained a special license. It was a cloudless blue day and the best hour of our marriage, I'm afraid."

A wrinkle flitted across Simon's forehead, and she knew he was feeling sorry for her. She didn't want his pity, however. Albeit short, her marriage was satisfactory in most senses of the word. She gained an aunt and a child and a best friend in Kitty. It was true that theirs hadn't been a love match—she understood that from her time with Simon—but they had been friends and companions at a time Edgar desperately needed one.

"Which is to say, I'd appreciate an overview of the ceremony as much as the marquis." She nodded at Simon.

Mr. Penroy paced back and forth, perhaps preparing a long speech, which was fine with her. The more time he took the better.

"Marriage is a commitment that should be entered into with much gravity. Months, not weeks, should be taken to consider the enormity of the promise one makes." Mr. Penroy stopped and looked pointedly at Amelia. "The ceremony itself, while enjoyable to plan for women like yourself, is a mere trifle compared to a lifetime vow. In fact, the matter ought to have been discussed with the couple before now. I should really check their appointment date, as well as go over the registry with you, in my office—"

Alarms went off in Amelia's head. Oliver would be in the office by now; he needed time to investigate the contents of the fireplace. The small pieces would prove difficult to decipher. "First, if you wouldn't mind." Amelia motioned to the nave. "It would be helpful for me, and probably Lord Bainbridge as well, to walk through the ceremony."

"Exactly so," added Simon. "I, like Lady Amesbury, would like to know what I am to do during the ceremony."

"Your task is simple." Mr. Penroy waved a hand toward the altar. "All you must do is walk up the aisle with Lady Amesbury. She will take your left arm, and you will walk last before the bride and groom. My job is the one that takes real preparation. I must give the homily, and I haven't even met the bride or groom."

"I understand, but could we attempt the walk up the aisle, as a sort of trial?" Simon asked.

"Yes," agreed Amelia, seeing how it would cause further delay. "It would be ever so helpful."

Penroy released a breath of exasperation. "Fine."

Simon held out his left arm, and she took it.

They started up the aisle slowly, methodically. Surreptitiously, Amelia looked for Kitty and Oliver and, when they reached the front, spotted Kitty near the left of the pulpit. Oliver was nowhere in sight. She turned to Simon and smiled. Oliver had begun his first investigation.

It was then that she noticed Simon's eyes. The church, harkening back to medieval times, was naturally dark, but his eyes were as green as the vales of Somerset. A new spark appeared, a flicker, like wind through leaves of a tree. One couldn't see the wind until it moved something or someone, and in this case, it was she.

A twist rippled through her chest, a quickening of her heart. It felt as if her life had led her to this very moment. No other time would have been right. Life was a twisted path that afforded many lessons, and sometimes it took many turns to find what one was looking for. It was Simon. Perhaps it had always been Simon. And it had taken her this long to find him.

Penroy continued, ignorant of the breath leaving her body. "The bridegroom stands to the right of the bride. The father stands just behind her so that he is ready to give her hand. Lady Amesbury, you will stand to the left of the bride, ready to take her glove."

"I will," Amelia murmured.

"I will as well," said Simon.

"You do nothing, my lord. It is only Lady Amesbury who waits for the glove. The vows are said, the ring is given, and the ceremony is over. Now, let us proceed to my office to discuss the registry of marriage."

It was only then that Amelia was shaken from her trance to see Mr. Penroy turning toward the vicarage, where Oliver was certainly sorting through the ashes of the fireplace. She called after him, "Wait! One moment."

He turned around.

She wracked her brain for something to say, some question that had been left unasked. But the last several minutes were a fog. She might have been standing at the altar of All Saints on Margaret Street, but her mind had been somewhere else. "Uh . . . uh . . . then we leave our posts?"

"Why yes, of course." Mr. Penroy turned and continued walking.

At this point, Simon tried a whistle and failed miserably. What came out was a hiss that might have come from a broken tea kettle. It wasn't even enough to catch Penroy's attention, let alone the attention of the intended receiver: Oliver Hamsted.

She frowned at Simon.

He looked as sheepish as a boy who has been caught taking a second dessert. "I told you I am an inadequate whistler. I said I needed a different signal."

Ignoring the complaint, Amelia grabbed his hand and pulled him down the aisle after Penroy, whistling all the way.

TWENTY-TWO

Dear Lady Agony,
   We know June is the best month to marry, but what of the day of the week? Can you give brides any advice?
   Sincerely,
   Wedding Day Decision

Dear Wedding Day Decision,
   I cannot, but perhaps this old rhyme can:
   Marry on Monday for health,
   Tuesday for wealth,
   Wednesday the best day of all,
   Thursday for crosses,
   Friday for losses, and
   Saturday for no luck at all.
   Yours in Secret,
   Lady Agony

Simon and Amelia had no choice but to follow Mr. Penroy into the vicarage. Upon entering, they continued making as much noise as possible. For Simon's part, he talked loudly, mostly about the medieval architecture. He praised William Butterfield's masterpiece and the gothic embellishments. Amelia, however, knew how to whistle and whistled loudly, also commenting on the prettiness of the stained-glass windows, illuminated by the afternoon sun.

Penroy looked at them curiously. He was a dull man without imagination, the type of person who did not ask questions about the color of the sky or the makeup of the stars. He was interested in that which involved himself and was unable to remark with any effect on the beauty of the church or the day.

Instead, he continued marching toward his office with a general murmur of acquiescence.

Amelia resisted hiding her eyes as they rounded the corner. The office door was open, but with relief, she saw that Oliver was not inside. The curtains, half open, afforded only filtered light, yet it was enough to take in the room. The fireplace was dark and unlit, and if Oliver had searched it, he left no evidence of himself behind. Their efforts to warn him must have worked.

They'd just entered the room when Oliver joined them, and Amelia wondered if perhaps he'd ducked out the moment before they arrived.

"You haven't seen Mrs. Hamsted, have you?" asked Oliver.

Amelia shook her head. "She is probably busily planning the number of orange blossoms to procure."

"Join us, Hamsted," said Simon. "Mr. Penroy was just about to show us where the attendants will sign after the wedding."

"Thank you." Oliver eyed the bookshelf. "I'll busy myself with these volumes if you don't mind."

"Go ahead," said Mr. Penroy with a hint of exhaustion. He seemed ready for the group to leave. "I cannot vouch for their quality. I haven't had time to go through them."

"You have your own belongings to consider, which I assume will be transferred to the vicarage in time." Amelia selected the chair across from Mr. Penroy, and Simon took the one next to her.

"I moved in my personal belongings immediately." He pulled open a desk drawer. "This is my home now. I must make it so."

Amelia had noticed. Although the books hadn't been touched, the desk was cleared, and Mr. Cross's favorite tins and particular prayer requests were removed. His newspapers were also gone, including the serial stories he followed so passionately. She glanced at the box of the fireplace, where ashes littered the floor. Thankfully it hadn't been cleaned.

"I am of the same mind." Oliver was still scanning the bookshelf. "I cannot feel comfortable without my things. Books, primarily. I especially enjoy a good novel. Have you read *The Mill on the Floss*? It came out in April in three

MURDER IN MATRIMONY 163

volumes." He pulled out one of the deep copper-colored volumes from the shelf.

Mr. Penroy's lip curled, showing his distaste for the comment. "I have no preference for sensational novels. That was Mr. Cross's area of indulgence, not mine."

Amelia remembered the fact with a smile. "He said if he didn't read for pleasure, he wouldn't be able to survive his line of work. He was fond of saying reality must be balanced with a healthy dose of fiction. It inspired him."

"If I am in need of inspiration, I turn to the Bible." Mr. Penroy said it as if it was the only thing one could do. "I cannot understand why the vicar would need any other book to occupy his time."

Amelia could think of several reasons but kept them to herself. Oliver was a bookworm and must have a reason for bringing up the work by George Eliot, so she encouraged the conversation. "I myself enjoy many types of fiction by various authors."

"I know you do," Oliver added. "Dickens is one of your favorites, and I wonder if he was one of Mr. Cross's as well from this collection of his work."

"He was. He followed several of Dickens's serials religiously."

Mr. Penroy hiked a brow.

"Excuse me, not religiously," Amelia corrected. "Regularly." It was one of the reasons she'd felt comfortable telling him about her secret pseudonym. He did not frown on penny weeklies or any magazine people read and enjoyed. "Life is a cornucopia of choices, Lady Amesbury," he used to say. "That kind of bounty is godsent." And oh, how she believed it, too. Her letters were as abundant as stars in the sky, each one with its own voice. She didn't have to like every one to know she was glad they existed.

"Books are expensive, and I do not believe in squandering money," said Mr. Penroy.

Amelia thought no money could be squandered on a book. Even if she didn't enjoy it, she usually learned something from it, and from that itself she gained enjoyment. But Mr. Penroy was correct about cost. Although the price of books had

164   MARY WINTERS

reduced dramatically over the course of time, they could still be expensive, which is one of the reasons Mr. Cross cherished the books he did have, rereading them many times over. In fact, she was surprised at the new book on the shelf.

"Some people think of books as an investment." Simon's tone relayed his belief in the statement. "They think books give you something more precious than money in return."

"I am not one of those people." Mr. Penroy glanced at his timepiece. "Now to the registry." He smoothed the paper on his desk. "If we may?"

Though it was a question, Amelia understood they had no option of declining. He covered the registry briefly, and when he was finished, Kitty was there with the curate, who looked fatigued. Amelia imagined that Kitty had him circling the church like a dog after his tail.

"Thank you, Mr. Dougal," said Kitty. "You have been entirely helpful."

"It was my pleasure." Mr. Dougal was audibly winded, and his cheeks were as flushed as the roots of his ginger-colored hair. He was a man who did his due diligence, however, and none could accuse him of shirking his duties.

Simon and Amelia thanked Mr. Penroy, and Kitty and Oliver did likewise. After another round of thank yous to the curate, they were gone and only waited to be seated in the carriage before asking Oliver for the results of his subterfuge.

Amelia had rarely seen Oliver so pleased. He was a distracted man with attention for only a book or his wife. Rarely did he draw attention to himself and could disappear from a party—most likely to glance at a library—without anyone noticing his departure.

But now, he smiled at their rapt attention, and Amelia thought he even delayed the telling of events to savor the moment, his efforts, or the information.

"Well?" Kitty pressed. "Did you find anything of importance?"

Still smiling, Oliver said, "You heard me mention the book titled *The Mill on the Floss*?"

Kitty waved away the comment. "This is not the time for one of your book reports. Lady Amesbury and Lord Bainbridge need to know what was found."

MURDER IN MATRIMONY 165

"It *is* what I found. Three new books among very old tomes. It must be important."

Kitty tapped his knee. "But the fireplace, Mr. Hamsted."

Oliver pulled a singed scrap of paper out of his coat pocket. "A handwritten note. I can make out the word *our*."

Simon, Amelia, and Kitty leaned closer, and Amelia could indeed make out the word also. "It's Cross's handwriting. But what does it mean?"

"It could be a reference to the church," Simon put in.

"True." Amelia squinted at the fragment. "But no word or punctuation mark follows it."

"Maybe it is a list." Kitty held up a finger. "I make lists all the time for my parties."

Amelia thought on the idea. It could be a list, but what sort of list ended with the word *our*? She returned to the book. "What of *The Mill on the Floss*? He wouldn't have splurged on himself."

Oliver cleaned his glasses. "I agree with you. The books in his collection were a decade old. Maybe someone loaned him the books."

"Maybe someone gave them to him," added Simon.

"Maybe Miss Rothschild," Amelia thought aloud.

"But she worked at the factory only a month." Kitty frowned. "I cannot imagine she had excess funds to purchase several expensive gifts."

A thought came to Amelia. "Such as the cross necklace she gave her mother."

Kitty gasped. "*Yes*."

Simon touched his chin. "Miss Rothschild might have been involved in something she shouldn't have been, something that earned her additional funds."

"But what?" Oliver asked.

"That is the question." Amelia glanced at the group. "It's one I'm going to put to her mother, who might have some idea where the money came from for her necklace. She had to wonder about it, given their reduced circumstances. Perhaps she asked."

"A solid plan," said Kitty. "We must go back to St. George-in-the-East."

166 MARY WINTERS

"*I* must," Amelia corrected. "You don't have to do anything."

Kitty reached for Amelia's hands. "After all you've been through, I would never desert you in your hour of need." Her blue eyes darted to Oliver. "Mr. Hamsted would not expect me to, would you, dear?"

Oliver rushed to assure them both. "Of course not. Mr. Cross was your friend and confidant, Lady Amesbury. After all you've told me about the situation, I think only you might be able to puzzle together the pieces of his death. If my wife can be of support, who am I to withhold her assistance?"

"She is indeed a great help to me. You all are." She shook her head. "How can I ever repay you?" She was overwhelmed by the support she felt in the carriage. Even Simon, who'd been so reluctant when they first met, was prepared to help her in every way. He was still overly cautious, in her opinion, but he was there for her in ways that she never expected.

"By your friendship—and esteem." Simon's voice dipped lower with the last word, and with it, Amelia's stomach.

"You have it," promised Amelia.

"I have a feeling you're going to rely on us all a good deal to get through these next few days . . ." Oliver was staring out the window distractedly. He pulled back the curtain so that they could see what he was seeing. His face revealed the hopelessness Amelia felt upon taking in the situation.

In front of her house was one, two, three carriages—and that didn't account for the family coming by train. Members of the Scott family were in various states of unloading, and Bailey, despite having his hands full, was taking a large trunk from Aunt Gertrude. As the carriage drew closer, Amelia heard her say it was impossible to find good poultry in the city, and she'd brought a nice duck for dinner. She only hoped the cook might know how to dress it properly.

While this comment was dreadful enough, still more dreadful was the fact that Aunt Tabitha watched all of it unfold from the front step. She stood as rigid as a watchtower guard, determined not to allow the enemy entrance. With her raven-handled cane gripped at her side, she made a formidable obstacle, but Winifred circumvented her. She ducked under her arm, running down the steps to greet Madge and Veronica Scott, whom she already thought of as family. Veronica, Amelia's mother, greeted her with a generous hug, and despite the chaos of the scene, Amelia felt herself smile.

Her smile was dampened, however, by the icy eyes of Tabitha Amesbury, which landed on hers at that very moment. Amelia's only relief was the necessary wait she must endure to get into her own house. Indeed, it might be several minutes before their carriage could unload, and she savored those moments like a prisoner's last meal.

"I suppose none of you wants to join me?" All at once, they spoke their excuses. "I do not blame you. I suppose I must face the lion's den alone."

The carriage inched forward.

It stopped in front of the house, and she sighed. "'Once more unto the breach, dear friends, once more.'"

TWENTY-THREE

Dear Lady Agony,

Are all brides doomed to wear white? My skin looks dreadful in the pale color, yet the dressmaker says it is all she sews. What is a woman to do? I'm to be married next June.

Devotedly,
I Prefer Colors

Dear I Prefer Colors,

I'm afraid brides continue to wear white for the time being. Although at one time, brides wore red, pink, blue, brown, or black, since the wedding of our great Queen Victoria, brides have shunned colors altogether. I'm sorry white does not agree with your skin tone. Perhaps ivory will agree better.

Yours in Secret,
Lady Agony

The first several minutes in the house, Amelia's attention was divided in multiple directions. Madge asked about her wedding dress, their mother wondered about tea, and her sisters demanded a tour of the garden immediately. It was her father, however, who drew her attention with his calm presence, and Amelia held out her arms to him. His quietness was a comfort to her, and she took in his warm brown eyes, so much like her own, and steady deportment with gratitude and relief. The entire house might be in a whirlwind, but with her father at her side, she could weather any maelstrom.

"First your rooms, then tea, then a tour." Amelia's eyes flicked to Madge. "Your dress will be fitted tomorrow, as well as ours."

"And where shall I put the duck?" Aunt Gertrude was a tall woman, as tall as Aunt Tabitha, and her loud voice carried above Amelia's head, filling the hallway.

"Follow me, please." The timbre of Aunt Tabitha's words determined her authority, and the two women set off in the direction of the kitchen while Mrs. Tipping showed the rest of the family to their rooms.

Meanwhile, Amelia prepared for tea in the formal drawing room, a large space that could accommodate everyone and more. Winifred trailed behind her, giddy with excitement. As her family trickled in, the room grew louder, and Amelia's heart grew full. Family would always mean noise to her, a cheerful din that couldn't be replicated in any of London's ballrooms. This was a different kind of noise, a happy noise among people who loved one another.

"How are the wedding preparations coming?" Mrs. Scott asked as soon as the tea was poured.

"I'm afraid I have sad news to report from the church." Amelia took a sip of her tea, knowing it was going to be a long afternoon with much conversation. "Mr. Cross was murdered after Madge left for Somerset. Mr. Penroy will be the new officiant."

"*Murdered*," repeated Amelia's sister Sarah with a gasp. Sarah looked the most like their mother, with fair brown hair and blue eyes that might be described as wistful. She was sensitive with a delicate constitution and preferred music to conversation. Amelia had seen her play the pianoforte for hours without speaking a word to anyone, living in the blithe music of her own making.

"There are lots of murders here." Unbothered by the information, Madge selected three lemon cakes. "Believe me. I've seen them—personally."

"London is a large city." Mr. Scott sought to soothe his daughter Sarah's nerves. "Much more happens here, good and bad, than our little village in Somerset."

"Mr. Penroy has a request of you and the captain." Amelia hid the next statement behind her teacup. "To meet at the vicarage before the wedding."

170 MARY WINTERS

Madge almost tipped her plate. "What? Why?"

"It doesn't surprise me that the church thinks you need more instruction," put in Amelia's sister Penelope, winking at Amelia. Penelope was the eldest Scott sister, and she and Amelia understood each other without saying a word. Penelope knew all her sisters intuitively. Having her present was as welcome now as ever. To survive the next week would take patience and empathy, and Amelia could count on her sister for both. Like everyone in the Scott family, Penelope was hard working, but she lacked the dramatic reactions some of the family fell prey to. If something must be done, she set about doing it without hesitation or fuss. Amelia appreciated the quality she sometimes lacked in herself.

"I don't need instruction." Madge pouted. "The captain and I love one another, and that's all the vicar needs to know."

"If only it were that easy, Madge." Amelia sighed. "Mr. Penroy is a young priest, and he has certain ideas that must be entertained. Not being known to you personally, and All Saints not being your home parish, he'd like time to acquaint himself with you and the captain. I'm sure that's all it is."

"I think it's a fine idea. What could be more natural?" Sarah was more inclined toward religion than the rest of the family, and it did not astonish Amelia that she would enjoy getting to know a priest. While the family was faithful, Sarah might be described as devout.

Madge sniffed at the idea, not bothering to hide her feelings. "How was the old priest killed anyhow?"

"He was murdered by a thief after the poor box. At least that is what they say . . ." Amelia allowed the sentiment to trail off, but her family, keen to her emotions, sensed a difficulty.

Madge put down her plate of cake. "You do not think so?"

Amelia noted Winifred's rapt attention and avoided an answer. "I don't know what to think. What I do know is that the meeting is to take place before the wedding, and I'm positive it will be easy enough to arrange between fittings and flowers and food arrangements."

"Of course it will be," said Mrs. Scott magnanimously.

At that point, Uncle Henry, Aunt Gert, and Aunt Tabitha

MURDER IN MATRIMONY 171

joined them in the drawing room, and Amelia was happy to see the duck no longer accompanied them. Uncle Henry was every bit as tall as the two women but differed in his round stomach and jolly face. He laughed easily and often, and it did not take much to entice a chuckle from his lips. He was her mother's brother, and their single resemblance was a divot in the chin which couldn't be mistaken for another's in a thousand years.

"Nothing stronger than tea, I suppose?" Uncle Henry said with a chortle. "But that's to be expected in Mayfair. Fine houses, fine manners—but where is the fine sherry, I ask you?"

That was put away days ago, thought Amelia. It was one of the first tasks she completed when she heard Uncle Henry was arriving with her parents.

"Satisfy yourself with a warm cup and a piece of cake, Henry." These instructions were given by Aunt Gertrude, who pointed to an empty chair. "Do not make yourself a nuisance."

Tabitha was pleased with the instructions, or at least her shoulders relaxed as she selected her own chair.

The subject of murder was dropped and not brought up again, and Amelia internally thanked her family. If Uncle Henry got ahold of the subject of murder, she wasn't sure how she'd get him off it. Instead, they talked of the wedding breakfast, and upon discussion, Aunt Tabitha came to realize Aunt Gertrude was an authority on food, menus, and gastric pleasures of every kind. She had someone to talk to who loved food as much as she did, and soon, they drew into a side conversation that couldn't be disturbed.

Meanwhile, Amelia and her sisters talked of dresses, and the men talked of horses. The women made plans to leave early the next day for the fittings. The dressmaker was scurrying to finish the final details and could not make the trip out to Mayfair. Amelia's mother and sisters were glad to go to the shop, for they had not been to Regent Street and looked forward to seeing the famous street on their excursion.

Glancing into their eager faces, Amelia looked forward to the trip too. They were much like herself, she imagined, encountering the variety that was London a little more than two years ago. So much had changed since then. She'd become a wife to Edgar, a mother to Winifred, and a pain in the side to Aunt Tabitha. She smiled. Yet so much remained the same: the unconditional love of her parents, the unwavering support of her sisters, and the comfort of having family in the house. Tomorrow would be a delightful day.

As good as their promise, the women were up with the sun the next day. The Scott family were early risers naturally, and staying in town could not change that. Instead of her morning walk, Amelia went directly to the breakfast table, where footmen were scurrying to finish laying the sideboard.

After they breakfasted heartily (all the Scotts were fine eaters), the women, along with Winifred, who wouldn't miss it for the world, set off for the dressmakers. Anita Hernandez was recently installed in London from Mexico and had a keen eye for fashion, which Kitty discovered immediately. After Kitty sang her praises to influential friends, the dress shop flourished, and Miss Hernandez relocated to Regent Street. Amelia felt fortunate she had committed to the order under a reduced timeline.

The small shop smelled of fresh starch and linen, and two front windows allowed ample light, even in the grayness of the early day. Later, sunlight would pour into those same windows, allowing for a genial warmth that couldn't be replicated in larger stores. Miss Hernandez cared for her customers the way some mothers cared for their children. Her first and last thought of the day was how to best serve them.

"Lady Amesbury, I've been expecting you and your family." Miss Hernandez rushed to greet her as soon as the door opened. Her dress was perfection, a light blue in Isabeau style with dark blue rosettes down the front. The color brought out the rich hues of her skin, not to mention her silky brown hair, which was parted down the middle and pulled away from her face in a severe chignon.

"Miss Hernandez." Amelia proceeded to introduce her family.

Miss Hernandez only had eyes for Margaret. She looked her

MURDER IN MATRIMONY 173

frame up and down. "You have gained weight since I measured you."

Amelia and Penelope snickered. Winifred covered a giggle with her hand.

"Those four pieces of cake, I wager," Mrs. Scott whispered.

Madge frowned. "It's been a very stressful time. Food calms my nerves."

"You know what calms my nerves, Miss Margaret? Girls who do not change weight after I make their dress." She flicked a finger. "Come."

Madge's gown awaited them in the dressing room. It was white satin silk with applique lace, fine yet understated compared to many other wedding dresses Miss Hernandez had done this season. Knowing Madge could not object to the design, Amelia released a sigh of relief.

Miss Hernandez's thoughts, however, were unreadable as she instructed Madge to allow her assistant to help her into the gown. She waited in the anteroom with them, her arms crossed, reserving judgment. A few minutes later, when Margaret appeared in the dress, Miss Hernandez smiled with pleasure. "The weight looks good on you. Your chest is not so flat."

"You look stunning, Madge!" Mrs. Scott exclaimed. "Simply stunning."

"I agree," seconded Penelope. "If I could have chosen from all the wedding dresses in the world, this would have been the one for you."

Sarah clasped her hands to her chest and sighed.

"You look very pretty," said Winifred.

Madge's eyes snapped to Winifred. "Do I?"

"Very much." Winifred seemed to sense a different question that hadn't been asked. She tilted her head in that way she did when she knew Amelia had something on her mind, her nose a perfect button.

Madge pulled lightly on the skirt.

Balderdash! She doesn't like it. Amelia rushed to agree with her family, assuring Madge it was the most perfect wedding dress she'd ever seen. "I've never seen a better fit or a more beautiful bride. Captain Fitz is going to be quite smitten." She

174   MARY WINTERS

hoped bringing up his name would remind Madge why she was wearing the dress in the first place.

Madge sniffed.

"You do not like it?" asked Miss Hernandez.

"Oh, I do." Madge stared at the dress in the glass. "I guess I never saw myself as a bride. That is all."

Miss Hernandez's dark eyebrows came together sharply. "It is not a question of the dress then. I'll give you some time with your family."

When the dressmaker closed the door, Mrs. Scott went to her daughter. "Margaret Ann, what's the matter?"

"Look at me, Mama." Madge was still staring into the glass.

Mrs. Scott gestured to her reflection. "I *am* looking, and you look beautiful."

"You know what I mean." Madge pointed to Winifred. "Even Lady Winifred knows what I mean. I am not a woman who wears dresses and tends houses. I am more comfortable in the shed with a hammer. What am I going to do when the captain finds out I can't cook soup?"

Amelia detected the panic in her sister's voice and rushed to ease her mind. She remembered her own raucous feelings the morning of her marriage to Edgar. One moment she'd been watering horses, and the next she was to be the wife of an earl. She'd almost run away that morning, but she was so happy that she hadn't. Marriage, she had found, wasn't based on soup alone, and no matter what the domestic magazines said, they would never adequately relay what happened between two people after they married. "Many women in London do not cook their own soup, and I am lucky to count myself one of them." Amelia smiled. "Captain Fitz is not marrying you for your cooking skills. He is marrying you for you."

"That's right," Penelope seconded.

Madge shook her head, and several fiery strands fell from her loose coiffure. "But why am I marrying him? How well do I know him? Not well at all. My head was turned by him, naturally. He is a good-looking man. But do I want to spend all the days of my life with him? Think of it. Every second from now until my last breath will be in his company."

MURDER IN MATRIMONY   175

Amelia frowned. "When you put it that way, any marriage sounds dreadful."

"Exactly." Madge crossed her arms. "Which is why I do not know if marriage is for me."

And there it was. The idea that Winifred had put in Amelia's mind days ago. Under the time constraint, the wedding arrangements were trying; delaying them would be more trying still. Then Aunt Tabitha must be considered. Picturing her face upon hearing the news of Madge's reluctance made Amelia's heart turn to lead. Yet, she would rather face all of it than see Madge miserable or Captain Fitz taken unaware by the situation. Madge was young, and London had perhaps gone to her head. Going back to Somerset might have changed things, changed her mind.

"Have you felt this way long?" asked Amelia.

Madge tipped her chin. "Ever since I put on this blasted dress."

So about thirty seconds.

"Margaret Ann, watch your language," Mrs. Scott scolded. "Children are present."

"Maybe it's the dress." Amelia knew how much her sister hated frills. Perhaps they were having an adverse effect on her. "Take it off. Then we'll talk."

"What about *our* dresses?" asked Sarah.

"We might not need them after all," Penelope muttered.

Mrs. Scott motioned to her daughters. "Come along, girls. You, too, Lady Winifred. We will try on our dresses while Amelia talks to Madge. She knows the situation best."

"But Mama—" Amelia started, but it was too late. They were gone. For better or worse, she would be the one to talk to Madge.

TWENTY-FOUR

Dear Lady Agony,
Before we married, my wife professed to enjoy the
smell of a cigar. She said she found the scent relaxing.
Now she nearly faints at the sight of one, and when I was
enjoying a smoke in the drawing room, she threw my case
into the fire. She said it was wrong, and she would not
have her draperies soiled. Isn't it she who did wrong to lie
to me in the first place?
Devotedly,
Young Husband

Dear Young Husband,
I advise you to give up the expensive habit immediately,
or, at the very least, find a less offensive place to take
your cigar. It was wrong of her to mislead you, yes, but
many ladies are in the custom of saying things they do
not mean when they are in love. Be lenient and learn.
Many are the lessons of early marriage.
Yours in Secret,
Lady Agony

When Magaret was out of her wedding dress and into her own clothes, she and Amelia discussed Captain Fitz at length. It was obvious Madge loved him, so Amelia was unsure of the problem. He enjoyed her company; he reveled in her beauty; he even found humor in her eccentricities. There could be no question of hardship. He had an adequate income and required no large dowry. What, exactly, concerned her sister? She put the question to Madge.

"I am not marriage material. I am who I am, and that is all."

MURDER IN MATRIMONY 177

"That's enough," Amelia promised.

Madge stubbornly shook her head.

Amelia tried a different approach. "Have you told Captain Fitz your concerns?"

Madge was immediate in her answer. "I couldn't."

"Why not?" Amelia pressed. "He is a reasonable man. I'm certain he shares some of your anxieties. No one is born to be a husband or father." She sat next to her sister on the small dressing bench. "I was terrified to meet Winifred. All the way to London, Edgar talked of his niece and how incredible she was. He adored her. I worried she would not like me, that she would resent my presence." Thinking back to the moment, Amelia shook her head with a smile. "As it turned out, my fears were unwarranted. When we met, I felt the concern we shared for Edgar. I couldn't imagine my life without Winifred now. I think most mothers feel that way."

Madge didn't speak for several moments. "You're right, Amelia. I never thought of you as motherly, but seeing you with Winifred has changed my mind. Your relationship is good. Natural, even. Nothing forced or put on, on either side."

"It is as if I've known her my entire life." Winifred was a subject Amelia could discuss at length but curtailed for the situation's sake. The marriage was to take place in less than a week. If Madge didn't figure out her feelings soon, they would face the consequences of inaction. "Will you talk to him then?"

"I will." Madge dipped her chin, determination overtaking her visage. "He's a sensible man, a strong man. He fought in the Crimean War. Surely my anxieties will be nothing in comparison."

Captain Fitz would be concerned, perhaps even hurt, but Amelia didn't see any other alternative. Honesty was a cornerstone of marriage. It might be an uncomfortable conversation, but one that needed to take place all the same.

With a plan made, Amelia joined her sisters, whose dresses were every bit as lovely as Madge's. Light blue was perfect for showcasing the Scotts' complexion and auburn hair, and Amelia quickly determined her own dress was as adequately made as theirs. After selecting gloves and bonnets, they were ready for a respite. Amelia was looking forward to a nice cup of tea when, with surprise, she noted the entrance of Mrs. Rothschild.

Mrs. Rothschild was collecting a donation for the Children's Society autumn bazaar, and Miss Hernandez committed to giving cloth and scraps for new dresses. Amelia scolded herself for not sending her own monetary donation and determined to do so immediately when she returned home. First, however, she was going to use the opportunity to ask Mrs. Rothschild about her daughter's recent gifts. Perhaps she knew the reason her daughter could afford them or another explanation that would account for the extravagance.

"Mrs. Rothschild," Amelia said. "It's a pleasure to see you again."

Mrs. Rothschild was likewise surprised to see Amelia but quickly overcame her alarm with a genuine smile. It was indeed the only warm spot of her personage, for she wore a long black coat, shabby and dull, that covered any detail that might lie under it. "Lady Amesbury."

"My mother and sisters are just there, looking at slippers." Amelia tipped her chin in the direction of her family. "They are from Somerset and not accustomed to so fine a selection as Miss Hernandez has here."

"I assume they find the city quite different from the country."

"Very much so," Amelia said. "I am glad we met today. First, I must promise my donation for the orphanage is forthcoming. With the wedding fast approaching, I haven't had the chance to send it."

The way Mrs. Rothschild accepted the excuse, with a barely perceptible nod, told Amelia she was accustomed to excuses.

"Second, I've had a question on my mind about your daughter Rose," Amelia continued.

The sadness of Mrs. Rothschild's life was so close to the surface that it flickered up in an instant upon the mention of her daughter's name. Her eyes shone with keen interest. "Yes?"

The shop door opened, and Amelia drew her into the corner. "I see you're wearing your beautiful necklace again." Indeed, it was the only item on her person that sparkled.

"I never take it off."

MURDER IN MATRIMONY

179

"I understand why." Amelia smiled. "It must have cost your daughter a good deal."

"A fortune, I am sure." Mrs. Rothschild touched the necklace as if to make sure it was still there. "Rose was considerate that way, too giving. Too kind."

"Yes, it was a very thoughtful gift." Amelia considered her next words a moment. "Before Mr. Cross's death, I believe she might have given him new books for his library. I noticed them on his bookshelf, and I wondered about the expense."

A furrow sprung up on Mrs. Rothschild's brow. "Books, you say?"

Amelia nodded. "A newly released set of three serials."

"That is curious . . . she gave Mrs. Hines a new cane as well." The furrow deepened. "Not just any cane. A walking stick with an ivory handle. Rose was proud of the gift and said Milly wouldn't be ashamed to be seen with it, even in the finest establishments." She blinked. "Lady Amesbury, how could it be? How could she have had the money to buy so many gifts?"

"It was my question as well." Amelia wished for answers, not another question. The cane confirmed, however, that Miss Rothschild had come into some money. Amelia just needed to know how. "Have you talked to her employer since the accident? Perhaps someone sent their condolences?"

"No, never, and I did not seek out an acquaintance. After her accident, I was angry. Resentful. She had worked so hard, and they seemed to care so little." She glanced at the window. "My husband said it was always the way in factories. People are little more than machines in them." Her eyes flicked back to Amelia. "He said Mr. Cross and I were wrong to encourage her to find work outside of the pub. Maybe he was right."

Amelia stepped closer. "This isn't your fault. You did what you thought was right by her, and so did Mr. Cross. You must stop blaming yourself."

Mrs. Rothschild averted her eyes, remaining silent.

"Would it be all right if I talked to your friend, Mrs. Hines? Perhaps your daughter told her where she received the money for the walking stick."

"What does it matter now?" Mrs. Rothschild's voice was cold and distant.

"I cannot say. All I know is that it is important." She didn't want to lie to Mrs. Rothschild after the woman had been so brutally honest, but she also did not want to raise another question in her mind. She had enough guilt to comprehend. "Does that make sense?"

She nodded.

"Do you have her address? I know she does not get around well."

Mrs. Rothschild gave her the information, and Amelia was saddened to learn Mrs. Hines lived in the rookery not far from the public house. Kitty could not join her on this expedition. Amelia and Oliver were on the best of terms, and she did not want to jeopardize that. Yet she wasn't so dull as to go alone to that area of town. Simon would have to accompany her.

Thinking of him brought a new warmth to her face. At All Saints on Margaret Street, they had shared a moment that had her considering the future. Would Simon ever marry? Would she? They both had problemed pasts, but she wouldn't have changed hers for all the gold in Egypt. Every moment had made her into the person she was today. He'd told her he cared for her, and that was enough.

Wasn't it?

Considering her sister's wedding and Mr. Cross's murder investigation, she would have to let it be—for now. But she hoped not forever.

She bid goodbye to Mrs. Rothschild. Then she and her family left the shop, handed their packages of gloves and hats to the footman, and ascended the carriage steps. After final alterations, the dresses would be delivered tomorrow. Amelia only hoped they would still be needed after Margaret talked to Captain Fitz.

"And how are you feeling, dear?" her mother asked Madge once they were safely tucked into the carriage. They were three to a side, and it was a tight fit. Amelia was grateful Winifred was next to her, for her smallness gave them more room.

"Not great," Madge said in brutal honesty. Amelia wished

MURDER IN MATRIMONY

181

she had a soupçon of consideration for other people's sensibilities, which were often more delicate than her own. As it was, their mother's face fell at the remark, and Amelia tried to repair the damage.

"She'll feel better once she talks to the captain." Amelia attempted a cheerful smile. "It will calm her nerves."

"I've never had a case of nerves in my life." Madge's tone was prideful, and Amelia, too, was proud of her strength, but at this moment, the reminder was unwelcome to their mother, and Amelia wished she'd kept the proclamation to herself. "But I do want to speak to the captain," Madge continued. "Will you accompany me, Penelope? They won't let you go anywhere by yourself in the city, and Amelia has too much to do."

"Of course I will." Penelope noted Sarah's crestfallen face and added, "Perhaps Sarah might join us?"

"Good idea," said Madge. "You two talk between yourselves while I discuss a few things with the captain. You know," she added in a low voice, "personal things."

"Gracious, Margaret Ann." Mrs. Scott clasped her hands on her lap. "Please remember our dear Winifred."

Winifred, who was sitting between Amelia and Madge, giggled.

When they arrived at the house, Amelia was pleased to see Simon in the entryway. She was not as pleased, however, to see Uncle Henry with his hand on the shoulder of the marquis, as if they were bosom friends and not new acquaintances.

She took a steadying breath and handed her parasol to Jones.

"You see, I am a connoisseur, if you will, of the happy cordial, and I feel obligated to supply the house with the liquor which it seems bereft of." Uncle Henry had ample side whiskers, and as he leaned in, they nearly brushed Simon. "I cannot imagine a house in all of England that deprives its inhabitants of the enjoyment of sherry, can you?"

"I cannot." Simon checked his timepiece. "And at this hour."

Amelia bit her lip to contain her smile. It was only teatime.

"Quite so," said Uncle Henry. "Do you have any idea where I might find a good Spanish sherry in London?"

Simon shared the name of his favorite establishment, and

Amelia lowered her lids at him. Blast Simon for giving up the information. At this rate, Uncle Henry would be snookered before dinner.

Uncle Henry set off for the mentioned place immediately, and once he was gone, Amelia pulled Simon into the morning room. "I hope you're pleased with yourself. I hid the sherry before Uncle Henry arrived for a reason."

"I apologize." The wry smile on Simon's lips betrayed his true feelings on the matter. "The man was determined to go, and he being your relative, my only thought was to assist him."

She admired his empathy for Uncle Henry, and perhaps there wasn't a man or woman alive who didn't need a glass of sherry after a day of planning Margaret Scott's wedding. Heaven knew, she was looking forward to one—after she paid a visit to Mrs. Hines. She must go today if she was to resume preparations tomorrow. "I need to visit Mrs. Hines, the woman who was attacked after her shift at the pub. Mrs. Rothschild said her daughter gifted Mrs. Hines a cane. The problem is her address. She lives on Old Nichol Street."

"Old Nichol Street," repeated Simon with new stress in his voice. "Of course I will go, if you are asking."

"You believe I would enter the rookery without an escort?"

"I believe you would do whatever you thought would help solve the murder of Mr. Cross." He raised a dark eyebrow. "Am I wrong?"

"No, I suppose not." She returned to the entryway, where her family members were quarreling over tea. Her mother requested a cup of the forfeiting liquid, as did her sister Penelope, but Madge wanted to depart for the captain's townhome straightaway.

When Amelia and Simon joined them, the family lowered the din to a murmur but did not stop talking completely. They eyed Simon from a distance, as if he were a conjurer or trapeze artist in the circus, waiting for him to do something.

Amelia decided the family argument before introducing him. "Tea will not do any harm, Madge. In fact, a break allows time for contemplation. You make decisions too quickly as it

MURDER IN MATRIMONY

183

is, and this one requires reflection. Give your family an hour of refreshment while you consider the matter."

"You would not wait an hour before alighting on a task with the marquis. You would run down the street with him if you could." Madge bobbed her red head at Simon.

Amelia took the opportunity to introduce Simon to her delighted mother and sisters.

Simon made a perfect bow. "Good day, ladies, Mrs. Scott. It's wonderful to finally meet you. I have heard so much about the family."

"By the by, Madge, I am not running anywhere," continued Amelia. "Lord Bainbridge and I have a prior engagement." And by prior, she meant two minutes ago.

"One plans things, Margaret Ann," Mrs. Scott replied approvingly. "One does not fly from one task to the next."

"Please, enjoy a refreshing cup of tea, and send a note to the captain." Amelia was firm in her encouragement. "Do not pounce on him unaware. I will be back in an hour."

Simon waited until they were in his carriage before inquiring about her sister and the captain. "I trust the wedding plans are going well?"

"The wedding plans are progressing." She paused, wondering how much to share with him.

The pause was enough for him to find out the problem anyway. "She is anxious about marrying the captain?"

"It is not the captain who worries her. I think it is marriage itself."

"Why would that be?" He frowned. "If she loves Captain Fitz, marriage should not cause her anxiety. Don't you agree?"

"I do." Marrying Simon would be the least anxious task in the world. "If your assumption is correct, however, it may mean she does not love Captain Fitz, which is difficult to fathom."

"Is it?" Simon steepled his fingers. "Like a soldier, the captain came to her defense at a time when she needed defending. She'd been implicated in Mr. Radcliffe's death and was new to town life. He was her guardian and confidant. It is no surprise they grew close."

"You think circumstance had something to do with it?" she asked.

"I think it had everything to do with it."

"And they don't love each other?" pressed Amelia.

"I did not say that." He turned to her at the exact moment the carriage stopped, his eyes washing over her like foamy green waves. She imagined this is what it might feel like to stand on the bow of a ship, the sea spray on her face and that terrific scent all around her.

They watched each other silently, the word *love* taking a third seat.

"Perhaps they do love one another." He stared at her lips. "Perhaps they have loved each other since the moment of their meeting. Perhaps they wished to profess it but did not want to appear foolish. One loses a little bit of himself with life's disappointments and rejections. It does not take years to make a hardened man."

She did not know what to say. He did not look at her, and she could not tell if he was talking about the captain or himself. Felicity Fairchild had rejected him in the worst way, agreeing to marry him while pursuing a relationship with his friend. Then there was her own early indictment of him. She criticized him for not thinking of the woman he encouraged Edgar to seek out. Knowing Edgar was an ill man, he told him to find a woman who did not recognize his wealth or title and make her his wife. Only then could he be assured of Lady Winifred's future.

His advice had been based on his own experiences. He was hardened. But even the hardest person desired love. Didn't he?

Her eyes studied his. "Simon?"

He glanced at her lips, waiting.

She couldn't say it, and neither could he. But by God if she didn't feel it, in the core of her being, her love for this man. If only she could turn her feelings into words. Instead, they rode on with only the lightness in their hearts to keep them company while descending into the darkest parts of the city.

TWENTY-FIVE

Dear Lady Agony,
Churches send money to help those in distant lands.
Meanwhile, citizens of our own city wither away in
rookeries, unnoticed. The problem is not reported enough.
If it were, more might be done. Please mention it if you
have space.
Devotedly,
Rookery Woes

Dear Rookery Woes,
I always have space for this topic. I do not always have
advice for it, however. Perhaps its inclusion is its own sort
of advice. If the topic takes up more space in our papers,
it might take up more space in our hearts. We must, every
one of us, do more to assist those in need.
Yours in Secret,
Lady Agony

Bethnal Green had perhaps been green at one time. Indeed, it had housed large houses and gardens in the previous century. But now those were gone, and what was left was a tumble of ramshackle buildings that accommodated several more people than comfort allowed. The mulberry trees were still beautiful, however. Amelia noted a singular beauty as they approached the neighborhood, where the streets were so narrow Simon's carriage could not pass. They left it at the corner with the footman, walking to the tiny apartment where Mrs. Hines lived.

In a way, Mrs. Hines was fortunate. At least she did not have to share her small space. As they drew nearer, Amelia noted a door with six people tumbling out of it. From the doorway, a woman with sallow, sunken eyes despondently watched her five children leave with their father. Amelia did not follow her eyes. Part of her did not want to know where they were going. Part of her wanted to ignore what she saw.

But another part—perhaps the part Mr. Cross saw in her— forced herself to acknowledge their suffering. They were standing here, just as she was. They were different but the same in the most basic way. What she could do to help her fellow man she must consider. It could no longer be about only Mr. Cross. She must involve herself on the most personal level.

Simon must have sensed her thoughts or apprehension, for he placed an arm around her shoulders. "Are you certain you want to do this?"

She nodded. "I must. It isn't only about Mr. Cross anymore. Do you understand?"

Simon's eyes flicked from the street to the door to her eyes. "Yes, I believe I do."

Amelia took a steadying breath and knocked. Mrs. Hines didn't immediately answer, and for a moment, Amelia thought she was not home. When she finally came to the door, Amelia understood how difficult movement was for her. Mrs. Hines was a stout woman who wore a brace on one leg and used a cane to support herself. Not just any cane but the one Mrs. Rothschild described. It was so out of place in the apartment— the walls damp with moisture, the threadbare chair worn beyond comfort, and the kettle dented without repair—that it was the first thing one noticed.

The second was Mrs. Hines's eyes. They were the color of two obsidian rocks, blue to the point of blackness. She was not a happy woman, and it showed. If eyes were the windows to the soul, her soul was as dark as the night of her barroom attack.

"Mrs. Hines, excuse the intrusion." Amelia went about putting her mind at ease. "We are friends of Mrs. Rothschild. She gave me your address. I wondered if I might talk to you about her daughter Rose."

Mrs. Hines looked from her to Simon, and he bowed respectfully. She moved to the side, allowing them entrance.

MURDER IN MATRIMONY 187

Amelia thanked her, and she shut the door. She didn't ask them to sit, perhaps because there was nowhere to do so. A straw bed took up much of the room. Mrs. Hines stood next to the only window, affording them as much space as possible, and Amelia noticed a deep scar that ran along her jawline. The cut had been badly stitched and left a bigger mark than necessary.

"What charity are you with?" asked Mrs. Hines.

"None," Amelia explained.

"The church?" she tried again.

"No, but I am—*was*—a friend of Mr. Cross. He, like you, had been treated to a gift by Miss Rothschild before her accident."

"Rose was a good girl. A smart girl." Mrs. Hines lifted her chin in challenge, and the light from the window revealed the deep lines on her face. Despite being the same age as Mrs. Rothschild, she looked many years older, probably because of her poor living conditions and invalid state, which kept her indoors. "I would have sworn you were one of those do-gooders from the church. Mrs. Rothschild is always sending someone by with a basket."

"That's very kind of her," murmured Simon.

"Is it?" She snorted. "I suppose you would think so, but it doesn't have anything to do with me. She's only trying to ease a guilty conscience."

"For the accident, you mean?" Amelia pressed.

"She told you about it. Of course she did." Standing for long periods was not an option for Mrs. Hines, and she stumped over to the chair with her cane. Amelia went to assist her, but she shook her head, her jowls moving in protest. "You might not believe this, but I was a nice-looking sort with a decent figure and fine hair. I had all the good fortune in the world until I went to work for the Rothschilds. I should have found employment elsewhere. My sister told me so, but I wouldn't listen." She looked toward the window as if she wished she was outside right now. "Young women of a certain age don't take advice, and my husband didn't care either way as long as I was bringing in money."

"What about Miss Rothschild?" asked Simon. "Did she take advice?"

"Rose was set on leaving the pub after my attack. She was the one who heard me holler from the alleyway. She found me." Mrs. Hines's eyes, hollow and bottomless, turned away from the window. "I wish she hadn't. Maybe then she wouldn't have been set on finding work at the factory. She thought it could solve all the problems." She shook her head. "Youth is enthusiastic if nothing else."

"What problems?" Amelia couldn't presume to know the answer. Around every East End corner was a surprise, an education. Here was another lesson, and she awaited it, the hesitant learner.

Mrs. Hines turned quick and hard. "What problems? Stick around, and you'll see. You'll see what we see every day: crime, filth, decay. You can't blame Rose for wanting to leave."

Amelia had known the criticism was coming, yet still she bristled. "Miss Rothschild wanted a different life."

"A *better* life." Mrs. Hines's eyes lifted, and for a moment, Amelia could see the young woman she had been: high cheekbones, chocolate brown hair, and eyes not black but deep, dark blue.

"And who's to say she didn't have a taste of it." Mrs. Hines tapped her ivory-handled cane. "She gave me this. Until then I used a stick—there." She pointed to a piece of wood next to the cold stove.

"It's an exquisite—and expensive—article to be sure." Simon nodded with appreciation. "Did Miss Rothschild ever say how she came by that kind of money?"

"No, but I had an idea the factory manager had taken a liking to her. She was a good baker, like her mother. Before the public house was reduced to a barroom, she was her mother's right hand at the oven."

Mrs. Rothschild was an excellent baker. Amelia had tried her goods at the prayer meeting, and they were incomparable. If her daughter had an ounce of her skill, she might have been valued for her expertise—and perhaps well compensated.

The idea put into motion a plan of visiting Baker Biscuits.

MURDER IN MATRIMONY   189

If she could talk to Miss Rothschild's superiors, they might be able to confirm her position at the factory and whether it paid better than an entry-level position.

She could place a biscuit order en masse for the wedding breakfast. Tabitha would certainly frown upon the idea, but if Amelia didn't share it with her, she would be none the wiser. It would give her an excuse, if nothing else, for the inquiry. If she could gain entrance to the factory rooms, she might be able to ascertain where Miss Rothschild's windfall came from— and if it was obtained by legal means. She would also be able to investigate the factory. If something foul was going on, she could report her findings in her Lady Agony column.

"I'm certain you are right, Mrs. Hines." Amelia smiled. "Mrs. Rothschild is an excellent baker, and her daughter surely took after her. That kind of skill would be valued anywhere, but particularly at her place of employment. Did she say she enjoyed her time there?"

"Very much." If Mrs. Hines was impressed with the compliment or the smile, her face didn't show it. Her lips were pursed in a perpetual pout. "She said her employment proved some good had come of my attack and told me so by giving me the cane. She promised more gifts were to come, but I only wanted her friendship. That's all I ever wanted from her mother. Not her gifts. Not her charity. Not her guilt."

While Amelia had thought Mrs. Hines's attitude unkind and even belligerent, she now understood it in a new light. Mrs. Hines wasn't hostile; she wasn't unappreciative of the gifts. More than anything, though, she wanted friendship. Not pity. The real way to atone for the attack was to be a friend at a time when she needed one most. If Amelia could, she'd find a way to tell Mrs. Rothschild.

"I understand," Amelia said. "One cannot put a price on friendship. You've been very helpful, Mrs. Hines. We appreciate your taking the time to talk with us."

Simon seconded her statement. "Thank you."

The lines of her face softened, and although she did not smile, she lifted her eyes in acknowledgment.

They saw themselves out the door, and as soon as they

returned to Simon's carriage, Amelia voiced her plan to visit Baker Biscuits tomorrow. The afternoon was growing late, and she must learn if Madge's visit to Captain Fitz had been successful.

"I'll take Kitty with me to the biscuit shop, unless you'd like to go, too." Amelia adjusted her parasol on the seat next to her. "She might be better than you with domestic details."

"I don't doubt it." He smiled.

She returned the smile, but as they approached her house, the smile dropped from her lips. She craned her neck to see if her eyes were deceiving her. Indeed, they were not. Captain Fitz was beside the gooseberry bush, hollering up at an open window.

"Miss Scott, I did not mean what I said." Captain Fitz's hat fell backward, and he repositioned it. "Please allow me to explain."

"That's not something one sees every day," murmured Simon. "I am going to gamble and wager the talk did not go well."

She sighed. "Very perceptive. However, no amount of yelling will make my sister see him if she does not want to. We must talk to him ourselves."

"We?" Simon arched a dark eyebrow. "As you said, I'm not good with domestic details."

"You will not help me?"

"What would I say?" His voice grew more serious. "I cannot get in the middle of a man's affairs. He wouldn't like me to see him this way. It's best I leave immediately."

Amelia knew he was right. Later, when he was thinking clearly, the captain would regret Simon observing his behavior. "Fine. Tell your driver to let me out here so that Captain Fitz does not observe the crest on your carriage."

Simon did as she requested, and she was off to solve her sister's problems. She had the idea this is what Sisyphus felt every time he reached the top of the hill only to have the boulder roll down again. Life with Madge was like that lately. All sibling relationships had their ups and downs, however. She took comfort in the fact that Madge would do the same for her.

"Psst, psst," came a noise from the front door. Amelia looked and saw Winifred peeking behind the heavy mahogany door.

Amelia detoured from the gooseberry bush.

"I'm afraid I have bad news." Despite the foreboding words, Winifred looked quite interested and even excited by the development. "Your family is upstairs with Madge, who is laid out on the bed, proclaiming Captain Fitz no longer loves her and that she should have 'kept her big trap shut.' And Captain Fitz, despite being told by Jones that Madge is not here, will not leave the lawns. He is determined to clear up a quarrel they had at his house."

"What an ordeal." Amelia looked over Winifred's shoulder. "And Aunt Tabitha?"

"She is gone with Aunt Gertrude to Thames Street to buy roasted chestnuts. Gert—excuse me, Gertrude, could not believe they were as good as all that in the city, but Aunt Tabitha assured her that they were and took her directly."

Winifred's face was so animated and her eyes so bright, Amelia had to suppress a laugh and force herself to consider what was happening on her own front lawns. "Thank heavens for their absence. Keep watch, will you? I'll talk to the captain."

Winifred gave Amelia a small salute and closed the door.

Amelia cleared her throat to make Captain Fitz aware of her approach. "I am sorry I missed you, Captain Fitz. Won't you come inside?"

"Lady Amesbury." The captain released a breath and straightened his hat. "I am relieved to see you. You must understand I do not want any ill will between me and your sister."

Amelia noticed an older woman who walked her dog every day stop to listen. "Let us go inside, where we can talk privately."

He nodded, and she did not bother with the drawing room, which was too close to Madge's quarters. Instead, she led him to the library. She did not want him to overhear her sister crying. Whatever was causing her angst—and Amelia was about to find out what—needed to pass before she saw Captain Fitz again.

He took off his hat and passed his hand through his blond

hair. It looked wild and unmanageable, a little like the man himself right now.

"Now then." Amelia selected a chair and pointed to the green couch across from her. "What may I help you with?"

"Your sister came to see me, and it was quite evident that she was upset. She mentioned a dress fitting and corset and some sort of bustle, I believe." He shook his head, perplexed by the terminology. "So I said, it sounded as though all was coming along swimmingly, to encourage her, you understand, and she said that it wasn't coming along at all. It was a stupid gown, and she wanted nothing to do with it."

"I am sorry." Amelia tried to come up with words that would soothe his distress. "She despises formal affairs. They were infrequent occurrences in Somerset, and she's always questioned their necessity."

"Indeed, I do not like them either." His brow lifted. "I understood her dislike from the first moment I danced with her. I do not care what she wears to the wedding, and I proceeded to tell her so."

"And what was her answer?"

"It was positively bizarre. She said, I suppose you do not care if we have mutton for dinner every night either, and I said I enjoyed a good roasted mutton now and then, but I was not so very fussy. She turned on her heel and ran out of the townhouse. I followed her, but she will not see me." He pointed toward the ceiling.

Amelia smiled lightly. "You must be patient with my sister. This past month has been extremely trying for her. It must seem her world has been turned upside down, but I know she will settle into the idea. She cares for you very much."

"And I her, but I do not want her to settle into the idea. I want her to desire the marriage to me."

"She does." Despite her warring emotions, Amelia kept her face encouraging. "Give her time."

"With the marriage date set, my lady, how much time can we afford to give?"

TWENTY-SIX

Dear Lady Agony,
I have a large family and a small budget. Which meals go the farthest? Could you give me examples for breakfast and dinner?
Devotedly,
Mother on a Budget

Dear Mother on a Budget,
Let the children have porridge for breakfast. It nourishes the body and costs hardly anything to make. For dinner, stews are your best choice for economy. However, boiled lentils and haricot beans with chopped onions and bacon make a nice pie. Pudding always saves on the meat, so have plenty of it for the children at every meal.
Yours in Secret,
Lady Agony

The captain's question was a valid one, and Amelia pondered it most of the night. How much longer could they wait for Madge to reconcile herself to the wedding? It was evident it still caused her angst. During last evening's dinner, she stared at each course, moving the food around her plate. Everyone in the family noticed, except Tabitha and Aunt Gertrude, who were preoccupied with the fowl and roast chestnuts. Aunt Gertrude declared her admiration, which pleased Tabitha, and for the remainder of the evening, the women discussed the proper way to soak them. Meanwhile, Uncle Henry enjoyed his sherry in heavenly silence, carefully watched over by Mr. Scott, who read the papers. Amelia simply stared at Madge, looking for a hint to her feelings.

Eventually, she concluded nothing could be done about them and went to bed. Madge alone must make the decision. Her family had taken turns counseling her all afternoon—when she would talk. Much of the time she lay despondently on the bed or crying into her pillow. She could be irrational and hot tempered, certainly, but weepy was a side Amelia had never seen. She must admit she wasn't an admirer. She much preferred the Madge she knew: strong and determined. She hoped this was the Madge that awaited her the following day when she and Kitty returned from the biscuit shop.

They were on Mill Street, Kitty dressed in rose and Amelia in sea-foam green. The brick storefront boasted two bow windows for browsing and a door between them with a half-moon window. The smell of baked goods filled the store and perhaps several blocks, for the factory was the next building over. The factory was taller than Amelia imagined, and it was not hard to understand how a fall from an indoor ladder at that height could kill a young woman.

"Good afternoon." A clerk in his fifties, with a stylish mustache, greeted them briefly. He was attending a shopper who requested a halfpenny roll, which he procured for her to enjoy immediately.

Meanwhile, Amelia and Kitty inspected the biscuits displayed prettily in the front windows. At one time, biscuits were for sailors and seamen, nourishment that would keep during a long voyage. These, however, were much more than that. They might even rival some baked goods. Their variety was extensive, with many flavors and types, and the packaging tins were stylish. Any woman would be proud to carry them home from her shopping excursion.

With a sigh, Kitty picked up a mint green and pink tin. The words *Baker Biscuits* were etched in beautiful cursive letters.

"Have you ever seen such a variety of biscuits?" Amelia gestured to the display of baked goods.

"Never." She finished inspecting the tin and returned it to the table. "I understand how they mean to compete with Huntley & Palmers. They must be in high demand."

Amelia agreed. Two young women waited to be helped before themselves. The clerk worked quickly, perhaps understanding from Amelia's and Kitty's clothes that they were not from the

MURDER IN MATRIMONY 195

Southeast but West London. The discovery often led to proclaimed higher prices by shop owners or clerks, but if anyone knew how to negotiate for goods, it was Kitty. She would not be overcharged. Amelia never had to worry about being taken advantage of when she was with her.

When the women left with their packages, the clerk turned to Amelia and Kitty and thanked them for their patience. "I apologize for keeping you waiting. Have you been here before? I have not had the pleasure of assisting you."

Amelia understood he was trying to determine if they, like the other customers, lived in the area. She hoped they could use their unfamiliarity to their advantage. "We have not. We live in Mayfair."

"Welcome, welcome." He opened a glass-covered cabinet, and they understood they were meant to follow him. "Our biscuits are one of a kind. If you please, try a sample."

She and Kitty each took a piece.

"Very good." Amelia thought it was quite satisfactory, considering its mass production. But she didn't need samples; she needed entry into the factory. "I'm looking for something special. My sister is getting married next week, and I'd like my breakfast to be unique."

"Ah!" The clerk looked over his shoulder, making sure no other patrons had entered the store. They hadn't. "I have just the thing." His voice was lower, and his mustache twitched with excitement. "I do not have one here, but if you would permit me to step next door? The factory has something new you might be able to sample."

Amelia was eager for the chance to gain entrance to the factory. "Yes, something new is what I want. We will join you."

He tutted. "A factory is no place for fine ladies like yourselves. I will bring the samples here." He spread out his arms. "For your approval."

Amelia could do nothing but nod and agree.

After he left, Kitty said, "I wish we could find a way into the factory."

"But how?"

Kitty tapped her chin. "I can think of no excuse. Perhaps we might wander in accidentally?"

Amelia lifted her eyebrows.

"A stretch, to be sure, but what else?"

"I confess I don't know," Amelia admitted. "Maybe something will occur to us when he returns. Until it does, we can ask about Miss Rothschild. If he could describe her position, it might clarify the amount of money she received during her employment."

They were prevented from saying anything else by the clerk's arrival with a man of prestige, dressed in nice trousers and an aptly tied cravat. The sleeves of his shirt were rolled up, reminding Amelia of someone. Perhaps it was her grandfather, who used to roll up his sleeves in the same fashion when he sat down with her with a bag of marbles. In his hand, the man carried a silver tray, as decent as any Amelia might use for tea, with two frosted biscuits.

"Ladies, you are in luck. Not every day is the owner onsite." The clerk's voice quivered with excitement. "May I present to you Mr. Baker, of Baker Biscuits. I told him of your wedding breakfast, and he wanted to bring you the selection himself."

"I do not have the pleasure of knowing your names, I'm afraid." His step was light and his words well spoken. His manners did his trade justice, and Amelia understood why Mr. Cross had encouraged his parishioners to seek employment at his factory. He appeared to care a great deal about his work and workplace.

"I am Lady Amesbury, and this is Mrs. Hamsted." She smiled at Kitty. "We have heard extraordinary things about your biscuits and came to see—or should I say taste?—for ourselves."

Upon hearing the honorific, the clerk inhaled a breath, beaming at Mr. Baker, perhaps gratified at having brought the owner over for the titled visitor.

Mr. Baker's face was placid but pleased with the information. "And Mr. Jefferies tells me it is your sister, Lady Amesbury, who is to be wed?"

"Yes, it is." Amelia wished her voice was more confident. It sounded as if she answered the question with a question.

Luckily, Kitty, who excelled at events, picked up the strain of the conversation. "Lady Amesbury is hosting a breakfast

MURDER IN MATRIMONY   197

for her sister in Mayfair, and she requires the best for her party. I assume those are your best biscuits?"

"Not only the best, Mrs. Hamsted, but the newest of our offerings." Mr. Baker paused for effect. "Indeed, we have not placed them in the store for this very reason."

"They have not been sampled by London, then?" Kitty appeared quite interested and not just for the sake of the investigation. Her interest might have been piqued for a party of her own.

"No." A smile transformed Mr. Baker's face, displaying all the kindness of which he was capable. Amelia imagined this was the face he showed his children, or perhaps grandchildren. It was the face of a proud parent. He took pride in his work, and it showed.

Kitty, however, was not taken in by smiles or promises and remained businesslike. "I hope they taste as good as they look, then."

"I await your estimation." Mr. Baker held out the tray.

From the first bite, Amelia knew what she was tasting. Soft, sweet, singular. She glanced at Kitty, and Kitty was staring at her. Amelia knew they shared the same thought: these were Mrs. Rothschild's biscuits. The taste was so distinct that it could not be replicated except by the exact recipe. She must know how he acquired it and knew of only one way—or person, rather: Rose Rothschild.

"I am impressed, Mr. Baker," Kitty exclaimed.

"As am I," agreed Amelia. "I've never tasted anything quite like it. The biscuit, if it may be called that, is extraordinary. May I ask if it is a new recipe?"

"You may ask, but I will never tell." Mr. Baker chuckled. "If your reactions are an indication, I believe it will take London, nay the entire globe, by surprise."

The factory was planning on mass-producing Mrs. Rothschild's biscuits. The notion was as clear as the pleasure Mr. Baker took from their approval. The factory was expanding, and this recipe would ensure the business's success. Amelia knew of no other confection like it. But did Mr. Baker realize it was Mrs. Rothschild's recipe? She saw no deception in his face, no crookedness. He seemed genuinely pleased with the product and their reaction.

"If not the globe, at the very least my sister's wedding breakfast." Amelia attempted to share in his laughter. "I would like to place an order, if I may, for the party."

"Very good." Mr. Baker was a professional, and the chuckle faded away. Still his voice held a note of pleasure perhaps in knowing the recipe was approved by fine ladies of Mayfair. "I will bid you a good day and allow Mr. Jefferies to assist you with the order."

Amelia and Kitty thanked him, and Mr. Jefferies went to retrieve an order form from a cabinet. When they were alone, Kitty whispered, "They are Mrs. Rothschild's biscuits."

"I thought so, too."

"Rose Rothschild must have given them the recipe," added Kitty.

Amelia raised an eyebrow. "Or sold it to them."

"Of course!" Kitty exclaimed, and Amelia shushed her. She continued more quietly. "That would explain her influx of monies and extravagant gift giving."

"We cannot be certain without confirmation, which we might be able to obtain yet."

Mr. Jefferies returned with the form, and they quit the conversation. Kitty gave her a look that explained she was ready to do whatever Amelia needed to find further answers. What that was, however, Amelia did not know. The recipe was secret; nothing would be shared there. However, she might be able to ask about Miss Rothschild and her employment at the factory.

As Mr. Jefferies took down her address, Amelia introduced the topic. "I must ask, Mr. Jefferies, about the working conditions of the factory. It's a subject that concerns me. I'm certain you've heard the tales of horror that come out of some establishments, and I believe it was not that long ago that I read of a girl falling to her death here."

"There is no concern about Baker Biscuits. On that you have my word." Offense entered Mr. Jefferies' voice. "I know of the girl you speak, Miss Rothschild. She was young and impatient. Her fall was her own doing. She had no business in the upstairs office. She worked the ovens." He shook his head. "Some

MURDER IN MATRIMONY

199

factory girls believe they can do anything. The work has gone to their heads."

"The girl did not normally work upstairs?" Amelia kept her voice calm but just barely.

"No, never." Mr. Jefferies tipped his chin. "Miss Rothschild was employed in the bake rooms. She had no business in the packaging rooms."

If that was true, why was she in there in the first place? Amelia wondered. She could only suppose that Miss Rothschild needed something, and no one was present to supply it.

"You may be assured, Lady Amesbury, that Baker Biscuits is an esteemed employer," continued Mr. Jefferies. "I've been here for ten years, and I've always been treated like family."

"I'm glad to hear it." Amelia smiled. "Mr. Cross was a great promoter of Baker Biscuits. He was my pastor at All Saints on Margaret Street."

Mr. Jefferies put a hand on his heart. "Dear Mr. Cross. He was trying to make changes to help people in the East End. He will be missed here and everywhere."

Amelia was glad Mr. Cross at least had one business supporter.

"Indeed," agreed Kitty. "Did he recommend parishioners to the factory?"

"Several." Mr. Jefferies returned to his bill of sale with a sigh. "But many in the area do not want change. They want things to continue as they always have." He pointed to the date, and Amelia supplied it.

"The recipe won't get out before then, will it, Mr. Jefferies?" continued Amelia. "I hope I can be assured of its novelty."

"Oh, no." A cheerful smile overtook Mr. Jefferies' dark expression. "All recipes are kept under lock and key in the office mixing book. No one goes in or out of there except Mr. Baker."

Amelia indicated her satisfaction, and Mr. Jefferies continued completing the order. She gave Kitty a look that explained the next order of business. They must get their hands on the mixing book. It could confirm the biscuit recipe was Mrs. Rothschild's. But how? The only day the factory workers were not present for their double shifts was Sunday. *Tomorrow.*

They must break in after midnight.

TWENTY-SEVEN

Dear Lady Agony,
A good many women are taking up a habit reserved for men: the after-dinner drink. I've seen two women in as many months opt for a glass of port after a large meal. What is the reason behind it, and what if it continues? I cannot imagine the men want us drinking with them.
Devotedly,
Tea for Me

Dear Tea for Me,
Two women in two months? That is not many. From the tone of your letter, one would think women everywhere are assaulting the liquor cabinet. But to answer your questions, the reason is enjoyment, and the consequence is happiness. A drink after dinner hurts no one, only your sensibilities. Rid yourself of them, and all will be well.
Yours in Secret,
Lady Agony

Amelia returned from Baker Biscuits to find Captain Fitz and Madge in a tête-à-tête in the drawing room. It was music to her ears to hear them conversing like civilized adults. After finding Captain Fitz in the gooseberry bush and Madge upstairs shut away in her room yesterday, Amelia wondered if the couple would ever reconcile. Now it appeared the wedding would take place after all. *Thank heavens!* The tormenting hours had come to nothing.

"It's a good omen, isn't it?" whispered Mrs. Scott behind her shoulder.

"Gracious." Amelia jumped. "You startled me."

"You're not the only one who listens at closed doors." Her mother tweaked her arm. "I would scold you if I weren't doing likewise, but desperate times require desperate measures, as they say, and the situation is as desperate as any I've known. What would have happened if she called off the wedding?"

Amelia cringed. "I do not even want to consider the possibility."

"Lady Tabitha would have disowned you, and the Fitz family would have cut you." Mrs. Scott's face turned as white as the hand she brought to her mouth.

"I said I did *not* want to consider the possibility." Amelia heard a small laugh from behind the closed door and paused, listening. Her shoulders relaxed with the noise. "Did you talk to Madge today?"

"I did," confirmed Mrs. Scott. "When you left with Mrs. Hamsted, she finally came out of her room, completely ravenous. It was as if she had overcome an illness. She ate an entire plate of cold chicken, three biscuits, and two cherry tartlets. I asked her if she shouldn't resist, for the sake of the wedding dress, but she said Captain Fitz didn't care a fig about the wedding dress, and neither did she. As you can imagine, I went quite silent at the comment, but she continued by saying she'd had a fine letter from the captain, who would be calling upon her later." She pointed to the closed door. "They have been in there for half an hour, and I have heard only happy murmurings."

"And Lettie? Is she in there also?" Amelia hoped someone was present who could report back the generalities of the conversation. She needed assurance that the wedding would take place as planned and that the couple felt assured of their direction.

Mrs. Scott shook her head. "Lady Tabitha said it wasn't necessary. She said they are engaged and could enjoy a few moments of privacy." She looked over her shoulder. "As you know, she didn't witness the commotion yesterday, and perhaps Mrs. Addington did not tell her of it. Lady Tabitha has been so pleased with Aunt Gertrude's cookery that the two women have been exalting each other's recipes for the better part of an hour."

202   MARY WINTERS

Amelia smiled. "Aunt Tabitha will miss Gertrude when she leaves."

"Don't worry your head about that, dear." Mrs. Scott had the ability to make Amelia feel seven years old again and did so now with a simple tilt of her face. "Madge tells me that she and the captain will be living in London until a property becomes available. Aunt Gertrude plans to visit frequently."

Amelia squeezed the bridge of her nose briefly, convincing herself that having family nearby was good. She and Madge would be able to visit all the time. Every day, even. Aunt Gertrude would have an excuse to come to town. They all would. Amelia swallowed. She couldn't think about that now. She needed to think about the wedding. Once they were married, all else would fall into place. "Did she say that today? They will be married?"

Mrs. Scott put an arm around Amelia. "Of course they'll be married. Believe it or not, Madge's behavior is not unnatural. Certainly, she has been more vocal than most brides, but that's her way. You worry too much. In fact." Here, she pulled back, studying Amelia. "You look thin. What else is bothering you?"

"It's nothing, Mama." Amelia smiled. She was not thin. Many more catastrophes would have to befall her before she'd be considered thin. But her mother was right about her anxieties. While she felt closer than ever to finding justice for Miss Rothschild, she did not feel any closer to solving Mr. Cross's murder. She tried to tell herself that he would be happy. After all, it was news of Rose Rothschild that he sent through the curate. But what of him and his work? She'd never had a priest for a friend before, and she felt as if she'd let him down. If only she could find a connection between the two, she might bring them both justice.

Suddenly, the drawing room door opened, and Madge greeted Amelia. Her face was flushed so prettily that it reminded Amelia of the afternoons Madge spent behind the inn, chasing dragonflies. Amelia was often tasked with watching her, but she never minded the responsibility. Seeing her auburn curls bounce over her shoulders while attempting something so silly and futile was often the highlight of Amelia's day. Most times,

Madge convinced her to play also, and Amelia would lose whatever maturity she'd gained, feeling the same age as her sister in a matter of minutes. It was good to be a child.

Her sister looked almost childlike in her happiness now—delighted. Madge could be herself with Captain Fitz, and he could be likewise with her. She didn't need an elaborate wedding gown to make him think she was pretty, nor did she need decorative words to understand how he felt. It was the same feelings she and Simon shared, a giving of oneself to another without pretense. The idea made her want to run to Simon and declare her feelings for him. But they were aware of their feelings for one another. Even Aunt Tabitha had come to terms with them. It was now up to them to decide what to do with them.

"Amelia!" Madge declared. "I was looking all over for you."

"Good afternoon, Madge. Captain Fitz." Amelia bobbed her head. "I was at Baker Biscuits, placing an order for the wedding breakfast."

"I'm not sure if you know this, but Lady Tabitha despises factory-baked goods. I overheard her tell Aunt Gert *the most important aspect of a pastry is its freshness*." This she said with a deepness and vibrato intended to match Tabitha's voice.

"Yes, well. Time restraints and all. Is there anything else you need before the . . . day?" asked Amelia, avoiding the word *wedding*.

"We don't require anything." Madge raised her eyes in Captain Fitz's direction. "Do we, love?"

"The clothes on our backs would suffice for me." He chuckled.

Amelia could detect no lingering turmoil or hesitation between the couple, and she was thankful the difficulty had passed. Once they were at the altar, she would be able to release the last of her concerns. Until then, she would remain vigilant.

Her mother, beaming at the couple, appeared to have no such concern. She believed in her children with her whole heart. Nothing could dissuade her that they were the most wonderful people in the world. Everything they did was expected and

204 MARY WINTERS

celebrated. Amelia sighed. If only she could have the same confidence.

Alas, she did not.

When Captain Fitz joined them for dinner, the long looks and soft whispers between him and Madge increased. Most of the company felt as her mother did about the interactions: amused and charmed by the young couple. They were lenient of their indulgences, ignoring them altogether when necessary. Even Simon, who joined the party, seemed unaffected. But to Amelia, their activities betrayed a notion she could not put her finger on. Madge had been upset by her wedding dress. How could she completely forget her reservations in twenty-four hours? Madge was temperamental, certainly, but she must also suffer from amnesia to resolve the problem so quickly.

After dinner, Amelia forestalled going into the drawing room with the women, instead asking Uncle Henry for a glass of his sherry.

Uncle Henry blinked innocently. "Why do you ask me, dear niece?"

She leveled a look at him. "Because I was present when Lord Bainbridge told you the address of his favorite liquor establishment."

He laughed, placing his hands on his stomach. "Quite so. Quite so."

Then he motioned to Bailey, whom Amelia had made certain would accommodate her family. Apparently, this was one of the accommodations. He reappeared with the sherry and glasses on a tray.

Uncle Henry took the proffered glass and drank it down immediately. "I say, good man. Don't make yourself scarce just yet." Bailey poured him a second glass.

Amelia refrained from doing the same. Instead, she took a small sip and said to Captain Fitz, "I am pleased you and my sister are on better terms."

"I am pleased as well." The captain took a long drink. "I believe it was the wedding arrangements that had her out of sorts. Once we got those out of the way, she was her happy self again."

MURDER IN MATRIMONY   205

Amelia frowned. She had been the one to toil over the arrangements—she and Tabitha, to be honest. All Madge had to do was show up. But she understood how much Madge disliked formal gatherings. The idea of being the center of attention must have been unbearable to her.

"The dress, to be sure, the company, the breakfast," Captain Fitz continued. "They were overwhelming. Her wants are few and simple. I'm sure you understand, Lady Amesbury, being her sister."

"Indeed." Amelia opted for another sip of sherry, this one longer.

"A second glass, Amelia?" prompted Uncle Henry, only too glad to have a fellow imbiber at his side.

Simon raised his eyebrows at her. He was thinking about their upcoming midnight break-in at Baker Biscuits. She knew he was. "No, thank you, Uncle. The women are waiting for me. It was very good though."

"If you change your mind, you know where I'll be." Uncle Henry winked, and the action transformed his craggy face to one of mirth and happiness. He signaled for a third glass of liquor.

Simon followed her into the hallway. "I understand your hiding the sherry now."

"I thought you might."

Simon cast a glance at the dining room door. "He is an old man. What can it hurt?"

"Stay until he takes to the pianoforte, and you'll find out." Amelia crossed her arms.

"The drink will be conducive to sleep at the very least." His green eyes flickered with mischief. "No one will hear you slip down the servants' staircase and into my carriage."

Slipping anywhere with Simon sounded heavenly, and Amelia's shoulders automatically relaxed. But Baker Biscuits wasn't just anywhere. It was a stone's throw from danger and violence. She must keep her wits about her if they were to be successful. Tomorrow was Sunday. They had a single opportunity to uncover the information. If they didn't, they'd have to wait an entire week to try again. "Did Mr. Hamsted tell you he and Kitty are meeting us there?"

206   MARY WINTERS

"He did. You've formed your own merry band of misfits to do your bidding, haven't you, Amelia?" The words held no malice. They were tinged with excitement and anticipation and, dare she say, admiration?

"You are no misfit, Simon." She smiled. "You are one person who suits me completely."

He touched her chin. "And you me."

The next thirty seconds passed in a stolen kiss that proclaimed everything they hadn't. Love, passion, respect. All was conveyed by the warmth of his lips and the pressure of his hand on her back. He was her freedom and security, and if anyone had told her she could have both, she wouldn't have believed them until this very moment. She had never known this feeling. Not with Edgar, not with anyone. She was drunk on it, desiring another taste of him as a drinker did another taste of spirits. Knowing that her family and Aunt Tabitha sat only a staircase away, however, forced her to pull back. Now was not the time for admissions, but someday, and perhaps someday soon, it would be.

"Until tonight." Simon's voice was husky, and he held her for a moment longer, his hand snaking around her waist.

She whispered, "Until then."

He inhaled the scent of her before releasing her. Then she raced up the stairs, counting the steps so as not to fall down, back into his arms.

TWENTY-EIGHT

Dear Lady Agony,
    So many of your reports on London's businesses require discretion. Yet I cannot imagine a quiet quarter-hour in this city. You must conduct many of your inquiries at night. Do you?
    Devotedly,
    Night Owl or No

Dear Night Owl or No,
    Your question is an astute one. That does not mean I'll be answering it, however. I would rather leave readers unaware of my location at all times, even nighttime.
    Yours in Secret,
    Lady Agony

The night was cloaked in fog, which was excellent for break-ins but not so good for walking. However, Amelia had only to make it to Hyde Park, where Simon's carriage awaited her arrival. Standing in his great coat, his broad shoulders formed to the cut of the cloth, he watched for her, and when he saw her round the corner, walked toward her. He wasn't wearing a hat, and his black hair was sleek and shiny from the mist. His eyes were light, the color of green glass, and like a lamp, they led her to him.

"With the fog, I wanted to come to your house, but I didn't dare change the plan. I thought we might miss each other in a comedy of errors."

"I'm glad you didn't. The walk isn't far." She settled into the seat across from him. She was wearing the same trousers she wore the very first night she met him, and she caught him grinning, perhaps with the remembrance.

"I talked to Hamsted, and he is looking forward to our little adventure." He checked the driver's direction and sat back. "I fear he might become one of Lady Agony's ardent devotees. He mentioned writing an article on the poverty in the East End."

"That was my idea," explained Amelia. "When we visited Mrs. Hines, I had a notion of doing something. Not just donating money but contributing in some real way."

"You do contribute by bringing forward injustices in your column."

"When they suit, which is rare." Amelia sighed. "People have so many of their own problems to contend with. I am always dealing with them. It is hard to step outside one's daily concerns and commit to others' wellbeing."

He tilted his head, and a black lock of hair fell across his brow. "This murder—it has changed you."

Amelia took a breath, about to protest, when she realized he was right. "It *has* changed me. I feel different. I want to make a difference."

"How?"

"I wish I knew." She looked out the window, watching the large houses and fine shops disappear behind them. The streets narrowed, and the carriage felt large and ridiculous, and she looked forward to leaving it behind. When they approached St. Saviour's Dock, they did, meeting Oliver and Kitty near the River Neckinger, a name derived from the "devil's neckcloth." Thames pirates had been executed near the inlet until the eighteenth century. Although executions were no longer performed here, the river was deadly and rank with refuse. A slimy green film covered the putrid water, and the smell of dead fish rose up in phosphorous fumes.

Kitty kept her mouth and nose covered until they drew close to Mill Street. "A great area to stash the carriages but terrible for walking." Her words were muffled by her hand.

"Still, you look fetching doing so in that cloak," Oliver whispered.

Kitty, who wore a black cloak and hood over a nondescript outfit, chuckled.

MURDER IN MATRIMONY   209

Amelia ignored the exchange. This might be the one time where more hands meant more work, not less. The idea was to break up and search the two-story factory for, first and foremost, the mixing book. Once they were assured Mr. Baker was using Mrs. Rothschild's recipe, they would look for references to Rose or her unfortunate accident. They knew she worked in the bake room. They would start there and expand the search if time warranted.

The street was pitch black and afforded them no light for lock-picking, but it didn't matter anyway. The door had an additional bolt that appeared uncrackable. They weren't going in through the front door without a hacksaw.

Amelia glanced up, noting a broken pane of a window. While Oliver and Simon looked for another way in, she asked Kitty if she would be able to get her hand through the glass and open the window. She assured Amelia she would.

Kitty held up a hand. "I wore my torn gloves for that purpose. I knew they were still serviceable in some way." Yes, she loved clothes, but she detested waste and repurposed most of her articles. It was one of many reasons Amelia respected and admired her.

"You are the lightest, and I'm certain Simon or Oliver could lift you up."

"Not Oliver," Kitty whispered. "I love him dearly, but when it comes to strength, he has none. Save him for his intellect. It will serve us once we get inside."

Amelia called for Simon and told him the plan. Oliver argued at first, contending he should be the one to lift Kitty to the window. Simon proclaimed all he had to contribute was brute strength and to please allow him to do something. After a few moments of quarreling, Oliver acquiesced, and Simon easily lifted Kitty to the window above. She snaked her arm around the broken pane and unlocked the window. With an extra boost from Simon, she was in, with only a small gulp from Oliver when she landed inside with a thud.

The ten seconds they waited for her to open the back door were heart stopping. Oliver stared without blinking, and when it opened, he practically fell inside, hugging her to his chest

210   MARY WINTERS

and telling her how proud he was. "I had no idea you were so capable."

Kitty tipped her chin in Amelia's direction. "It isn't my first escapade with Lady Agony."

Amelia handed out four candles, and as Simon lighted them, their location became clearer. They were in an extremely tall room with wooden rafters. Upstairs were long packing tables and stalls where employees, most likely women and boys, packaged biscuits. The main floor contained the baking rooms. Long silver trays and an oven were just beyond her view. A single ladder led to offices and supply rooms.

Amelia nodded to it. "That must be where Miss Rothschild fell."

They were silent for a moment.

"I should go up," Amelia said.

"I'll go with you." Simon took a step closer to her.

"We'll check this room and the next." Oliver looked at Kitty for confirmation. She nodded, and the couples went off in different directions.

Slowly, Amelia made her way up the steep ladder. There were forty rungs at least, and despite not thinking herself afraid of heights, she felt lightheaded when she looked down. She focused on the upper rungs instead. When she neared the top, she paused.

"What is it?" Simon asked behind her.

She ran her hand across the rung. The wood was new, unblemished. "This is it. Where she fell."

"How do you know?"

She compared it with the one above it. "The wood is new."

"I believe you're right."

She continued up the remaining rungs, scanning the upper floor. Packaging tables, stands, and boxes filled the area. Here, workers packaged the goods for delivery and shipping. The space was the shape of a long rectangle, with one office, and she walked to it directly. It must be important to have its own door.

She tried the handle, but it was locked. She pulled two hairpins from the back of her head and felt several pieces of hair fall down her neck. She used one to create tension at the bottom

MURDER IN MATRIMONY

211

of the lock. The other she inserted into the top of the lock to move its pins. When they released, she turned the tension pin until the lock turned and the door opened.

Simon put a hand on hers. "May I tell you how intriguing I find you at this moment?"

She arched an eyebrow. "Yes, but quickly."

His bright smile flashed white in the candlelight, and they continued inside the room, which was small and contained a desk, chair, and cabinet. Amelia started with the desk while Simon examined the cabinet. The desk was orderly, and the lamp was full of oil, the wick newly trimmed. No stray papers or ledgers littered the surface. She opened the center drawer, and it was only deep enough to hold the simplest writing provisions—stamps, notepaper, a pen. She moved the paper, and two tarnished screws lay in the drawer. Nothing remarkable.

"I'm afraid, in terms of books, I've come up empty," said Simon. "Any chance it's in the baking room? That might be the usual place for a recipe."

"Mr. Baker wouldn't want secret formulas readily available to anyone." She shut the center drawer and opened the deeper bottom drawer. It contained only one item: a thick black leather book that read BAKER BISCUITS LONDON OFFICE MIXING BOOK. "It's here," she announced.

Simon joined her as she laid the book atop the desk, zeroing in on its lock. This one might not be so easily picked.

Perhaps seeing her look of consternation, Simon said, "May I?"

"You?" She couldn't keep the surprise completely out of her voice.

"I lived much of my young life on a ship with men of debatable morals." He crossed his arms. "You cannot believe I am ignorant of how to pick a lock."

She felt her eyebrows raise.

He held out a hand. "The hairpins, if you please."

She handed them over, and he went to work on the lock. It seemed impossible that his hands could be large yet deft, and she was mesmerized by the action. The lock sprung open, and she blinked. "I stand corrected, my lord. You are a regular cracksman."

212   MARY WINTERS

He took a bow, and she put the pins back in her pocket.

The book was old and its pages worn. Amelia carefully turned to the back of the book, where she wasn't disappointed. On the last page was a newly written recipe. She scanned the ingredients.

"What do you think?" prodded Simon. "Is this the one?"

"I believe so." She opened the drawer and drew out a pen and paper. "We must copy the ingredients to be certain."

"You will take them to Mrs. Rothschild, then."

"Yes. Right away." She paused as she was writing down the ingredients. Something about the recipe seemed familiar, but she couldn't say what. *Odd.* No one knew of the recipe except Mr. Baker and the Rothschild family. She shook off the thought, continuing to write as quickly as she could, stuffing the note-paper into her trouser pocket. Simon locked the book and returned it to the drawer. Then they crawled back down the ladder to find Oliver and Kitty.

They located them in the bake room. Oliver was studying the large oven, perhaps fascinated by the mechanics, and Kitty was bent over what appeared to be a ledger. When Amelia inquired, she explained, "It's a schedule. Miss Rothschild was working with a woman named Lydia Hinkel the day she died. They both worked the bake room."

"She might be able to tell us what happened," Amelia said.

"It's a person to ask at the very least." Kitty flipped to the front of the book. "Her address is listed here with the rest of the bake room employees. I suppose if one is ill, another can be called upon to fill in."

Amelia looked over her shoulder. There were about a dozen names on the list. "Good work." She glanced at Oliver. "Did you find anything of interest?"

Oliver glanced at them. "This oven is quite interesting. I imagine it puts out a hundred biscuits or more at a time. Can you imagine? Hundreds of biscuits a day! The room must get very hot with the ovens running from sunup until sundown."

Amelia was not surprised by the observation. He indeed was a scholar and almost everything interested him. Perhaps his next tome would be on biscuit making. The idea brought a smile to her lips.

MURDER IN MATRIMONY

Kitty asked Amelia if she and Simon had any success, and Amelia gave the Hamsteds the new information. Kitty wanted to inspect the recipe, but Simon cautioned them against staying too long. Now that the recipe was copied, they could view it any time.

"Our candles are burning low," he said. "We should go."

Amelia agreed.

"We can leave out this window," observed Kitty, motioning to the window in the room. "As Oliver said, the room must become stifling, so no one will be surprised to find it unfastened."

They agreed, then blew out their candles and slipped out the window into the dark night air.

TWENTY-NINE

Dear Lady Agony,
  My response did not appear last week, nor the week before. I assumed you respond to all letters. Do you?
  Devotedly,
  Nowhere to be Found

Dear Nowhere to be Found,
  It's my dearest wish to respond to each letter, but as much as the paper has enlarged my space, I cannot answer every correspondent. If you respond with Second Request, I will be sure to answer you in the very next column.
  Yours in Secret,
  Lady Agony

Miss Hinkel lived with her parents in a house on Hare Street, and Amelia and Kitty were glad to find her at home on Sunday afternoon. It was her only day off, and Amelia hated to interrupt her rest but hoped Miss Hinkel might be able to provide an account of Miss Rothschild's last hours at Baker Biscuits. Amelia needed to know more about the Rothschilds' biscuit recipe and how it found its way into Mr. Baker's hands. She guessed it was by Miss Rothschild herself, who was perhaps compensated for the information. She was also interested in the fall and what the young woman was doing upstairs when the bake room was downstairs.

These questions and more were on her mind as she and Kitty were situated in the cramped front parlor while Mrs. Hinkel went to fetch her daughter. The girl was younger than Amelia imagined, no more than eighteen years of age, with a waifish figure and large gray eyes that stared at them with wonderment.

MURDER IN MATRIMONY 215

Miss Hinkel almost missed the well-worn seat of her chair as she sat down. "How do you do?"

"Very well, Miss Hinkel. My friend and I are glad to meet you." Amelia nodded at Kitty. "This is Mrs. Hamsted, and I am Lady Amesbury. We are friends of Mrs. Rothschild."

"Rose's mother," the girl said. "I know her."

Mrs. Hinkel interrupted to ask if they would like tea. "I was just putting the kettle on."

"Thank you, Mrs. Hinkel." Kitty smiled graciously. "That would be lovely."

"I am sorry for your loss." Amelia wasn't certain how friendly the two girls were, but they were the only females listed in the address book of the bake room employees. Perhaps this was enough to make them associates, if not cohorts. "I understand you worked with Miss Rothschild at Baker Biscuits."

"Thank you. Unlike most of the girls, who worked in the packaging room, we worked in the bake room." Miss Hinkel tipped her face toward the window, and the angle gave it a jaunty look, full of dignity. "We were working together the night of her accident."

"I'm glad you bring it up, Miss Hinkel, because I did not like to recall the uncomfortable moment upon just meeting you."

"Such a tragic affair," added Kitty.

Miss Hinkel jerked her head, perhaps surprised by her choice of words. Accidents were common occurrences in London's factories. To describe it as a tragedy might be taking it too far in Miss Hinkel's eyes.

"You mentioned that you were working together that day," Amelia continued.

"That night," corrected Miss Hinkel. "We sometimes worked evenings."

"The newspaper account said that she fell off the ladder," said Amelia.

The hardness and perhaps wiseness of Miss Hinkel came through in a harsh breath. "I read that too. What you didn't read is the rest of the story. She was working on a special recipe for Mr. Baker and had been working sixteen-hour days for a week. I know she was tired, fed up. She told me so. She said she might not come back to work the next day. Turns out, she didn't know how right she was."

Mrs. Hinkel padded in with the tea things. She had a heavy footstep, and the teacups shook in their saucers with the motion. As Mrs. Hinkel poured out, Amelia noted the biscuits were from Baker Biscuits. She recognized the tin from the shop.

When Mrs. Hinkel left, Amelia picked up the conversation. "You weren't there when she fell?"

Her gray eyes narrowed, and the thinness of her face became evident as the skin stretched over the prominent cheekbones. "I was told to go. The ovens would be running only the new biscuit. Nothing else was to be produced that evening, and God forbid they pay a person for a minute they're not working."

Amelia thought it interesting that she was dismissed for the evening. As the girl said, she was told to leave. Perhaps it wasn't a coincidence.

Amelia took a biscuit. "Was anybody else with her at the factory?"

Miss Hinkel slurped her tea. "Mr. Baker had been there and left. I remember because he'd never been at the factory past dark, and that night his oil lamp was burning. Those important sorts never stay for the real work."

Amelia supposed they didn't. Indeed, the clerk was happily surprised to find him there the day they visited the storefront. He might not have any idea how hard Miss Hinkel or anyone else worked to keep up day-to-day operations. "I assume Mr. Baker left the work to you and Miss Rothschild." She paused. "Do you know why he wanted her, specifically, to bake the new recipe?" Amelia hoped to confirm that recipe was indeed Rose Rothschild's mother's and no one else's.

Miss Hinkel put her cup back in the saucer. "Rose was a good baker. She was new to the factory, but everybody understood the fact. There was no one Mr. Baker trusted more with his new idea. He was sorrier than most by her accident."

He must have been devastated, thought Amelia. Here was a girl he trusted more than any other to make the special recipe. After her fall, he must have entreated someone else to ensure the recipe was properly prepared. "I trust the recipe continued. Whom did he select to continue the work?"

"Not me." Miss Hinkel snorted. "Any of the bakers might have finished it once Rose had it perfected. I heard it's to be put in the store next week. Until then, we're not to talk about it with anyone." She frowned. "I hope you won't mention it. I need my job, and I only meant to answer your questions about Rose."

"We won't say a word," promised Kitty. "You've been a great help to us."

"Mrs. Hamsted is right. Thank you."

After thanking Miss Hinkel and her mother, they retreated to Kitty's carriage. When the door was closed and the steps put up, Kitty released a long sigh. "Our conversation was not as fruitful as I anticipated. What now?"

"We gained information, perhaps just not the information we wished for." Amelia tried to keep her voice patient, but her patience was running thin. She, too, wanted answers—all of them. "We know Miss Rothschild was alone the night of her death. We also know Miss Hinkel might have been sent home for this very reason."

"But as she said, they don't pay her to stand around." Kitty shook her head, and her blonde curls bounced beneath the pink satin ribbon of her hat. "If she had no work to do, they wouldn't allow her to stay. Mr. Baker seems like a generous man, but he has a business to run."

"And he was a favorite of Mr. Cross." She glanced out the window. The streets were narrow, and the noise palpable. A loud buzz of shouting was rising above the din, and she wondered what it was about. "We cannot discount him entirely, however. I'd like to talk to him about the accident if nothing else."

"How do you propose to do that? You already committed to four dozen biscuits. Must you buy four dozen more?" Kitty pressed her lips together to keep in a laugh.

"I confess I don't know . . ." The sentence trailed off as she craned her neck to look around the passing street corner. The problem causing the disturbance came into view. It was the

Plate & Bottle. The building was succumbing to flames. "Kitty, stop your driver!"

Kitty did so quickly. "What is it?"

A line of men with buckets were attempting to douse the fire, but from the rise of their voices, they were having little success. They were shouting at one another to bring the water faster, but the task was impossible. The buckets were coming as quickly as they could.

"Amelia?" Kitty's position in the carriage did not afford her the advantage of a view of the street.

"It's the Plate & Bottle. It's on fire." She looked at Kitty's wide blue eyes. "It appears the arsonist has been successful."

"No!"

They waited only for the driver to put down the steps before descending. The driver had stopped away from the busy thoroughfare, and they had to walk several blocks before they could survey the damage for themselves.

It was catastrophic. As they grew nearer, smoke infiltrating their nostrils, Amelia saw the kitchen was no more. The windows had been shattered, perhaps by an explosion, and a hole stood in the pub where she and Simon had danced not that long ago. She covered her mouth, not sure if she was going to cry or be sick to her stomach.

Nearest the pub was Mr. Rothschild, who continued to demand water despite the futility of the effort. He had serious gray side whiskers and a prominent brow. If not for the emotion in his voice when he spoke, Amelia would have thought him brutish. He glared at the fire brigade even as they started to put out the fire.

"You got your way, didn't you, old Cross?" He opened his arms above his head. "The pub is no more. A present sent down from heaven."

"Mr. Rothschild!" Mrs. Rothschild exclaimed. "You must not blaspheme."

"Pray for me. Pray for me as you did our daughter. I would rather be dead than living." He looked at his wife, whose face was stricken with disbelief. Her shoulders drooped, and her stature seemed to shorten before Amelia's eyes. She stumbled backward, visibly shaken by his words. It was only then that he reached out and grabbed her arm to prevent her from falling. Her chest began to heave as the tears she'd held back began to roll down her cheeks.

The worst being said, Mr. Rothschild took pity on her, drawing her closer to him. She sobbed into his shoulder, and Amelia saw that his eyes were moist, too. His life's work had gone up in smoke. The fire would be put out (Amelia could see hints of it already), but the damage was done. Amelia didn't know if they'd ever be able to recover from it.

"The poor Rothschilds," whispered Kitty next to her. "Haven't they been through enough? Why must they continue to suffer?"

Amelia couldn't answer her question, nor could she confront Mrs. Rothschild about the recipe her daughter sold to Mr. Baker. Not now, perhaps not ever. The woman had no idea what her daughter had done. If she had, she would have known where the money came from for the gifts. "Come along, Kitty. Let us examine the recipe ourselves. We never had the chance last night, and there is nothing more to be done here."

Kitty nodded, but the look of consternation didn't leave her face. She was angry with the situation, and so was Amelia. She wished to help, but she didn't know how. There was one thing they could do, however, and that was examine the solid evidence they did have: the biscuit recipe.

THIRTY

Dear Lady Agony,

It is time to retire to my parents' country house, where I will be with my family until next spring. I cannot say I'm looking forward to it. There will be no escape from their company. What suggestions do you have for keeping sane? I will take any and all recommendations.

Devotedly,

Time for Torment

Dear Time for Torment,

Time with family might seem like torment, but there will come a day when you would walk through muddy fields without shoes to find that kind of torment. It seems impossible now, but trust me. It will come sooner than you think. Until then, bring plenty of books and take plenty of walks. They have saved me from despair many times.

Yours in Secret,

Lady Agony

Amelia had hidden the copied biscuit recipe in her library's secret compartment, where she stored readers' letters, and she and Kitty went there immediately upon returning to her house. Upstairs, the drawing room was buzzing with rankling relatives, and Amelia paused only long enough to hear Aunt Gertrude insist on a joint of mutton for Henrietta's arrival this evening. She would hear of nothing less for her and her four boys after traveling from Frome.

With a shudder, Amelia replaced her parasol in the stand. She couldn't imagine what the evening held for her, and by the sympathetic look in Kitty's eye, she, too, was imagining the worst.

"I am serving veal if you'd like to join me and Oliver," whispered Kitty.

"It's tempting, to be sure, but I am needed here." Quietly, Amelia tiptoed to the library so that no relatives would overhear them, but she couldn't evade them completely. Uncle Henry was standing near the half-full sherry decanter when she entered the room.

"Good afternoon, ladies. I said to myself, here is a decanter gone dry. Why not refill it with the sherry your good Lord Bainbridge recommended? No, you need not thank me. Please, it is *my* thank you for inviting us to stay with you in London, which is no small gift." Uncle Henry threw out his hands. "You have a beautiful home, Amelia, if I may call you that in company. I speak for myself and the entire family when I say we are glad to be here."

Amelia could only smile. She loved her family and her dear uncle Henry. Sure, he drank too much and was a little rough around the edges, but he was a kind-hearted and generous man. He didn't say things he did not feel, and though she'd heard her home spoken of highly many times, it didn't have the impact his words did just then. "And I am glad to have you here—everyone. I've missed you all so very much."

He tipped his chin with satisfaction. "I imagine you and your friend came in looking for a little privacy. I'll leave you to it." He started to walk toward the door and then paused. "I'll just take a cordial of this to go if you don't mind." He poured himself a tipple. "Mrs. Hamsted." With a bow, he was gone.

"Your family is so *interesting*," proclaimed Kitty.

"Thank you . . . I think." Amelia locked the door so that no one would descend upon them unannounced, which was a real possibility. Then she opened the secret cupboard, found the copied recipe, and settled into the green couch with Kitty. She unfolded the square and examined the ingredients. Besides flour and butter, a substantial amount of caster sugar was involved, an ingredient not widely used. It was what gave the biscuits their light texture and sweet taste, a simple but novel idea when compared to the biscuits brought onto ships and packaged for long journeys. They were little more than taste-less rations to keep men's stomachs full.

"Sugar," said Kitty, repeating the conspicuous ingredient. "That is what makes the difference—that and the lightening agent listed here." She blinked. "If they ice them, as suggested, just imagine the difference. Biscuits will be served alongside cake and other desserts. It will transform teatime as we know it."

"I think so, too. Mrs. Rothschild's recipe will make Mr. Baker a very wealthy man."

"What he paid for them, whatever it was, will be nothing compared to his return on the investment." Kitty put a hand to her heart. "If only Mrs. Rothschild knew."

"We must tell her. Tell *him*," Amelia added through gritted teeth. "He cannot think what he has done is fair."

"No indeed." Kitty shook her head. "How could he? Miss Rothschild bought some books, a necklace, and a walking stick. They are a pittance compared to his future profits."

Amelia stared at the recipe, wishing it hadn't come into the wrong hands. But wishing didn't make it so. Mr. Baker had the recipe. He planned on mass-producing the biscuits. He would have never agreed to her order otherwise. He anticipated their grand reception at her wedding breakfast and their subse-quent demand. To be hailed as a success in Mayfair would certainly secure their future. When she considered it, she herself might have unwittingly contributed to their assured triumph.

She sighed.

A dusting of flour from the factory bake room covered a corner of the paper, and distractedly, she swiped at it with a finger. Then stopped.

Something was coming into focus. She continued to stare at the words on the paper, trying to make it out.

"What is it?" asked Kitty.

"I don't know—yet." Inadvertently, she had pushed the white powder over the *fl* in *flour*, and when she did, it spelled the word *our*. Our. The same word as the scrap of paper in Mr. Cross's fireplace. The paper hadn't been a letter. It hadn't been a note. It had been a recipe.

MURDER IN MATRIMONY   223

She glanced up at Kitty, whose face told her everything she needed to know.

"My God! Mr. Cross had the recipe."

Amelia believed even Mr. Cross would have forgiven Kitty's use of the Lord's name in vain, for the idea was so striking, so certain, that her hand began to shake. "That's why it was burnt in his fireplace. No one else could possess the recipe if it was to be produced in bulk. It must remain a secret until Mr. Baker reveals the original."

"*Tomorrow*," exclaimed Kitty.

"Yes, tomorrow. Which is why something must be done today."

A soft knock came upon the door. "Psst . . . Amelia. Are you in there?"

Amelia started at the sound of Winifred's voice. "One moment. I'm coming." She tucked the recipe into her desk drawer and opened the door. Winifred glanced behind her as if to ensure no one was following her.

"I hope I'm not interrupting," said Winifred.

"Never." Amelia pushed open the door wider. "Come in. Mrs. Hamsted and I were only looking for a quiet space to converse."

"Good day, Mrs. Hamsted." Winifred bobbed a curtsy. "You won't find any upstairs. Aunt Tabitha and Aunt Gert are debating the cooking of meat in no uncertain terms. One believes in roasting it and the other in boiling it. I guess there is a great difference in the taste of the meat." Winifred shrugged. "But that's not why I'm here. I'm here because I'm looking for Madge. Have you seen her?"

"Not since this morning at breakfast." Amelia had seen her eat enough ham to feed a small army and wash it down with three cups of tea. She took it as a sign of her improved mood. "Is there something I can help you with?"

"I don't need her for anything." Winifred blinked her big blue Amesbury eyes. "I only wondered where she was. She and I talked of walking to the park after breakfast."

Amelia went about soothing the girl. "I'm certain she would have liked to—heaven knows she doesn't want to bother about

224   MARY WINTERS

the wedding. But she has several last-minute alterations to tend
to, not to mention her meeting with Mr. Penroy. She missed
an entire day with the dress debacle, and now she must make
up for it."

"I'm sure you are right." Winifred scrunched up her button
nose. "Only, I'd hoped she'd be free by now."

"She most likely will be occupied the remainder of the day."
Amelia smiled. "Are you certain you don't need me?"

She returned the smile, shaking her head. "No. Miss Walters
is waiting for me in the music room. Good day, Mrs. Hamsted."

"Good day, Lady Winifred." Kitty sighed and smiled as the
girl left. "You are very lucky, Amelia."

"I remind myself of that fact every day." Amelia, too, still
smiled at the door. When Edgar became ill soon after their
marriage, she knew they would never have children. He would
never risk passing on the degenerative disease. Yet, here was
Winifred, who felt as close as her own daughter. Life had a
way of working out beautifully.

She turned back to Kitty. "Now what to do about this recipe?"

Kitty stood. "We must confront Mr. Baker. It is the only
option."

Amelia stood also to stop her friend from making a
dangerous decision. Oliver had just become used to the idea
of Amelia being Lady Agony. She couldn't risk Kitty—or any
of her friends—doing something rash. "Today is Sunday. Mr.
Baker won't be at the factory."

Kitty smoothed her pretty pink garibaldi blouse. Her skirt
revealed a matching pink petticoat that went with it beautifully,
and on her hat was a feather the exact same color. "We shall
go to his house then."

"We cannot be certain he is the one who burnt the recipe,"
cautioned Amelia. She also wanted to confront Mr. Baker, but
if he was the murderer, she didn't want to put Kitty in harm's
way. And it was true that they didn't know if he was the culprit.
He was Mr. Cross's friend. Mr. Cross had referred parishioners
to his factory. Would he really murder a friend and priest for
money?

The answer had to be yes. Many horrible deeds had been

MURDER IN MATRIMONY   225

done for the sake of money. It was the reason money was considered the root of all evil. It had the power to persuade people, all people. Young, old. Rich, poor. East London, West London. If only she could be certain. If only she could have proof of what he'd done, she'd be more confident of her direction.

Kitty flung up her hands. "What else?"

"I need to think on it." Amelia put a hand on her friend's arm. "You and Oliver discuss the matter, and we will come to a decision."

"Yes, Oliver." Kitty blinked. "He is so bright. He will have many ideas on how to proceed."

"Indeed." She walked her to the door. "He will appreciate your coming to him with the problem." *And me for keeping you safe*, she silently added in her head.

While her friend was taking the short walk home to consider the matter, Amelia understood what she must do. More than once, she'd tried to confirm the person in Mr. Cross's office the day of his murder. No one had been able to tell her who it was. The time was blocked out, after hours, but no name was written in his appointment book. But if she went back to the factory, through the window they'd left open, she might be able to locate Mr. Baker's calendar. As a man of business, he certainly had one. If his time was blocked, she could be more certain of her next action.

The trouble, however, was that she would have to enter the factory in daylight on a Sunday. She couldn't wait until tonight. Tomorrow was the wedding. It must be done now. She saw no way around it.

In her room, she put on her drab mourning hat with veil, as she did the night she went to the Plate & Bottle with Simon. Trousers couldn't be worn in this instance, but she had a billowy gray walking dress that disguised her shape. After donning it, she slipped down the servants' staircase, motioning to her footman Bailey.

She whispered the street name, and his eyebrows rose questioningly. Then he went to the groom and gave the order to ready the carriage, acting no differently than if she were calling on the Queen of England. She mouthed the words *thank you* as he assisted her into the carriage.

He dipped his chin. "Of course, my lady."

Perhaps because it was daylight and the carriage conspicuous, the minutes passed like hours. At every turn and every stop, she anticipated her detection. But eventually, the driver arrived at the neighborhood, parking several streets away from the factory. There was no time for dissemblance or clever excuses. She was here, and all that was left was to climb into the open window.

While Mill Street itself was not abandoned, Baker Biscuits' storefront and factory were. The lack of commerce helped her clandestine operation, but it did not mean she could avoid detection entirely. Her carriage was noted by a man in a stall, perhaps a traveling stationer, who sold writing paper, envelopes, and small prints. The man immediately inquired after her needs, but she dismissed him with a shake of her head, keeping her eyes focused on the ground.

Bailey took several steps forward, and if Amelia's ignoring the seller didn't work, Bailey's size and countenance did. He was her youngest—and fiercest—footman. He was strong, capable, and discreet.

She turned the corner and was suddenly alone. Mill Street was dark, overtaken by the tall buildings and low fog. No vendor nor seller nor child attended the area. Taking a steadying breath, she remembered why she was here: Miss Rothschild and Mr. Cross. Their fates were tied together, and she would untangle the mystery, for it was the only way to bring their spirits peace—and justice.

The ground floor window was open, just as they'd left it hours before, and Amelia crawled through with some difficulty. The pane was heavy, and she had to raise it with one hand while hoisting herself up with the other, landing on the floor with a graceless thud.

Though it was daylight, the room was dark, and she chided herself for not bringing a candle. However, once she was out of the oven room, into the lofted area, she could see again. The space was improved by several long windows, and the light hung between the floor and wooden rafters, a dusty sunbeam landing on the ladder.

She navigated the ladder carefully. Simon was not behind her; he would not catch her if she fell. Until then, she hadn't realized how much she relied upon him being there.

It made her extra cautious, and each step was slow and methodical. She forced herself not to rush, not to anticipate the appointment book. As she approached the new rung, thinking of Miss Rothschild as she did, she noticed the screws that held it in place. She couldn't *not* notice them. Shiny silver screws. She inhaled a quick breath. Except for the sheen, they matched the ones in Mr. Baker's desk drawer.

Rose Rothschild hadn't fallen.

Rose Rothschild had been murdered.

THIRTY-ONE

Dear Lady Agony,

Have you read about Mary Jane Harrison, who went to work at a biscuit factory, by the request of her mother, only to be assaulted by her employer once they were alone? After struggling against him, stumbling into the knob of a door, she returned home with a terrible pain in her side. Six weeks later, she is dead and the employer fined only three pounds. It was said an abscess on her liver caused her death, either by the violence or natural causes. The deputy coroner gave the employer the benefit of the doubt, deciding on natural causes. At seventeen years of age, though, how could it be?

Devotedly,
Doubting Delilah

Dear Doubting Delilah,

You have every right to doubt the shameful outcome. I have also read the sad story of Mary Jane Harrison and the turmoil she suffered for six weeks before dying. The pain in her liver ended her employment and eventually her life, but nothing can stop the deplorable actions of some men, except what we are doing here, which is to discuss them, question them, and refute them. Audibly, deliberately, and without shame. Until justice is served, it is our only matter of recourse.

Yours in Secret,
Lady Agony

Amelia finished climbing to the second floor. Of course Rose Rothschild was murdered. She was a young woman with something valuable, and it was unsurprising—perhaps

MURDER IN MATRIMONY   229

even predictable—that someone took it from her. Mr. Baker gave her money. He was not completely without charity. To be able to say he paid for the goods was gentlemanly. Just, even. Amelia imagined this is what Mr. Baker told Mr. Cross when Mr. Cross confronted him. He was an honorable man, a good man. He would never *steal* from a woman.

Yet when Miss Rothschild demanded more money, as she must have, he refused. A factory girl could have an accident without incident. No one would question the death of a poor girl from the East End falling clumsily to her death. Mr. Baker had removed the screws from the ladder, and then what? Did he call to her? Did he hide one of the ingredients? Whatever brought her up the ladder was important enough to make the towering trek.

Unbeknownst to him, however, Cross had taken down the recipe for collateral, perhaps when Miss Rothschild gave him the books. When she died in an accident of convenience shortly thereafter, Cross must have confronted him. Amelia remembered the biscuit tin on Cross's desk. It was proof Mr. Baker had been there. Everyone who knew the recipe must be killed. A breath hitched in her throat. Including Mrs. Rothschild. *The Plate & Bottle fires!*

The tragedies—all of them were connected. And they were all realized because of the narrow slip of newsprint Cross had left for her. A feeling of peace coursed through her. She had discovered the answers to the mysteries that had plagued her head and heart. Mr. Baker had killed Miss Rothschild and Mr. Cross. Retrieving the screws and the appointment book would provide evidence of the facts for the police.

Amelia was surprised to find Mr. Baker's office door open and glanced over her shoulder. Perhaps someone did work in the factory on Sundays. *Surely not Mr. Baker.* Quickly, she skimmed the papers on the desk, then the center drawer, grabbing the screws and tucking them into her pocket. If he kept an appointment book, it wasn't here. She opened the deep desk drawer.

The black leather mixing book was gone.

Her heart dipped into her stomach. Had she not put it back?

230   MARY WINTERS

Quickly, she retraced the previous night's steps in her head. She was certain that after copying the recipe, she replaced it in the drawer. Which could only mean one thing. Someone else had taken it.

"Looking for something, Lady Amesbury?" Mr. Baker stood at the open door.

Terror, panic, then preparation overtook her. She'd navigated high waters before and could do so again. She only needed to breathe and remember herself.

"Mr. Baker. Thank heavens you're here." Amelia lifted the veil of her hat. "I was worried about tomorrow's order— woman's nerves, you know—so I came to the shop, but it was closed, and then I came here." Even to Amelia's ears, the excuse sounded feeble, but it was something, which in her opinion, was always better than nothing.

"I was notified of a break-in last evening. I have been here all morning."

"You were?" Amelia swallowed. "Dear me. I hope nothing was stolen." Inadvertently, she glanced at the empty drawer.

Mr. Baker took a step forward, and his heavy footfall echoed in the room. "Tell me why you are really here."

"Why, as I said, my nerves over tomorrow's wedding break- fast might be understandable under the circumstances—"

He cut her off. "Do not try to pass off your Mayfair manners on me. I know you are here for the biscuit recipe. You glanced at the drawer it was in just now."

"I certainly did not."

"And you were a favorite of Mr. Cross's," he added.

"How did you know . . ." The question faded from her lips. That's where she recognized him. He didn't remind her of her grandfather; he was the man in the back of All Saints on Margaret Street with his sleeves rolled up. He was speaking with Mr. Cross when she entered the church the morning of his murder. Mr. Cross must have delayed the meeting until that evening, when he could speak to him in private. She no longer needed the appointment book. She knew it was Mr. Baker.

"You see?" His smile was cunning. He was as clever as any East End fence. "You are not the only one who can travel across

MURDER IN MATRIMONY

town. When you came with your stylish friend, I had hoped it was only an extravagance of an overdone wedding breakfast. But when my man told me there was a break-in last night, I suspected a connection. I've been awaiting your arrival."

There was no use dissembling. He knew, and they were alone. She might not get out of the situation alive, but she would get out of it with the truth. "Mr. Cross was your friend."

He shrugged. "He sent me workers with the souls of angels. How could we not be friends?"

He did not admit to the murder, and she needed him to. "He thought you were helping people find decent work, but you were only helping yourself."

"Who else would I help?" He walked to the desk, and as he grew closer, the practiced manners fell away. He had no need for them now. He was not a gentleman; he was a crook. "Who is there to help *me*? You?" His chuckle was harsh. "No. Not you. I've come up from nothing, like everyone else in my factory. But I grow tired of work. I deserve a rest."

"Which is what the recipe would allow," supplied Amelia. "Why you stopped at nothing to obtain it."

"Miss Rothschild came to *me*, sold it to *me*." He shook his head, and a shock of dull gray hair fell over his forehead, making him appear older than she realized. "I hired her to package biscuits. She insisted I try her mother's recipe, and I did. It was good, and I bought it. I did nothing wrong."

"Except kill her."

He seemed genuinely insulted by the accusation. His small eyes, marred by wrinkles, widened at the acknowledgment. "Her death was an accident. She fell down the ladder."

"She indeed fell—because of you." Amelia was surprised, too, by the strength of her own voice. Miss Rothschild's murder would be acknowledged. It would not be forgotten like so many others in the area.

He leaned over the desk between them, and she instantly leaned back. He sat down in the chair across from her with a laugh. "That's what's wrong with women like you. You have too much time on your hands. What possible reason would I have for murdering Miss Rothschild?"

"I don't need a reason. I have these." Amelia pulled the screws from her pocket, shoving them forward.

The laughter stopped abruptly. He knew he'd been discovered. "Miss Rothschild was a street urchin and cheat. I gave her money, and she wanted more. When I refused, she tried to take back the recipe she gave me—just like I knew she would. I planned for it, removing the screws from the ladder. She took her life into her own hands when she decided to climb up that ladder and steal it from my office. If you knew the East End better, you would understand the truth of it."

She knew it was about money but was glad to have it confirmed. "It is not cheating to demand what you're owed. The recipe was worth much more than you gave her. You knew it. She knew it. Mr. Cross knew it."

"Cross knew nothing!" Mr. Baker's voice boomed. "Holding church services in the area did not make him one of us. Nor did his little society. He grew up in affluence. We were lucky to grow up at all." His voice turned gritty. "So save your moralizing for your friends in Mayfair. We do what we must to get by."

"And Mr. Cross did what he had to do, which was to write down Mrs. Rothschild's recipe."

"I burned that," he shot back automatically.

"Was that before or after you murdered him?"

"After." He was visibly agitated and stood from his chair. Instantly, she tucked the screws into her pocket. "He refused to give it to me, so I struck him with the clock and took it myself. I changed the time and took the poor box, to put the police on the wrong trail. The peelers will believe anything, and I couldn't risk our meeting being connected to his death." He stepped from around the desk. "Cross was the one who told the girl to ask for more money. But she didn't ask. She demanded. She said her mother would continue to make the biscuits at the Plate & Bottle if I didn't give her ten thousand pounds—after she'd promised me her mother would retire the recipe. Ten thousand pounds! She was an urchin, I tell you. A blackmailer."

He had to prevent Mrs. Rothschild from making the biscuits,

and the only way to do that was put an end to her oven, if not her. With Rose Rothschild gone, it was the only thing left to do. "She might have blackmailed you, but you killed her, her priest, and burned down her family's business. What does that make you?"

He grabbed her arm, hard. "A smart man."

She dug her heels into the floor. "Not so smart. If something happens to me, the recipe will be known to all. I left it with a friend who will know what to do with it."

"When they find you, which will take a while. You must know what the Thames is, my lady. It will take some time for you to wash up on shore."

He was old but strong. In his youth, he'd probably wrestled many men on the brutal streets of East End London. She twisted like a wildcat to get out of his claw-like grip. He took an umbrella from the stand by the door and hit the back of her knees with it. She buckled long enough for him to get her through the office door, and in a moment, she was before the ladder, thinking of all the people in her life most dear.

Tabitha, Winifred—Simon. She wished she'd told him that she loved him. She wished she'd told him every day for the last three months. How foolish she'd been to hold back.

"Don't take another step, Baker." Simon was there at the bottom of the ladder with a shooting rifle. "I'm warning you."

It was as if she'd wished so hard, she'd manifested him, and she blinked twice to make certain he was real. He was. In his black frock coat, which must have concealed the rifle, he looked the navy captain he'd once been. Kitty and Oliver, who had, like good students, figured out her plan to investigate alone, stood next to him.

"I'll push her." Mr. Baker's voice was raspy. "I swear to God I will."

"If you do, I'll kill you dead." Simon's deep voice cut through the charged air with eerie calmness. His eyes were focused on Mr. Baker, like a hunter's on a deer.

Had he his umbrella, Mr. Baker might have been able to make good on his threat. But as it was, Amelia knew she could overpower him. The problem was they might both fall over, and she couldn't live with his blood on her hands. Mr. Cross wouldn't want it, and neither did she.

So they stood at an impasse. Or so she thought. Until another man's voice surprised her from behind.

"Lady, what have I told you about the East End?" Isaac Jakeman tsked. "I say, 'stay home in Mayfair,' but you do not listen."

"You're late." Mr. Baker loosened the grip on her arm. "You were supposed to be here fifteen minutes ago to throw this chit in the Thames."

"Ah, but there is one problem." Isaac Jakeman stepped closer, taking Amelia's arm as if it was part of a criminal transaction.

Mr. Baker's brow furrowed. "What is it?"

In one swift motion, Jakeman pushed Amelia toward the office. "I like this chit more than I like you." He grabbed Mr. Baker's arm instead. "Lower your gun, Sir. I am for the lady."

Seeing the truth of his words, Simon lowered the gun.

"What is this? Here now. Did she pay you? I will pay more." Mr. Baker tried pulling away, but it was no use, and he knew it. Isaac Jakeman had no doubt killed his fair share of men. Resisting or retaliating would ensure his own demise. Jakeman had no qualms about hurting the older man. He held the belief of an eye for an eye.

"No, she did not pay. But you will pay whatever the lady wishes." Jakeman looked at Amelia and smiled. "What do you wish for, Lady?"

In a moment, she knew. What could be done—must be done—for the Rothschilds and the East End. It was almost as strong as her wish to tell Simon she loved him, and she voiced it immediately. "I wish for Baker Biscuits to give the proceeds from the new biscuit to Mrs. Rothschild and her charity."

"An admirable wish." Jakeman dipped his chin. "You were not jesting when you said you wanted to help Wapping."

"I meant every word, Mr. Jakeman. I promise."

He held her eye for a moment, then shook the arm of Mr. Baker. "See? She calls me Mister. Why wouldn't I like her better?" He didn't wait for an answer. "Now, I want you to promise the lady and her friends here that the proceeds will

MURDER IN MATRIMONY 235

go where she wishes. You will put them in writing for your partner, and in turn, I will not cut off your head. You will rot away in prison like the rest of the cheats on the East End."

"How could you, Ike?" Mr. Baker's voice was hoarse with emotion, and for a moment, he looked like an older version of the younger man. "You and I are the same."

"You are not the same," Amelia spat back. "You are nothing like Mr. Jakeman."

"There, you see? We are quite different." He nodded at Simon. "Now then, we have some business to commence. Would you like to join us?"

Kitty put her hand on a rung. "We would."

Oliver put his hand over hers. "Let's find a constable, shall we? I think they have matters under control, and Mr. Baker must be taken into custody."

Kitty met Amelia's eye, and Amelia nodded her agreement, giving her a weak smile. She should have told her friend the plan, but in her own defense, she had no idea Mr. Baker would be in the factory on a Sunday.

Kitty took Oliver's hand then but not without a parting word. "If you ever try something like this again, Amelia, I won't bring Mr. Hamsted and Lord Bainbridge. I'll bring Lady Tabitha."

The name echoed in the rafters, reminding one and all that there were things scarier than men and guns, and it was Aunt Tabitha.

THIRTY-TWO

Dear Lady Agony,
Tell it to me short and straight, like cupid's arrow. Do
you believe in love at first sight?
Devotedly,
Reader in Love

Dear Reader in Love,
In a word, dearest reader—absolutely.
Yours in Secret,
Lady Agony

While Mr. Baker signed his half of the proceeds over to the Rothschilds, Oliver and Kitty Hamsted found a constable who eagerly took down the accounts of the murder of Rose Rothschild and Mr. Cross. They had the evidence from Rose's murder—the screws—but the evidence from Cross's murder was yet to come. The officer thought it very probable that Mr. Baker kept the poor box from the church, and the Metropolitan Police would be able to substantiate the claims quite quickly. The time of death had been mistaken because of the clock but also the fire, which kept the body warmer than it would have been without it.

Before the officer's arrival, Isaac Jakeman had quietly left the same way he came but not before receiving Simon's eternal gratitude and a genuine handshake. Amelia owed him her very life, and she told him so. He shrugged off the kindness as commonplace, but she knew it was not. Anyone in his position would have done what benefited himself. Instead, he'd put her wellbeing before his own, and for that she would be forever grateful.

Amelia's carriage waited on a side street, and before climbing inside, she apologized to Oliver and Kitty for taking it upon herself to investigate without her friends. Oliver said he understood why she had done it but implored her to come to all of them next time, to which she replied, she hoped there wouldn't be a next time.

Alone in the carriage with Simon, Amelia recalled her fervent desire to tell him she loved him. They had said very little, and it seemed her feelings filled the space between them. So thick were they that they might have broken them into a thousand pieces with a word, and no matter how she thought to begin, she couldn't quite start.

As they grew closer to Mayfair, however, she knew she must. Once she returned, all the obligations would return with her, and she might lose her nerve. The girl who moved to London two years ago wouldn't have waited one day, but she was more careful now. Too careful. She must act, even if it was too sudden or soon. She opened her mouth and took a breath. "Simon—"

"Amelia," he said at the same time.

They shared a small laugh.

"I defer to the lady." Simon flourished a hand as if to allow her passage.

She mustered her strength and started again. "When I was standing at the top of the ladder, one person came to mind. It was you."

A timid smile flitted across his lips.

"I had a single regret, but a considerable one, and if I would have plunged to my death, it would have gone with me to the grave." She swallowed, willing herself to continue. She could do this. She *must* do this. Even if it was not the right time or place. Even if it wasn't customary or condoned. She had been honest with her readers when it was hard; now she must be honest with Simon. "I've longed to tell you something for a while, and I know I shouldn't, but it is always this way with you. I must say what I believe."

"You can say it now," he said quietly.

"It feels as though every moment of my life has led me to you, each stone laid at my feet in the hope of finding you. And when I did, it felt as if I was home for the very first time. I never want to leave this place of you and me." She took a breath, and the next words came out as easily as a breeze in April. "I love you."

"Amelia." His hands cupped her face, and his green eyes searched her own. He must have seen the raw honesty in them, and in the next breath, an emotion had been unlocked, and he whispered, "My pride has made me foolish and reticent. But I, like you, can no longer keep silent. You must know I love you too."

He kissed her tenderly, then hugged her to his chest. She swore she could feel his heart through his coat, beating hammer hard. He kissed her neck, and as she released a little sigh of pleasure, he snaked his arm around her, pulling her closer. When their lips met again, their desire was more fervent, as if they both knew the moment must end but didn't wish it to.

Amelia felt the carriage come to a stop, and they broke apart.

"Ours has been a patient path, but I have lost my patience. I do not wish to go on as before. I can't." He grasped her hand, glancing out the window, then at her. "Would you ever consider . . . I mean, under the right circumstances, would you consent to . . . marry me?"

This was a surprise, in timidness and honesty. She answered with the same honesty and without thinking. "Under any circumstances. Yes, I would marry you."

He released a stream of air. "That is a relief. I thought you might be against it because of Winifred. But you must know I would raise her as my own daughter. I understand that's how you feel for her, and I hope to one day as well."

"Oh Simon," she exclaimed and gave him a brief kiss on the cheek. "How could I ever be against us?"

"If Lady Tabitha objects, if she insists you remain an Amesbury—"

She squeezed his hand. "You have forgotten one thing. She is the most Amesbury of the Amesburys. To be mistress of home and hearth again must be her secret and most ardent wish."

"I did not consider that point. She has lived here most of her life, and I cannot imagine she enjoys sharing. She again would be the matriarch of the Amesburys, but we would bring the name merit with our raising of little Winifred."

MURDER IN MATRIMONY 239

For Winifred to have a father figure such as Simon Bainbridge in her life was almost too much to hope for, and Amelia loved him even more for his words. He didn't regret raising another man's child. He looked forward to it and the life they could give her. Her heart swelled with admiration, and she was about to show him how much when Bailey set down the carriage steps.

"We will make plans, after your sister is married," Simon added quickly. "Is that too soon?"

"I would marry you today if I could," she whispered, and they shared a secret smile.

Then Bailey opened the door, and Aunt Tabitha was walking toward the carriage. Alone. Without a shawl. Pointing at her with her raven-headed cane.

"What in heaven's name?" Amelia wondered if the trouble at Baker Biscuits had followed them from the East End already.

"You don't think her ears are *that* good, do you?" Simon jested. "She couldn't have heard me from inside the house."

She shook her head distractedly. "Something is wrong. Very wrong."

Her feet had only touched the ground when Aunt Tabitha proclaimed, "Your sister is missing."

"Which one?" Amelia asked.

"The red-headed menace, that's which one."

Oh dear.

"Good day, Lady Tabitha," murmured Simon.

"It's not a good day, Lord Bainbridge. In fact, rarely is it a good day when Miss Margaret is expected to do something rational."

"What is it, Aunt?"

"She missed her final wedding dress fitting," Aunt Tabitha announced.

Dread, panic, fear. Those were the emotions that coursed through Amelia's body in immediate succession. Why had Madge missed her appointment? The wedding was tomorrow. The answer was simple and immediate. There wasn't to be a wedding. She knew it as well as the grip of her own parasol. Here she thought the couple had overcome their obstacles and

240 MARY WINTERS

resolved any difficulties. Her absence proved how much she knew. And yet . . .

"Oh Amelia!" Mrs. Scott was joined by Penelope and Sarah. "Have you heard? Margaret is missing."

"I told you! I told you this morning!" Winifred trailed fast on their heels.

Simon touched her shoulders. "No matter what has happened, we will overcome it—together. You need never be alone again."

Aunt Tabitha tilted her head ever so slightly, perhaps cognizant of a change in the relationship. She wasn't unpleased, however. In fact, she appeared grateful for his assistance.

As for Amelia, the palpable relief she felt in her heart came out in two words. "Thank you."

Her mother and sisters were talking at once, giving different accounts of Madge's whereabouts. She listened to all, regarding some and discounting others. When they finished, she had one question that would answer all others foremost on her mind. "Where is Captain Fitz?"

The din of noise around her went perfectly silent.

"Captain Fitz?" Mrs. Scott repeated after a moment. "Why, we haven't seen him either."

Knowledge fell slowly, like a mist turning into rain. It was one thing if Madge was missing. It was quite another if they both were.

"I will call on Captain Fitz if you'll allow me your carriage," said Simon. "Be sure I'll return with news."

Amelia agreed, ushering her family into the house. In a matter of weeks, Amesbury Manor had become one of the busiest—and perhaps noisiest—houses on the block, and Amelia could not admit to being sad about it. Although a new problem had befallen her, the noise and food and drink brought her much comfort. It was no longer a house of mourning. It was a house of life, and difficulties were proof of it. Human beings were fallible, but that didn't mean they were any less loveable, including Madge. Amelia only wanted the best for her, and she and her family waited on a word from Simon to know the extent of the problem.

It came forty-five minutes later, after Winifred had eaten the

MURDER IN MATRIMONY

241

last strawberry tartlet on a hastily made tea tray. Simon entered without waiting for Jones to announce his arrival, and Amelia braced herself for the news. He looked grave, and his eyes darted to hers for permission.

She dipped her chin in acquiescence.

"What is it, Lord Bainbridge?" asked Mrs. Scott. "What did the captain say?"

"I'm afraid he said nothing, Mrs. Scott, because he wasn't there." He glanced at Amelia, and she knew the case at once. "Captain Fitz and your daughter have eloped."

THIRTY-THREE

Dear Lady Agony,
A young man's disappearance in Clonmel was lately
noted by his distressed mother and father. It now appears
he took all his possessions and ran away with the family
cook to America. Can you imagine anything worse? And
such a disgrace to the family! I do not blame them if they
never allow him into their home again.
Devotedly,
Disgraced is Deserted

Dear Disgraced is Deserted,
I can indeed imagine worse things than elopement but
will refrain from naming them, lest I grow morbid, and
marriage is such a happy topic. Even in America.
Congratulations to the bride and groom, wherever they are.
Yours in Secret,
Lady Agony

Aunt Tabitha was astonished by the news of Captain
Fitz and Margaret's elopement. The Scott family not
as much. Amelia felt some alarm but only for a moment,
and then it passed like so many Scott family emotions. She
knew her sister was displeased with the wedding arrangements.
The day she put on her dress was perhaps the worst of it, but
Amelia had seen early signs of her reluctance. She had returned
to Somerset, and after leaving the city, submitting to a large
party—even one of her own making—must have been more
than she could bear.

Several covered mouths and shy smiles passed among the
Scott family. Aunt Gertrude laughed aloud; Aunt Hen slapped
her knee; and Uncle Henry went as far as to say he didn't

MURDER IN MATRIMONY 243

blame the couple. Only Aunt Tabitha decried their selfishness, and Mr. Scott was quick to agree with her. His spirit was perhaps the lowest of the group, and Amelia went to him, assuring him all would be well. The banns had been announced for three weeks. It wasn't so much an elopement as a private wedding.

"But the expense. The trouble. The *waste*." Mr. Scott inhaled a breath. "I apologize for my daughter's behavior, Lady Tabitha. I mean to repay every farthing you've spent on preparations."

"It is not your fault, Mr. Scott." Lady Tabitha's voice was gentler than Amelia had ever heard it. "I do not blame you."

The quietness of her voice was felt by the entire room, and it fell still and somber.

"What if it wasn't wasted?" Simon asked.

All in the room turned to Simon with blinking sets of eyes. In the midst of the unexpected news, they'd forgotten him in the doorway.

Amelia stared at him most interestedly. Could he mean what she thought he meant? *Never.*

He came to Amelia's side in three large steps.

"I've been silent on a subject too long. But today, my heart found its voice, and I cannot keep from singing. I would declare it from the chimney tops if I could." He grasped Amelia's hand and squeezed it before allowing it to drop. Then he turned seriously to Mr. Scott. "I am in love with your daughter, and she is in love with me. I wish to marry her, and we'd like to do so now, with your permission. I can obtain a special license today. Everyone she loves is here and my family as well. We need not wait until spring. We need not wait another moment if no one objects." Here, he glanced at Lady Tabitha.

"You will have no objections from me," Tabitha said slowly. "I know of your mutual affection." Her voice lowered. "If you recall, you confirmed it once."

Amelia's cheeks flushed at the remembrance of Aunt Tabitha finding them in an embrace in the library several weeks ago. Amelia knew her own heart, but Simon and Tabitha had taken more time to acknowledge the relationship. But from all accounts, they had.

"My concern," Aunt Tabitha went on, "has always been for the Amesbury name, and you, Lord Bainbridge, do it no disservice by marrying Edgar's widow."

"And caring for his niece—which we wish to do," he added. "She will retain every virtue of this great family, and with time, I hope, acquire some of mine."

Winifred exclaimed in happiness.

Simon returned to Mr. Scott.

"You need not my permission, Lord Bainbridge, although I appreciate the kindness." Mr. Scott was a quiet man, and his words had none of the excitement of the women in his house. He turned to Amelia. "My daughter is more than capable of making her own decisions. You need only ask her if she wishes it. If she does, nothing in the world will prevent her. Count on it."

With all grace and sincerity, Simon clasped her hands. "My dearest Amelia, will you marry me?"

Her heart hadn't prepared her for the words nor for the actions of her family. In silence, they awaited her answer. Aunt Tabitha looked upon her with a generous smile. Winifred grasped her hands in front of her in joyful anticipation. Her sisters exchanged the word *finally*. For it had felt like she'd been waiting for this moment forever, a second chance at happiness and with a man that loved her not for what she could do for his family or fortune but for herself absolutely. She and Simon had no secrets. Their dreams and desires had been laid bare. They had agreed, they had disagreed, they had fallen in love for better and worse.

Now she turned from the others to Simon, to his green eyes which belied his early feelings of tenderness. It was where she wanted to live. In them, she saw all she wanted to be—could be—who he believed she was already. Honesty, tolerance, compassion, and a man who believed in the same directly by her side.

"Yes, Lord Bainbridge, I will marry you."

With this, Winifred squealed in a way only girls in their tenth year could do. She ran to Amelia and hugged her, and it was the first of what she hoped was many family embraces. Amelia and

MURDER IN MATRIMONY 245

Simon both reached down to surround her with love and affection while the rest of her family joined in congratulations.

Uncle Henry elbowed Mr. Scott. "I say, that's one way to save the wedding breakfast—and the champagne."

They exchanged a laugh and a handshake. Then Uncle Henry proceeded to shake Simon's hand, giving him a healthy pat on the back and promising him a darling bottle of scotch as a wedding gift. "Although it was promised to Captain Fitz, he's not here, so you might as well be the beneficiary."

Amelia took the opportunity to speak to Aunt Tabitha, who was looking upon the scene with what might be called a whimsical smile if Amelia didn't know her better. As Amelia approached, she straightened her countenance, and she was the serious and intelligent woman Amelia had come to know and respect.

Tabitha extended her hand. "Congratulations."

Amelia took it warmly in both of hers. "Do you mean it, Aunt?"

"I do." Tabitha's eyes were steady and sincere. "I am an old woman, but I am not blind to young happiness. You are courageous and know your own mind. I esteem that in any woman but especially of your tender age. I suppose, at one time, I wanted you to follow in my footsteps, if I am to be honest."

Amelia raised her eyebrows.

"Not that you could have filled them, mind you." Tabitha raised her eyebrows in return and then lowered them with a flicker of a smile. "For so long, my single object has been the preservation of the Amesbury name and fortune—perhaps because of the family's *mis*fortunes. I can see now that family is so much more than that."

"Truly?" Amelia could not keep the pleasure out of her voice.

"Truly." After a moment's regard, she continued more evenly. "You and your family have shown me it and more, which I will share with you on another day."

"Another day when we are still the closest of friends," Amelia pressed, wanting a promise from a woman who had become so much more than an aunt.

"No dear, not just friends. *Family.*"

EPILOGUE

The next morning, Simon and Amelia were married and enjoyed the wedding breakfast that had been planned for Captain and Margaret Ann Fitz. There was little difference in the taste, but it was perhaps all the sweeter because of the surprise. In a peach-colored gown with few adornments (there hadn't been time, and she'd never cared for frills), Amelia sat next to her handsome groom, who was also dressed sensibly. Only the fragrant orange blossoms in her hair belied their morning marriage, which took place without fanfare at All Saints on Margaret Street. Indeed, one bride and groom had been supplanted with another, and the ceremony went on as planned.

Except for the small bouquet of white lilies at the altar. No one could explain who brought it or how it reached the church. But Amelia thought she knew. A sense of peace pervaded the sacred space, falling upon her and Simon like a benediction as they exchanged vows. She had solved the murders of Mr. Cross and Miss Rothschild. No one could bring those two most important people back. Indeed, she would live with Mr. Cross's absence forever. But what she had done for Wapping—for his most beloved poor—made his life, in fact *her* life, more meaningful. It taught her she could make a difference; she only needed courage.

"If I could make a toast to the bride and groom," announced Uncle Henry.

Everyone found their glasses.

"Wait!" came a loud voice from the stairwell. "Uncle Henry, please wait!"

A murmur snaked through the crowd, growing louder as the voice approached the drawing room. Then Madge and the captain appeared, and the room fell silent.

"Captain and Mrs. Fitz, my lady," announced Jones, out of breath.

Amelia and Simon stood.

"Oh, Amelia!" Madge ran toward her with open arms. "I'm so glad I didn't miss your wedding day. Please forgive me."

And as families sometimes do, without resentment or reason, Amelia did, returning her embrace. "Of course I do."

Captain Fitz and Simon shook hands.

"Well then," said Uncle Henry in a jovial tone. "We have two happy couples to celebrate today, and I'd like to thank His Grace for supplying an inordinate amount of champagne which now seems entirely appropriate."

Simon's father, the duke, dipped his head, smiling.

Uncle Henry raised his glass. "To the Scott family, who has gained two sons worthy of their fair daughters. And to the Bainbridge and Fitz families, who have gained daughters who are as dear to me as my own."

Amelia raised a glass, her eye meeting her sister's. Many changes had occurred in their lifetimes and still more were to come. Technology and industry had changed everything, especially social classes. The popularity of her agony column was a testament to it. Correspondents were looking for new ways to navigate a world where people of trade and commerce not only contributed to the country's wealth but had a share of it. That was new and, in Amelia's opinion, about high time.

Amelia had been a countess by marriage only, but Simon made her feel like royalty every day. People could say what they pleased, but times had changed, and she had changed also. More importantly, perhaps, so had Simon. As they clinked glasses, he no longer looked at her as the widow of his best friend. He looked at her with respect and devotion and pride.

When he drew close and declared his love, her breath hitched, for it was as courageous an act as it had ever been. The world might have changed, but love never would. It was the constant that would keep them and the world together forever.

Acknowledgements

What goes through an author's mind when she starts a book? For me, each novel is different. A thought, a place, even a word can spark my imagination. This time, while reading a Victorian newspaper called *Lloyds Weekly London Newspaper*, I came across an article I could not stop thinking about. It told the story of a girl named Mary Jane Harrison who, at seventeen years old, went to work at a biscuit factory on the advice of her mother (see the letter that begins chapter 31). The biscuit manufacturer attacked her when they were alone, shoving her against a doorknob, and she died, after much suffering, six weeks later. The manufacturer was not jailed; he was fined three pounds. The girl's death bothered me, and I wondered why there are so many bad people in the world. It was at this same time, however, that I came across an article about a very good person, the Reverend Charles Lowder, who was sometimes dubbed the Slum Vicar for his work in the East End of London. As I read more about the man, I came to the realization that had Charles Lowder known Mary Jane Harrison, he would have helped her, and thus the story of *Murder in Matrimony* was inspired. It took many turns, and in no way do the characters in my book represent the two lives mentioned. But I wanted to acknowledge both of these real people who ignited my passion for this book.

I'd also like to acknowledge Julian at All Saints on Margaret Street in London, whose assistance with forms of address was especially helpful. I'd like to thank editor Laurie Johnson and the entire crew at Severn House for their invaluable support. Thank you, also, to my agent, Amanda Jain, who is so good with all the details. Finally, thank you to my family for their unceasing love and encouragement.

And to you, dearest readers. Thank you for welcoming Lady Agony and her advice into your hearts.